MW01257926

WHITE ANGEL MURDER

A Thriller

Victor Methos

I hate mankind, for I think myself one of the
best of them, and I know how bad I am.
—Joseph Baretti

San Diego, California

The coppery stink of blood hung in the air like a strong perfume.

Jonathan Stanton felt the coolness of the kitchen linoleum against his back as his nostrils filled with the scent. His vision was blurry, and only faint echoes rang in his ears, but he knew no one was near. He felt the calmness of the house now, the quiet. His gun was heavy in his hand and he didn't think he had the strength to lift it.

He glanced down and saw black blood pouring out of him and onto the floor, spreading into a wide circle around him. His shirt clung damply to his ribs, and urine trickled down his thighs as he lost control of his bladder. His vision was cloudy past a couple of feet and he didn't know what, or who, was there, but there was no movement. His head fell back and his eyes began to close.

Stay alive. Stay alive. Don't fall asleep.

But all he wanted to do was sleep. It would be a simple thing to do, like falling onto silken sheets and wrapping them around himself. The softness would kiss his skin and then, there would be nothing.

His eyelids grew too heavy to keep open and darkness enveloped him.

Crash!

Cold air flowed over his chest. His lids opened, but his eyes had rolled back into his head and they twitched and fluttered.

"He's conscious!"

He felt lightness, a floating sensation, as if he was hovering, and he thought of his mother. She had soft hands that smelled of lavender. She had passed too soon from breast cancer and he had watched her forgiving smile as she withered away in a hospital bed with clean white sheets. She held his hand as much as possible those last few days and they watched reruns of old television shows. He would tell her about his day and the mundane things that happened.

"It's trivial stuff, mom."

"No," she would reply. *"Nothing's trivial, sweetheart."*

One day, she couldn't speak. And the day after that, her soul was lifted from her body like fog over a still river at sunrise.

"Wake up, Jon. Jon! Stay with me. Jon!"

A gasp of warm air rushed into him. Stars sparkled above as his stretcher rattled out of the old house and to the ambulance. The twirling red-and-blues of the police cruisers caught his eye as he vomited blood and it spewed from his nose.

"He's bleeding out! I need an IV now. What's his blood type?"

"No time. Grab a type O bag and get it going. We're losing him."

1

Four days had passed since anyone had seen Tami Jacobs.

She worked the night shift as a server in a small barbecue restaurant just outside La Jolla. Tim Piggeneli, the owner, had been calling her cell phone and leaving messages, and after two days, his calls went straight to voicemail.

The apartment complex she lived in was known to house young men and women who had come to southern California in search of the life they had read about in books or seen in movies—the life that had died out with the older generation, supplanted by a new generation marked more by apathy than a love for the ocean.

Tim assumed she had enough money to live for a while and would surf and get stoned and have sex with the ever-present beach bums. In a few months she would come back, nearly broke and begging for her job. That sort of thing occurred often, and he usually accepted the kids back. He had been in the same position when he moved here almost thirty years before and wished desperately that someone had given him a helping hand when he'd needed it.

Tim sat in his office at the back of the restaurant. It was a tiny space cluttered with papers and empty boxes. The room was too small for the bookshelf against the wall filled with culinary books, and the guitar and amp stacked in the corner. He picked up the phone and called Tami's boyfriend, who also worked at the restaurant, and asked if he could make sure she was okay.

Two hours later, Jimmy Arnold pulled into a parking space at her apartment complex. He had been dating Tami off and on for over a year and wondered what he had done to make her ignore his calls. They'd had a domestic violence incident three months before, but that was old news. The district attorney's office had dropped the case when Tami refused to cooperate. It was a minor scuffle, Jimmy decided, and one the law had no business investigating.

He tried her cell phone again.

"This is Tami. You know what to do."

He went up to her apartment and knocked. He pounded on the door and shouted into the peephole. He waited patiently another five minutes and then made his way back downstairs.

The manager was in the first apartment, and Jimmy stood next to his car and smoked a cigarette before walking there. A pool was in front of the building, but it was empty, with garbage and old toys strewn in the deep end. Weeds had overtaken the small gardens and an old tricycle sat on the grass, the red and white paint faded and chipped.

He knocked, and a man with a massive belly hanging over his belt answered the door. He wore shorts, a T-shirt, and sandals.

"Hi, I'm Tami's boyfriend, in 2-F. She's not answering her door. You mind openin' it for me?"

"Can't do it."

The man went to shut his door, and Jimmy blocked it with his foot. "Hey, man, I just wanna make sure my girl's all right. She mighta passed out or somethin'."

"Sorry. Now take yer foot out."

"She smokes, man. If somethin's lit up there, ya know... could burn shit up. Come up with me. If she ain't in, we'll leave. Or can you at least call an ambulance or somethin' so they can check on her?"

The man appeared to think about it and then said, "Wait here."

A moment later, the man came back wearing sweats, and they headed to the second floor. He opened Tami's door with a master key and called out her name. No answer. They stepped inside.

The apartment was warm and all the windows were closed. It

smelled stale, like dust, and Jimmy saw half a sandwich on the coffee table.

The manager was saying something, but Jimmy walked down the hallway and looked into the bathroom. Her hair dryer was out, and a photo of him and his black lab was taped to the mirror. He stepped into the hallway and saw her bedroom door was shut.

"Hey, she ain't here," the manager said. "Let's go."

Jimmy ignored him, walked to the bedroom, and opened the door. The manager came over and looked in. He stood frozen a while, and then ran to the bathroom and vomited.

2

Police Chief Michael R. Harlow sat in a patio chair and raised a glass of orange juice to his lips. The balcony of the small apartment overlooked Ocean Beach Park, and he listened quietly to the waves lapping the shore.

Early in the morning, the only people out were joggers and dog walkers. The sun was a golden orb in the sky, and he slipped on his sunglasses so he could watch its rays reflect off the water.

"It's small," he said, "but the view makes up for it."

Stanton sat down in the chair next to him but didn't respond.

"Can I ask you something, Jonathan? You left homicide for your family, and now your family's gone. Why didn't you ever call me?"

"I don't know," Stanton said. "Just never seemed right."

"You could've pushed papers at a desk. You didn't have to quit."

"Melissa wouldn't have gone for that. She knew what it was like, the not having me around."

Harlow nodded. "How is she, anyway?"

"The divorce gets finalized next month. There's a waiting period. She's going to get married as soon as it goes through."

"I know. I got an invitation to the wedding." He shook his head and chuckled. "The balls on her."

Stanton leaned back and stretched his legs. The sunlight warmed his bare calves. "What is it you want, Mike? I know you're not here to hang out."

It was too quick, Harlow thought. He wanted to save the meat of the conversation for when Stanton was relaxed and comfortable. He wished like hell Melissa was still around.

"We're starting a new division. Cold-case homicide."

"I read about it in the *Union-Trib*. They had photos. I didn't think I'd ever see you shaking hands with a fed."

"You gotta cut deals in this day and age if you want to get things done. It's not like it was when you and I were coming up. Everybody's into this collaborative bullshit. Drug enforcement, the DA's office, hell, even the Navy's got a piece of this thing. But believe it or not, it's actually looking good. We got a nationwide database that searches prints, DNA, facial recognition... the feds let us use their labs in Virginia. It's not all bad."

"Sounds like you got everything you need."

"No, not everything." Harlow finished the rest of his juice and set the glass down. "I'd like you there, Jonathan. I need you there. The senior guys don't want it, and the greens can't do it. I need someone with experience. That's you."

Stanton looked down at a scar on his chest, just under the collarbone. His former partner, Eli Sherman, had put a couple of slugs into him two years prior.

"Yeah, I've got experience."

"What happened with Eli," Harlow said as calmly as possible, "was unavoidable. It was like lightning or a shark attack. No one could see it coming."

"He ate Sunday dinners at my house every week. Did I ever tell you that?"

"No." Harlow looked out over the water.

"The newspapers were right. If anybody should've seen it, it was me."

"Fuck the papers. They're bottom feeders. Your worst days are their good days. They live off misery. Nobody cares about them."

Harlow felt the blood hot in his face. He could still see the headline of the *Trib*:

KILLER EMPLOYED WITH SAN DIEGO
PD FOR TWELVE YEARS.

"I heard you're teaching at a community college. Is that really where you want to be?"

"I like teaching," Stanton said.

"You can make a difference here. The division's brand new. No ground rules yet. You could help set those. Bring closure to families."

"What's the criteria to screen a case?"

"Has to have no active leads and be older than one year. A lot of it'll be drug killings, deals gone bad, bank robberies, things like that. But some of it'll be different. Some of it'll be the real sick ones. Jon, you and I both know that if the case is open, *he's* still out there. He's still looking, and he's still watching, and he may not even know he's killing them himself, much less anyone around him. Not until he screws up. I need someone like you for those."

Stanton stared into the distance.

He's much darker, Harlow thought. *Darker and with sun-bleached hair. He's taken up surfing again.* "I wouldn't ask this from you if I had any other options. Lord knows you have every reason to say no and tell me to shove it. But this isn't about me."

"You've got everyone you need. I don't think I could bring anything to the table."

"That's not true." Harlow saw a young lady in skimpy shorts and watched her run by. "You got something, Jon. Whatever it is, it helps."

"Didn't help me with Eli."

Harlow leaned forward, taking a long while before speaking again. "Do you remember the Tapia case? The pedophile?"

"Yeah."

"You got him quick. What was it, like, three days? After you left the force, he was interviewed for an unrelated case. Insurance fraud or something. He said he had planned another victim that day. Had him picked out and everything. He was going to pick him up at his school early by wearing a fake badge and uniform. The same day, Jon. You stopped that. You can make a difference in people's lives. I know that's why you became a cop. That's all I'm saying."

"I'll think about it."

Harlow rose, pushing his sunglasses onto his forehead. “Call me. The unit gets up and running Monday morning.”

Harlow pulled his Mercedes out of its parking stall and turned onto Grand Avenue. A billboard near the stoplight featured a young girl in cutoffs and a see-through shirt. Her thumb was tucked into her waistband, and she was pulling her shorts down, revealing her hips and lower stomach. The ad was for vodka.

He dialed a number on his phone.

“Hey, Chief.”

“He’s going to be joining, Tommy. Make sure everybody’s on their best behavior. Any jokes or comments about Sherman or what happened and it’s your ass.”

“I understand. How’d you get him to come back?”

“Don’t worry about that.”

“Does he know what we’re doing?”

“I don’t think he would come if he did.”

3

Harlow sat at the large circular desk he'd had custom designed by a young sculptor making a name for himself in the San Diego art scene. Calls had been placed to the papers and a few blogs the day he bought it, every story emphasizing the fact that he had paid for the desk himself. The photo in the *Trib* showed the sculptor sitting at the desk with Harlow sitting on the edge, in the foreground.

The desk was clear except for a computer, a legal pad, and a box of files. The box had been pushed to the edge of the desk, as far away from him as possible. A large white label across the top read "TAMI CRYSTAL JACOBS" in red permanent marker.

His phone buzzed.

"Yes?"

"Chief, Melissa Stanton here to see you."

He paused. "Send her in."

His office door opened and a woman entered and sat across from him. She wore tight spandex capris and a Gold's Gym tank top. He rose and shut the door before sitting back down.

"I'd heard you were a personal trainer now. How's that going?" he asked.

"Make more money than I ever did in a uniform."

"I bet. How you been, Melissa?"

"I'm good. Not great, but good."

"I got your wedding invitation."

"Are you going to come?"

"No," Harlow said, leaning back in his chair.

"The mayor's going to be there. So is the lieutenant governor. My fiancé is in the legislature."

Harlow wondered whether she saw the struggle on his face as he realized why he had recognized the name on the invitation.

"Don't worry, Mike. If you decide to show up, I won't think less of you."

"Well, maybe. You know, for appearances' sake."

"Sure."

"So"—he crossed his legs—"what can I do for you?"

"Jonathan called me. He said you offered him a job yesterday."

"And?"

"And he intends to take it. Why can't you stay the hell away from him, Mike? You don't need him."

"I do need him. We're starting a new unit. I've got good cops here—don't get me wrong—but they don't have that one thing. That ability to get into the heads of these sonsabitches."

"You nearly got him killed last time."

A vein flared in Harlow's neck, but his face remained passive. "I did everything I could to protect him," he said. "Before and after."

"Oh, please. You had a psychopath as one of your detectives, and in all those years, you never saw it? How many brutality complaints did Eli have? Thirty? Forty? Jonathan only rode with him for a couple years. It was your responsibility."

She calmed herself and looked out the window. Harlow could see she was staring at a tree swaying slightly in the breeze, highlighted by a streak of black exhaust from a semi on the road.

"He talked to me about him once," she said. "He thought something was really off about Eli, and he didn't trust him anymore. That's why Eli shot him. Jonathan put it together."

Harlow put his elbows on the desk and made a dismissive motion with his hands. "The past is the past. What do you want from me?"

"I want you to be honest with him. You don't give a shit about giving closure to those families. This unit is for you to erase some black marks in your career for when you throw your hat in the ring for commissioner. You're using him."

"Nobody put a gun to his head," he said louder than he would've liked. "And what do you care? You left him when he was dying in the hospital."

"That's not true, and you know it."

"So it didn't get finalized until two years later. So what? You as good as left him in that hospital bed. You think he doesn't talk to me?"

A knock came at the door, and Tommy poked his head in.

"Chief, got somebody here from Channel Four wants to talk to you about the Cold Case Unit."

"I'll be right there."

Melissa rose and walked toward the door. "If you hurt him again, I'll make sure you're held accountable for it this time. I swear it."

As she walked out, Harlow stood and straightened his tie. He checked his underarms for pit stains and used a mirror he kept in his desk to make sure his hair looked good. He then walked toward the front of the station to meet the television crew.

4

It was 6:30 p.m. on a Saturday when Jonathan Stanton walked into the San Diego PD headquarters on Broadway. The building had recently been through a renovation, and the exterior looked clean and white, the tinted windows freshly washed. The surrounding area was grass and trees and clean sidewalks. Stanton didn't remember it being that clean a few years ago.

Night security checked him in and gave him a temporary employee pass to use on the elevators. He went to the fifth floor and turned down the hall.

The Cold Case Unit had been set up in five empty offices and a large conference room. The space recently housed two other units that had been moved a floor below.

A man in uniform nodded to him and looked down at the small box Stanton was holding. His framed degree, a PhD in psychology, lay on top. "You're Detective Stanton?"

"Yeah."

"Got your own office next to the chief. But he wasn't expectin' you till Monday."

"Just came to set up early. Didn't want to bother anyone."

The man mumbled something and then said, "Follow me." He led Stanton down the hall and past an enormous number of cubicles. They stopped at a large door with a keypad on the wall. "Combo's five twenty-one. Got it?"

"Yeah."

The door clicked open, and they went in. The offices were furnished with glass desks and leather furniture. Stanton looked into each one as they passed them. They had well-manicured plants in the corners and a piece of abstract art hanging behind each desk.

They walked through the conference room. Stanton counted

at least twenty high-backed leather chairs, and a large flat-screen TV at the front of the room was hooked up to a laptop. On the other side of the room was a floor-to-ceiling map of San Diego.

"Your office is that one there."

"Thanks."

The man left without saying anything more, and Stanton entered his new office. He placed the box on the desk and sat down. One wall was a thick window looking down on Broadway. Cars passed on the street below, and he watched them a long time.

A computer was on the edge of his desk against the wall and he turned it on. The screen flashed and prompted him to enter his password. He entered it, and an error message came up: "Password Expired. Please see the administrator for a new password."

He leaned back in the seat and closed his eyes. It felt strange being here, as if he had come into someone's home uninvited. Stanton began unpacking his box and hanging up his degrees. He took out two photos and put them on his desk: one of his sons, nine-year-old Mathew and four-year-old Jon, and one of his mother with his father, and his sister, Elizabeth. He stared at Elizabeth a long time.

His father had been a psychiatrist and was displeased when Stanton chose the police academy rather than going to medical school after earning his doctoral degree. A PhD and MD, his father had told him, would make him invaluable as a researcher to any number of universities lucky enough to have him.

The day he told his father he was joining the police academy, all his father said was, "Son, power, no matter how nobly it's applied, eventually corrupts."

After unpacking, he sat down. He looked out the window again, and a man with a vacuum stepped into the room. The man checked the garbage can and glanced passively at Stanton before exiting the room.

Stanton took a deep breath and decided to leave.

It was dark by the time Stanton pulled to a stop in front of a large house. Two stories with a wide lawn. A Mercedes parked in the driveway. Through the kitchen window, he saw a man, a woman, and two young boys eating dinner. They were talking and laughing, and the woman occasionally rose to get another dish or fill someone's glass.

He walked to the door and knocked, a large manila envelope under his arm. Melissa answered with a smile on her face that quickly faded when she saw him.

"Hi," he said.

"Hi."

He pulled out the envelope and handed it to her. "A few things. Some jewelry I found when I moved."

She looked through the envelope. "Jonathan, you can keep most of this stuff. I gave it to you."

"No, some of it's family heirlooms. It should be in your family."

Just then, a small head popped around the corner, and Mathew ran out and threw his arms around his father. Four-year-old Jon stood at the corner and didn't move.

"Hey, Dad," Mathew said.

"Hey, squirt. How was the game?"

"We lost by two goals."

"You'll get 'em next time."

Lance, Melissa's fiancé, came to the door and stood behind her, resting his hand softly on her shoulder. "How are you, Jonathan?"

"Fine. Thanks."

Lance cleared his throat. "So what's up?"

"He was just dropping off some of my stuff," Melissa said. "Why don't you join us for dinner?"

"Yeah!" Mathew shouted.

Lance said, "I'm sure your dad's got more important things to do than have dinner with us. Don't you, Jonathan?"

A long silence passed as the men stared at each other.

"Sure," Stanton said.

"Come on, Matty. Let's finish up supper. Good to see you, Jonathan."

"Yeah. I'll see you later, squirt."

"Bye, Dad."

Melissa stood at the door until they were out of view in the kitchen. She stepped outside, folding her arms though it wasn't cold.

"He misses you," she said.

"I know. I wish I could see him more."

"Jon Junior misses you too. He just doesn't know how to show it."

"He's angry with me. He thinks this is my fault."

"That's not true."

After a brief silence, Stanton said, "I'd like to take them more, Mel. I don't see them enough."

"They're going to have a new life. Lance is going to be a big part of that life, and they need to spend a lot of time with him. I think every other weekend is appropriate."

Stanton looked at his shoes. They were worn and hadn't been polished in a long time. He noticed that Melissa was barefoot and had painted her toenails black.

"I should go. Kiss the boys for me."

"Jonathan," she said hurriedly as he turned to leave, "I know I can't talk you out of that job. But be careful."

"I will. Thanks."

As Stanton got into his car, he looked through the window at the family having dinner; they were laughing and joking around again. He started his car and pulled away.

5

When Stanton walked into police headquarters on Monday morning, he stopped at a vending machine and got a Diet Coke. He wore old khakis and a blazer he had dug out of his closet. After work, he would have to go to the Fashion Depot and pick up a couple of suits.

He went to the fifth floor, which was buzzing with activity. Detectives with their suit coats off and their sleeves rolled up ran around making demands of assistants and secretaries. A few uniforms were wandering around, rubbing elbows with the detectives and swapping war stories.

He walked to the large door and entered the code. It clicked open, and he stepped inside. The space was quiet, unlike the rest of the floor. He could hear someone speaking in hushed tones on a telephone in one of the offices.

"Jonathan!" Harlow shouted from across the hall. The chief came over and shook his hand. "I'm so glad you said yes. We're going to do some real work here, Jon. God's work. Come on. Let me introduce you to everyone."

The conference table had an ample supply of bagels and coffee spread over it. Three men and a woman sat at the table, speaking quietly with each other. They stopped and looked at Stanton when he walked in. Harlow motioned to a seat near the head of the table, and Stanton sat down.

The chief took his position at the head and quietly glanced over everyone. "I can't tell you how happy it makes me to see these faces around this table. You five are the best at what you do. I've never served with better cops in my career. There'll be more coming, but you were the ones I wanted, the ones I needed right away. I know this isn't grade school, but I want to go around the table and have you introduce yourselves. Where you're from, family, all that bullshit that you would have to get out in small talk. Let's start with you, Chin."

An Asian man with glasses and a finely cut suit straightened in his seat and said, "I'm Chin Ho. I'm from San Francisco PD. Got transferred down for this unit. Originally from Korea. I have a partner, and he's moved down with me too. He's a lawyer."

Harlow looked at the next man, tall and black with an iPad on his lap.

"Nathan Sell. San Diego PD. Divorced, no kids."

The third man, white and overweight, wore a black suit and white shirt.

"Philip Russell, FBI. On loan to the unit. Single, no kids."

The last was a slim woman with shoulder-length hair.

"Jessica Turner, LAPD. Single, one child."

Stanton cleared his throat. "Jonathan Stanton. I'm... I guess I'm with San Diego now. Going through a divorce. Two sons."

"Good," Harlow said. "Now we're all friends." He reached for a bagel and placed it on a napkin in front of him. "I've talked to each of you individually about what we're doing and what's expected of you. If you have any questions, now's the time to ask."

Nathan raised a finger, and Harlow nodded to him.

"Who's the unit commander, Chief?"

"I am. That's why you're set up next to my office. I want everything reported and run through me."

Jessica asked, "What's the budget for this unit?"

"As much as we need to get the job done. We got grants from the city, state, and federal governments. But like I said, everything goes through me. No one buys so much as a paper clip without me knowing it. But I'm not going to micromanage. Submit a report of what you need directly to Tommy, and as long as it's reasonable, I'll have the money to you within one day. I'm putting a lot of trust in each of you, and I expect you to take that trust seriously." He looked around the table. "Anything else?"

"How are cases assigned?" Stanton asked.

Harlow shifted in his seat. "I'll pair the appropriate case with the right investigator. You don't start another case until the one assigned is solved or it's dead. Either way, it then shifts from this unit to archives."

Clever, Stanton thought. Every year the unit's cases would shrink, and people would assume it was because they were being solved.

"Anything else?" Harlow looked at each person. "Good. Let's start with assignments." He pressed a button on a sleek gray phone set up on the conference table.

"Yeah, Chief?"

"Tommy, get me the assignments."

"You got it."

While they waited for Tommy, the group quietly read emails or checked phone messages. Jessica took a cup of coffee and asked if Stanton wanted one, but he declined.

"He's Mormon," Harlow interjected.

"Oh," Jessica said. "That's interesting. Why the Diet Coke?"

"It's a gray area in the church," Stanton said.

The door opened, and Thomas Sanchez walked in with several uniforms carrying boxes and thick three-ring binders. They spread everything on the table, shoving the food out of the way, and left the room with a nod to Harlow.

"Chin." Harlow passed two binders over. "Todd Grover. He was a liquor store owner that was robbed in oh four. They got off three rounds during the robbery and one hit him in the neck. He died in the hospital. Only thing he gave us was that they were African American, young, and one had a tattoo of some sort on his hand."

Harlow pointed at one of the boxes. "Nathan, that's you. Alberto Dominguez Jovan. He was leaving a strip club and flirting with one of the dancers in the parking lot when some other patrons began talking shit to him. He asked them what their problem was, and they showed him with two slugs in the head. Got at least twenty witnesses and two suspects that went nowhere."

"Got it, Chief," Nathan said.

"Jessica, this is yours." He handed her a binder and a small box with a DVD and a folder in it. "James Damien Neary. Stabbed in the heart while walking home from a Walmart. He got back to his apartment and, for whatever reason, didn't call an ambulance. Died there. No leads."

Harlow pointed at a box at the end of the table. "Philip, you got Rodrigo Carrillo. Gang member. Shot to death sitting on his porch in a drive-by."

There was one final box, and Harlow hesitated before putting his hands on it. He grabbed it by the sides and pulled it close, staring at the name.

"Jonathan, you got Tami Jacobs. Twenty-three-year-old waitress. It's... it's pretty bad."

He pushed the box to Stanton and then looked at everyone again before standing. "All right, we've got a lot of work to do. Tommy's your point man on everything. Once a week, we have meetings on Monday morning to go over our cases. You may be working them alone, but you're not alone. We've got a brain trust on these cases." Harlow glanced at his watch. "I'm not expecting miracles, but I am expecting results, even if it's nothing more than declaring the case dead and moving it to the basement. Now, do what I know each of you is capable of doing, and let's have some of these bastards stay in our concrete hotels, courtesy of the California taxpayer. Our system's burdened by too many obstacles and loopholes as it is, but we can make it better and give our kids the future they deserve."

Stanton glanced around the table and saw that no one had noticed the prepared stump speech, one intended to be given at a lectern before an audience.

When the chief had gone, everyone gathered their materials and headed to their respective offices. Stanton stayed, got a bagel, and spread warm cream cheese over it with a plastic knife before heading to his office.

Jessica threw away her paper plate and napkin in a trash bin in the hallway. "Sorry about the coffee."

"It's okay." He noticed for the first time that she was wearing one pearl earring in her right ear and nothing in her left. Before he could ask her about it, she walked back to her office and shut the door.

Stanton finished eating and took the Jacobs box into his office. He placed it on the desk and pulled out the first three-ring binder.

6

Stanton read that Tami Jacobs had originally been from Iowa. Her parents were both custodians, one at a high school and the other at a grammar school. Her mother committed suicide when Tami was nine years old, and her father died eight years later, on the night of Tami's high school graduation. He was driving drunk and careened into oncoming traffic. He survived for six days in the hospital, with massive brain swelling, before the family decided they needed to cut life support.

She had two siblings somewhere, brothers. Stanton wondered whether they felt the tug of guilt in their bellies from not being able to save her. Brothers were often the *de facto* protectors of the only female in the family.

There was a photo of her with her family when she was in her teens. She wore a University of Iowa sweatshirt and was hugging someone Stanton guessed was her grandfather. Short blond hair and deep blue eyes were set in a thin face that seemed to constantly be smiling. Her legs were long, and she had slim hips. Stanton knew instantly why she had come to California.

He didn't need to look at her bio to know she was an aspiring actress, waiting tables until her big break. At some point, the cold detachment of reality had fallen on her, and she realized that even if she made it, it was still failure. Hollywood was a zero-sum game.

She was an A student in high school but moved to West Hollywood after her father's death. No college transcripts were in the files.

Tami volunteered on the weekends at a senior center. In the box were printouts of emails she had written to her grandfather in Iowa and some from the patients she had befriended at the center. He pulled out one of the emails. He hesitated before looking at it, as though he needed to ask permission first.

i hope you are doing good poppy! im great here. the beach is next to my house and i surf all the time! I miss you guys. i wish i could come home and visit but its pretty crazy with auditions and everything :(

but i'll come as soon as i can. i have a audition tomorrow for a commercial for lotion. its not much money but it would be my first commercial!!!

wish me luck poppy! tell everyone hi for me!

loves and kisses

After a year in West Hollywood, she moved to a cheap apartment in La Jolla. That was where the monster found her.

Stanton checked her criminal record and found twelve arrests in a three-year period: three for driving while intoxicated, six for public intoxication, and three for disorderly conduct in a public place. Stanton knew from his uniform days and a stint on the DWI squad that for every DWI, there were at least seventy nights that she drove drunk but wasn't caught. With three on her record, she was likely a bona fide alcoholic.

She had a boyfriend: James Christopher Arnold. Stanton called the two phone numbers listed for him and both times got a message letting him know the number had been disconnected. There was a brief official statement taken on the day her body was discovered, but it was less than three paragraphs and didn't give any specific details about her life.

He flipped through some of her mail: credit card statements, bank statements, and utility bills. He came to a copy of her work schedule printed from an online calendar and looked at the day of her death. She had been scheduled to work that morning, but the rest of the days that week were all evening shifts. Alcoholics were notoriously bad at morning shifts, and waitresses' schedules were usually flexible. If she was working that morning, it meant she had to be somewhere that evening.

The homicide report was twelve pages with a fifteen-page supplemental report. The case had been worked by two detectives, both under thirty years old. The necessary information in the report made up about two pages. The other ten or so were filler, an attempt to cover up the fact that they had nothing to go on. There was no mention that Tami was to work the morning shift the day she was killed.

Stanton pulled out the first photo from forensics, and it sent a shock through his body. He dropped it and looked away. It had been too long, and he hadn't prepared properly. He looked out the window. A taxi was waiting on the curb outside, so he watched it a few moments before turning back to the picture. He stared at it and then took out the coroner's report and placed them side by side.

The brutality of the killing made him think of an animal attack, and one line in the coroner's report stuck out: "Feces found in the subject's esophagus matched the feces found on the bedsheets."

He pushed the coroner's report away and stared at the photograph a long while before putting it back in the box.

Stanton went outside and decided to walk around the block. The weather was hot, and sweat began to form on his forehead. A little café was nearby, and he went there, sat down in a booth, and ordered a turkey sandwich with gazpacho.

A couple was sitting near him. They were older and weren't speaking to each other. The man was missing a finger on his right hand, and his nails had grit underneath them. His dentures were lying on a napkin, and he gummed some soup as his wife ate a thick hamburger. She looked at Stanton and then away.

"I forgot to ask if you want anything to drink," the waitress said as she placed his sandwich on the table.

"No, water's fine." Stanton stared absently out at the street, watching people walk by, enveloped in their own lives and oblivious to those around them. Tami had been that way.

He paid for his food without eating and left the café.

7

Stanton drove to Interstate 8 and headed northwest to La Jolla. It was evening, but the sun was still out, and the freeways were not as packed as they would have been an hour earlier.

He had read everything in the box and looked at most of the forensic photographs. A video was in there too, but he couldn't watch it yet. The coroner's report was detailed, even to a fault. Stanton knew the pathologist that had performed the autopsy had a daughter Tami's age.

There was still some daylight left when Stanton pulled to a stop in front of the Ocean Vista Apartments. The coroner had placed Tami's death at around one in the morning, at least four days before she was discovered by her boyfriend. Maggots had been found at the scene, excellent for determining time of death, as the incubation period in the egg and the hatching process were the same length of time from one specimen to the next.

It would have been better if Stanton had gone there at one in the morning and seen the apartment as the boyfriend had seen it that night. But it was currently rented, and he didn't want to impose on the tenants any more than necessary.

Some mention was made of a manager having found the body along with the boyfriend, but when Stanton knocked at the leasing office, which was just one of the apartments, a woman answered and said the previous manager had moved out. Stanton walked upstairs to 2-F and knocked on the door. A slim male in cutoff shorts answered, an unlit cigarette dangling from his mouth.

"Yeah?"

"I'm Detective Stanton with the San Diego Police Department. I think we spoke on the phone." Stanton had called ahead and made sure the tenants understood the police were coming.

They would be more at ease when they had the opportunity to hide anything they might not have wanted him to see.

"Oh yeah." He lit the cigarette. Stanton guessed it was an attempt to cover the strong odor of marijuana pouring out of the apartment. "So you just, like, wanna look around, right?"

"Yeah."

He opened the door. "All right, cool."

A young girl, maybe eighteen, was on the couch. Her eyes were rimmed red and she had a piercing through her nose. She stared absently at Stanton but didn't say anything.

"So, why you wanna look around again?"

Stanton ignored him and began to his left, behind the door. He ran his eyes along the baseboards and then up the wall. The glass kitchen table had only two chairs. *The Anarchist Cookbook* was open on a page showing how to tie a grenade to a fence with a piece of rope so that the pin would pull when the fence gate opened. Out of the corner of his eye, Stanton saw the boy glance at the girl; they had forgotten to hide the book.

The kitchen was small, and a microwave was bolted above an oven.

The day the police arrived, half a sandwich had been found on a coffee table, with large bite marks that didn't match the victim's. The killer had made himself a meal before leaving.

Stanton ran his eyes past the kitchen into the living room. The carpet was tattered, and cigarette burns adorned it like spots on a leopard. He noticed the sliding glass door. The frame looked worn, an off shade of gray. But the lock was new chrome.

"Did you guys replace the lock on the sliding door?"

"No," the male said. "Why?"

"Is that the same lock as when you moved in?"

"Yup."

"How long have you lived here?"

"'Bout seven months."

Stanton walked down the hallway and the male followed him. They went into the bathroom, and Stanton glanced quickly at the bathtub. He then moved to the bedroom. The door was open, and he stood in the entryway.

A single bed and a nightstand, clothes strewn on the floor, one window overlooking the parking lot. He sat on the bed. The closet was full of sneakers and tank tops. A few posters of women in bikinis and others of Bob Marley were nailed up. No stains were on the carpets, other than from cigarettes, and nothing was on the walls or ceiling. The room now held only ghosts of what had happened.

Stanton sighed. "Thanks for letting me look around."

"No worries. Hey, why were you wanting to look around anyway?"

"Someone came through here once that I wanted to see. But they're gone."

8

Stanton went into a little barbecue shack as soon as they opened at nine in the morning. He had been waiting in the car for twenty minutes, watching surfers on the beach pack up their things and head to their day jobs.

The shack was much bigger than the exterior let on, with at least twenty tables and a few booths. A large bar stood at one end and the kitchen sat to the right of the entrance. The bar was dark with few windows, most of the illumination provided by neon beer signs throughout the space.

"Can I help you?" a young girl asked.

"I'm looking for the owner."

"Tim? He's in the kitchen. I'll get him."

Stanton sat at the bar. He ran his fingers along the top and felt the notches from drunks slamming bottles down too hard. A small bowl of peanuts was next to him with a bottle cap inside.

"How's it going?" Tim was tall, with a prodigious belly and thick arms. He towered over Stanton and was wiping his hands on a rag. He threw it over his shoulder.

"Good."

"I'm the owner. What can I do for you?"

"Jonathan Stanton. I'm with the San Diego Police Department. I'm doing some follow-up on Tami Jacobs."

"I smoke a joint in the back, and you roll up in minutes. Beautiful young girl's raped and killed, and you can't find who did it?"

Stanton saw the anger in the man's face and said, "The department's got its head up its rear most of the time. That's why I'm here. I'm gonna find who did this." The cadence and volume of his voice matched Tim's.

"I hope you do, but I ain't got that much to tell you. Police already talked to me when it happened."

"I know. But there was something I wanted to ask you about."

"What?"

"You had her on the schedule to work a shift the morning she was killed. I don't see her as a morning person. Did she always work them?"

"No, her shift was nights. If she was working morning, means she traded shifts with somebody."

"Do you know who?"

"Been too long, man. Couldn't say."

"Any way you could find out?"

He folded his arms. "I don't keep schedules for longer than a few months. Probably deleted it."

"Could you check anyway?"

"Yeah, I guess I could."

Stanton placed his card on the table. "Thanks. Please call me if you find that name."

9

The body had stiffened to the consistency of a two-by-four.

It lay in the sand, one arm up, reaching for help that had never come. The surf rolled in on the beach, and the sun was rising above the horizon, painting the ocean a soft hue of orange.

A group of sand crabs were crawling over the corpse, and Maverick "Hunter" Royal kicked them off with his wingtips. One fell near him, and he crushed it. A blue gelatin splashed up over his pant leg. "Shit."

"Hunter, what the hell you doin' here?"

Detective Daniel Childs walked next to Royal and folded his massive arms, which he liked to show off with skin-tight shirts, seemingly not noticing the body two feet away.

"Danny boy," Royal said. Then he sang, "Oh Danny boy, oh boy."

"Cut the shit, Hunter. What's going on?"

"Just doing some reporting for the fine people of San Diego."

"You're not a reporter. You're a damn parasite. And how'd you find out about this so fast?"

"I got my sources. And a hundred thousand daily readers disagree. I am a reporter."

"Piss off. And if you messed with my crime scene, I'm taking you to the cage for the night."

He held up his hands. "I didn't touch anything."

Royal walked away, just far enough for Childs to think he was leaving, then turned toward the body. He pulled out a small camera and began taking photos. There was a particularly good one of Childs snapping on latex gloves as he examined the victim's head up close. *Even if he is a prick*, Royal thought, *I'm still gonna make him look good.*

He took about twenty photographs and turned to leave. Two uniforms leaned against a cruiser next to his Viper. One of them ran his hand over the hood, leaving prints, and looked inside the sports car, checking the door to see if it was unlocked. Royal would have to pay back that little disrespect. Maybe make something up about the officer getting sex from hookers instead of taking them in. They all did it anyway, he figured.

When he got closer to his car, he saw that one of the uniforms was Henry Oleander. Royal nodded to him, and Oleander said something to the other officer, causing him to walk away and go farther down the beach.

"What's up, Hunter?"

"Henry. How's the missus?"

"Good. We're having our second kid soon."

"Congrats."

"Yeah," he said, looking over to Childs. "So, you want a line?"

"What've you got?"

"How much?"

"Something I can sell to the *Times* or *Examiner*, thousand bucks. Something I gotta put on my blog, hundred bucks."

"There was a murder couple years back. Young girl named Tami Jacobs. You remember it?"

"Yeah," Royal said. He had paid five hundred dollars to be let into the apartment to snap a few photographs before the medical examiner's body movers took the corpse. It'd been a shit storm when the San Diego PD saw photos of their crime scene all over the web the next day.

"Been assigned to the Cold Case Unit. Guess who's the detective? Jonathan Stanton."

"No shit?"

"No shit."

Royal pulled out a wad of cash from his pocket. He gave five hundred-dollar bills to Henry and said, "Five now. Twenty more if you can get me the files of everyone in Cold Case."

"How would I do that?"

"Figure it out. You're a smart boy. They gotta eat sometime, right? They don't live in their offices, and I bet they don't take their personnel files with them when they leave."

"Yeah, I guess so. I'll see what I can do."

"Good." He slapped the officer's arm on the stripe.

Royal climbed into his Viper and turned the key. The engine roared to life. He peeled out of the parking lot and blew a kiss to Childs as the detective yelled something about impounding his car.

10

Stanton finished reading all the emails they had gathered from Tami's account. She'd kept a MySpace page, never bothering to update to Facebook. There were photos of her with different groups of people, mostly at bars and on the beach. One was at Mardi Gras in New Orleans. A slow country song that Stanton didn't recognize was playing on her page, and he listened to it once before muting his computer.

Already afternoon, and Stanton had been in the office for seven hours. He called Melissa to speak to the boys, but there was no answer. The voicemail said to leave a message for Melissa and Lance Jarvis. He hung up.

Jessica walked by the office and glanced in. She stopped and took a step back, poking her head through the doorway. "Hey," she said.

"Hey."

She came into his office and collapsed on a chair with a loud sigh, looking out the windows. "Nice view."

"It's not bad. How's Neary going?"

"Not good. Totally random from what I can tell. Talked to a girlfriend he had that said he wouldn't've hurt anybody. No criminal history, no major debts, nothing." She saw his PhD on the wall. "I heard you had a doctorate. What are you doing here?"

Stanton shrugged, lifted the Jacobs box, and placed it on the floor. "Don't let it shock you," he said.

"What?"

"Neary. The randomness of it. Some people only want to add chaos without getting anything in return."

"I've worked Robbery-Homicide in LA for two years. Randomness doesn't shock me. It's meaninglessness that does. Whoever did this did something horrific and against his interests that probably didn't even bring him any pleasure. I don't understand it. And you didn't answer my question. Most cops daydream about an exit strategy, and you've got one hanging on your wall."

"It's not as simple as—"

His phone rang. He answered it and heard the front-desk receptionist's voice tell him he had a call from a Tim at the Barbeque Pit.

"Send it through." He paused. "Hello?"

"Hi, is this Jon?"

"Yeah."

"Jon, Tim, from the Barbeque Pit."

"What can I do for you, Tim?"

"Well, turns out I did have a schedule from back then. Must've hung on to it 'cause I thought you guys would want it, but no one asked me for it."

"I'll send someone down to pick it up."

"It's an Excel spreadsheet. I just emailed it to you."

"Thanks."

"All right, man. You find that cocksucker, you pop him once for me."

He hung up, turned to his computer, and then remembered he didn't have a new password yet to log in to his email from his office. The network administrator was on vacation.

"Do you mind if I check my email on your computer?"

"Sure," Jessica said.

Her office was easily half the size of his, with no windows. But the walls were covered in photos. One of a young boy in a soccer uniform, standing with one foot on a ball.

"Your boy?"

"Yup." She closed a few windows on her screen. "All yours."

Stanton logged in to the San Diego PD server and went to his account. He had two hundred thirty-seven unread messages. Most were updates, questions about holiday and overtime pay, and announcements for birthdays and retirements. Tim's was at the top of the list, and he clicked on it.

In the body of the email was a name: Kelly Ann Madison. Next to that was a phone number. Stanton opened the attachment and saw the schedule. It covered a period of three months, and Tami had worked only evenings. The day she had been killed was the only time she was scheduled for a morning shift. Kelly had been scheduled to take her evening shift.

"My sister watches him during the day," Jessica said.

Stanton turned to her. "I'm sorry?"

She was sitting on the edge of her desk, staring at the boy's photo. "I was just thinking out loud."

"Must be hard not to see him as much as you'd like."

"It is. I think you said you had some?"

"Two boys."

Stanton put Kelly's phone number into his phone's contact list and rose to leave. "Thanks for letting me use your computer."

"No problem. Hey, I'm starving. Do you want to grab something to eat? Maybe we can swap notes on our cases or something."

"I can't right now. How about a rain check?"

"Yeah." She looked at the floor. "I was just thinking we might both be hungry. No big deal."

"Are you free tomorrow?"

"Sure."

"Tomorrow, then."

"Sure, tomorrow."

Stanton walked to his office and shut the door. He pulled up Kelly Ann Madison on his phone and dialed the number.

11

Stanton sat in his car in the parking lot of the Westfield UTC mall. Night had fallen, quieting the city. The high-pitched squeal of a siren would occasionally break the silence then trail off, and the silence would return, only to be broken again a little later.

His window was down, and the air was warm and smelled slightly of exhaust. But a breeze was blowing, so he leaned back and let it blow over his neck and down his collar.

A few people left Nordstrom and walked to an Escalade parked near him. They were females, teenagers, white and rich with empty looks on their faces. They seemed the type whose boredom would drive them to do things their parents had tried to bribe them out of because of their station in life.

The driver reminded him of a case from long before, another rich young white girl who had begun dating an Hispanic ex-con. She had met him through correspondence while he was incarcerated at the California State Prison in Los Angeles County. When she was at a party at his house, he'd allowed all the partygoers to gang-rape her on the futon in the basement.

"Detective?"

Stanton turned to see a young girl standing by his car, far enough away that her face was only shadow and her hair glowed under the parking lot lamps.

"Yes."

"Can I see your badge?"

"Sure." He reached into his pocket, brought out his shield, and offered it to her through the window.

She approached close enough to look at it. "Okay. Thanks."

"No problem."

He stepped out of his car and shut the door. Leaning back against the driver's side, he took out a small notepad and a pen.

His iPad was far superior at organizing his notes, but there was something about the paper and pen that he needed. When he saw a full pad and had to go to another one, that told him progress was being made and the notes would somehow lead him to what he was looking for. Sometimes when he went through them again, it felt as if he were using a map rather than just wandering aimlessly.

"So," she said, "you wanted to talk about Tami?"

"Yes. Do you remember much about her?"

"Yeah, she was cool. She was real sweet, ya know? Like if I needed a ride or to borrow some money, she would always do it. Even if I called her at, like, three in the morning, she would gimme a ride." She pulled out a package of cigarettes and lit one, let the tobacco burn and crinkle, and moved a strand of hair away from her face with her pinkie.

"What would you guys talk about?"

"I dunno. Stuff. She really liked surfing, so she was always talking about that. She really wanted to go to Australia and surf. She said she was saving money for it."

"She had a boyfriend named James Arnold. The numbers we had for him are disconnected. You have any idea where he is?"

"Oh yeah. You don't know? Jimmy died."

"When?"

"Like... maybe three months after those other detectives talked to me."

Stanton's pen stopped moving, and he lowered the pad. "What other detectives?"

"The two that came and talked to me after she was... after she passed."

"Do you remember their names?"

"No, and they didn't gimme their cards. I thought that was weird 'cause cops always leave their card, right?"

"Can you describe them?"

"Um, one was Mexican, and the other was a white dude. Kinda cute. I think he was flirting with me."

Stanton flipped to an earlier page in his notepad, where

he had written some names. “Francisco Hernandez and Taylor Stewart?”

“I guess. I really don’t remember.”

Stanton put the pad in his pocket and asked, “Is there anything you can tell me that can help me find who did this, Kelly?”

“I don’t think so. I just knew her from work, ya know?”

“Did she have any other friends that you know about?”

“Not really. She said she didn’t like other girls. But there was this guy she was kinda hanging out with. She didn’t want Jimmy to know about it ’cause he was real jealous. I think the detectives already talked to him.”

“Do you remember his name?”

“No, but I know he was a cop, if that helps.”

12

Stanton awoke and felt his sweaty shirt clinging to him. He sat up in bed and pushed himself against the headboard, feeling the firmness of the wood against his back. A glass of water sat on the nightstand next to him, and he took a long drink, the warm water beginning to taste like dust. The clock said 11:13 p.m.

He rose and put on sweatpants and a zip-up Nike jacket. His sneakers were under the bed, and he pulled them out and slowly slipped them onto his feet. There was something in the purposefulness of it that he wanted to feel right then, but he wasn't sure why.

Sleep wouldn't be coming tonight—at least not for another four or five hours. He took a diet cola out of the fridge and headed to his car.

The city was lit neon blue in the darkness, and the streets were still crowded from restaurants and bars and clubs that catered to nighthawks and the young. Palm trees lined both sides of the road, appearing like giant dandelions against the backdrop of the moonlit sky.

He remembered the city from when he was young. They had traveled a lot in his youth, his father working his residency for two years in Montana and two years in Buffalo before moving to Seattle. He liked Seattle for the first month he was there. After that, the gray skies and constant dampness discouraged him, and he grew depressed. His fifth-grade teacher recommended medication, but his father, a psychiatrist, refused.

"Only as a last resort," he would tell his mother when she pleaded with him to put their only son on antidepressants.

The depression eventually grew so pronounced he could no longer get out of bed. They used medication, but it only numbed him further.

His parents coddled him, threatened him, bribed him, and

finally attempted to physically move him out of bed in the mornings. Occasionally, he was in bed for seventy hours or more at a time. He had lost so much weight his mother was concerned he would starve to death, so she would bring cake and chips and steaks to his room and feed him while she spoke about ordinary things that had happened during the day.

His father would try to hold therapy sessions but could never get him to open up enough to help him. Eventually, his father left him alone.

The only comfort Stanton found was in his friend Stacey. She was Mormon and saw his pain when she came to visit him once to bring his homework. She invited him out to "family home evening," and for whatever reason, he went. The family was sweet and welcoming and did not judge or care where he had come from or what he had done. It was the only glimmer of happiness he had in those times.

His parents had to travel a long road toward accepting that their son had mental health issues, and Stanton remembered that night clearly. He was awakened by something and saw his mother sitting on the edge of the bed, softly crying into her hands. His father sat next to her, his arm around her shoulders. The next day, his father began applying for jobs in California. He found one in the ER at UC San Diego Medical Center.

His father was the staff psychiatrist for the emergency room from nine at night until seven in the morning. He evaluated and decided the proper course of treatment for anyone coming through the ER who was determined to need a psych eval. Primarily, it was the homeless. They would be let out onto the streets and told to come back at certain times for their medications, but none of them were able to keep track of when to return. The next week or month, they would be back in the ER because they had walked into traffic or jumped off a building or were beaten up or stabbed or shot. Dr. Stanton had once told his son, "You know the world is truly going to hell when the mental institutions are closed and the prisons are full."

Stanton's mother enrolled her son in surfing lessons the week they moved to San Diego. The sand and sunshine and crisp blue water revived him, and his mother told people he was like a different child. But the scar of that severe depression never left him, and he carried sadness in his eyes for the rest of his life.

Stanton arrived at his office shortly before midnight. The security guard was dozing and didn't bother to feign attention when he saw him. Stanton took the elevator and then regretted not taking the stairs. The exertion would've helped him, and he needed to try to exhaust himself so he could get some sleep later in the morning.

Nathan Sell was in his office, and Stanton nodded to him as he made his way down the hall to his own office. Jessica was still there as well, watching DVDs of recorded interviews.

"Hey"—she paused the DVD—"what are you doing here so late?"

"Couldn't sleep." Stanton stepped into her office and sat down across from her. The chair was thickly cushioned and warm, and he realized how much he would've liked to be able to sleep. "I didn't know there were any witnesses."

"Just over twenty people were in the area. No one saw or heard anything. Couple of 'em look like they know more than they're telling us. I'm going to hit them up tomorrow." She took two ibuprofen from her drawer and washed them down with a Crystal Light. "How's it going for you?"

"I need to talk to the original detectives that worked the case. A few things aren't adding up."

"Like what?"

"They talked to a coworker that they never put in their reports."

"Hmm... Well, everybody's got their own style."

"I guess." Stanton hesitated about telling her the victim might have been seeing a cop. Police were ravenously protective of their own, and he didn't want to seem as though he was smearing a cop's reputation if he didn't have to.

"Can I ask you something, Jonathan? Something personal?"

"Sure."

She played with her pencil, tapping it lightly against a stapler on her desk. "I knew Eli. We'd worked a case together, a kidnapping where the perp came down here from Watts. In that time that he was your partner, did you ever—"

"No."

"Me neither. I know they say psychopaths can be charming, but I always thought if one was in my life, I would know. I would just know."

"How long did you know him?"

"It wasn't for very long. Just work related." She bit her lip. "But he asked me out."

"What did you say?"

"I said no. But not because I wasn't attracted to him. I was literally just too busy at the time. If I'd had fewer cases, I would've taken him up on it. When I found out what he did to those girls... I can't tell you how sick I felt. I thought about quitting the force."

"You have nothing to feel sick over. There was a part of him that was human. That was the part that was likeable and friendly. But there was the other part too. It was a fight for him, but it had nothing to do with you." He stood up. "I better get going."

As he left, he heard the DVD come back on, a male voice adamantly denying having seen anything. He turned to look at her, but she was already focused on the screen.

13

Stanton left the office at three in the morning and was back at nine. He began placing calls. Taylor Stewart was in Iraq on active duty, frontline infantry in the army's third infantry division. Stanton called the local recruiting office and got the numbers for Army Investigative Command and the local JAG office. Both offices said they couldn't help him unless he had an official subpoena or writ. He knew the army ignored writs and subpoenas from state judges. It would have to be a federal judge, and he would need a good reason. So far, he had none, other than a name left off a report.

Francisco Hernandez was different. Human resources told Stanton that Hernandez was still with the police department but had been transferred to Vice a year before. Stanton contacted the section chief at Vice and was told a meeting could be set up, but it would take some time and would have to be outside the city.

He put his feet up on the desk and noticed the scuffs along the edges of his shoes. They reminded him that he still needed to buy a couple of suits, and he suddenly felt awkward in his worn-out sports coat.

A thought kept recurring to him as he sat there: what if Eli was responsible for this girl as well?

Eli Sherman's victims had been young blondes and brunettes, but the killing pattern didn't match. Stanton knew firsthand that Eli didn't like blood. Eli had once nearly fainted at the scene of a suicide where the victim had shot himself with a 12-gauge shotgun. Eli's two known victims had been strangled and the bodies covered, indicating a last vestige of shame and guilt.

Stanton had not thought about Eli Sherman in a long time, and all the events and feelings he had buried came rushing back, as if a dam had been broken and a flood was enveloping everything in its path. He remembered Saturday morning racquetball at the gym. Eli was so competitive that Stanton had to let him win occasionally so it wouldn't ruin his day. After their workouts, they would shower and talk about women and kids and where they wanted their lives to take them.

Stanton also remembered the night Eli had nearly killed him.

They had finished a long day working a drive-by shooting. Stanton was in a fight with Melissa. Like most of their arguments, it was over something so minor he couldn't remember what it was.

Eli's home was a large two-story house in the suburbs. He had gotten a deal on it because the elderly woman that owned it had no children to leave it to. She wanted a quick infusion of cash to spend traveling to the places she'd always wanted to see.

Stanton was going to spend the night at his partner's place to give Melissa a chance to cool off. They drank soda and ate steak and potatoes. Eli, always respectful of Stanton's beliefs, never drank alcohol or swore in front of him. He even refused to drink coffee, and Stanton always appreciated him for that small courtesy.

When they had finished their meal, they watched a boxing match on television and then went to bed. Stanton was to sleep in the guest bedroom, but there were no pillows on the bed. He went upstairs to check the hall closet.

Stanton pulled out two pillows and was about to shut the door when he noticed something tucked behind a neatly folded quilt. He pulled it out: red silk panties. Stanton grinned, about to tease his partner that a woman had forgotten her underwear. Then he noticed another pair and third pair behind that one. He pulled them all out. Twelve total. They had been covering something, and Stanton picked it up. It was a little tin box, black with a design of a flower on top. Inside were photographs, a necklace, and a ring. The photos were of women with pale, detached faces, crying into the camera. Police could identify only two of the victims. They were the ones whose deaths Eli would later be prosecuted and sent to prison for, narrowly avoiding the death penalty through a plea bargain.

When Stanton turned around, Eli was behind him, wet and naked from the shower, a .40-caliber Smith & Wesson in his hand. He raised the gun and shot twice without hesitation. The impact threw Stanton backward and over the balcony railing onto the main floor. The fall knocked the breath out of him, and blood cascaded out of his chest and onto the carpet. He tasted the warm thickness of it in his mouth and began to choke.

Eli rushed down the stairs.

Stanton, unable to breathe, saw his holster hanging from a chair in the kitchen with his suit coat. Blood poured down his legs as he rose and sprinted for it. As soon as he felt the weight of steel in his hand, he turned and fired three shots. He missed twice, but the third bullet hit home as Eli fired and missed.

He remembered the clink of the cartridges against the linoleum before the world dimmed and went black. He woke up in an intensive care unit, hooked to an IV and a ventilator.

Tami Jacobs was likely not a product of Eli's pathology, but the possibility couldn't be excluded. The murder had happened at the same time that Eli was hunting and in the same general area. Stanton would have to see him to find out for sure.

14

The flight to Del Norte County was brief. Stanton read a book on the history of the Middle Ages. The man next to him slept and snored. At one point, the man's head collapsed backward, his mouth opening to reveal four gold teeth and a thick white film on his tongue.

Stanton was surprised by how easy it was to secure funding for his flight. He'd simply phoned Tommy and told him why he needed to go. Two hours later, a receptionist dropped a ticket onto his desk. Normally, he would have had to pay for it and then fight for months to get reimbursed by the department, if he ever got reimbursed at all.

When he exited the plane, he headed straight outside. The Del Norte County Airport was small but well kept, and he was impressed that no garbage littered the sidewalks outside, as with larger airports. He found a taxi at the curb.

"Where to?" the driver asked.

"Pelican Bay."

Pelican Bay State Prison was termed a "supermax" facility, a prison within a prison. Inmates were segregated and units separated to a degree of the highest level of security within the Department of Corrections. The designation was given only to those facilities housing prisoners considered a threat to national or international security, those too dangerous to attempt rehabilitating.

"Why you headed out to the prison, my man?"

"Just need to talk to somebody."

The driver nodded as he turned right at an intersection without looking for anybody coming from the left. "Had some homies up there myself. Back in the day. Some near twenty, maybe twenty-five years ago."

"Oh yeah? What were they in for?"

"Pssht, all sorts o' bullshit, you know. Robbery, dealin' drugs, attempted murder. You run wit' them gangs and go out and rob somebody, they add damn near ten years to your sentence." The driver pulled out a lighter and held it in his hand. "So who you talkin' to out here?" With his other hand, he pulled out a small pipe from the ashtray, wafting the unmistakable smell of marijuana. "You mind?" the driver asked.

"I'd prefer you didn't."

The driver shrugged and put the pipe back. He took out a flask from his pocket.

"My old partner."

"Partner? Like business partner or somethin'?"

"No, I'm a cop. He was my partner."

The driver slowly lowered the flask and placed it on the passenger seat. He unwrapped a piece of gum and put it in his mouth. He didn't speak the rest of the time they drove but mumbled the fare when they stopped outside the prison gate.

"Wait for me here," Stanton said.

The facility was massive. Buildings were spread out over a large clearing in what was essentially a forest. He stood near the entrance almost ten minutes, pacing back and forth, before going in.

He walked to the X-shaped cluster of white buildings. Electrified barbed wire fencing surrounded them, and a small box was bolted by the entrance. He pressed a button.

"Yeah?" a voice bellowed.

"Detective Stanton, San Diego PD. I have a visit scheduled with Eli Sherman."

"Yeah, I got you."

The gate slid open. Stanton stood a few moments, staring at the white steel door a guard had opened. The man had a rifle slung over his shoulder and he motioned with his head for Stanton to enter.

Prison, any prison, had a smell to it: sweat and flatulence and rotting food and rotting flesh. The corridors and reception area held only the slightest trace of the zoo contained a few hundred feet away.

The front-entrance guard gave Stanton a visitor's pass and led him to a small room. He was seated on one side of a glass partition on a cold stool bolted to the floor. Phones were mounted on both sides of the thick glass, and he pulled out a small digital recorder and started it.

Stanton ran his hand along the glass and then over the concrete border. The ceiling had exposed water pipes and he followed them with his eyes to each wall. Three other stools and glass partitions were in the room, but no one was using them.

A bolt on a door on the opposite side of the glass slid open and the metal hinges creaked. A muscled guard with tattoos running up his forearms walked behind a handcuffed Eli Sherman, the handcuffs connected to chains that ran around his ankles. The guard sat him down and then held up his hands, indicating ten minutes, and Stanton nodded. The guard went back out through the door and left them alone.

Sherman was in a yellow jumpsuit and white shoes with the laces removed. His hand went to the phone, and he put it to his ear.

Stanton picked up his receiver and could hear his old partner's breathing through the earpiece. "How are you, Eli?"

"You never ask a prisoner how they are. Then you put them in the position to either lie or talk about how miserable they are, and they don't want to do either. You're supposed to say, 'How you holding up?' or 'How are they treating you?'"

"How are they treating you?"

"I was raped my first night here. Do you know what it's like to be raped, Jon? I bet you don't. Two inmates paid a guard off with some weed, and they were given a half hour with me. They took turns."

"I'm sorry," Stanton said.

"*You're sorry*?"

"I didn't put you in here."

A long silence fell between them.

"What the fuck do you want, *Detective*?"

"I want to talk."

"You haven't been here for two and a half years, and now you want to see me? Bullshit. Did they find another one of my bodies? There are more, you know."

"I know."

"Are they still looking?"

"I don't think so. Not in San Diego County. I heard they had a task force in Los Angeles."

"I heard that too." Sherman spread his legs wide and leaned back. "So you got a few minutes. What do you want to talk about?"

Deception or circumlocution, he knew, wouldn't work. He would have to take a bold stance and stick to it. "Did you kill a girl named Tami Jacobs? Blonde, twenty-three. A small apartment in La Jolla. It would've been about a month before you went in."

"You really think I'd be honest with you if I had?"

"Yes, I do."

He grinned, exposing yellowed teeth. "Why?"

"I don't know. Pride, maybe."

"Maybe."

"Do you remember it?"

"I would need to look at a photo."

Stanton pulled out a manila envelope he'd brought and removed a photo of Tami in her University of Iowa sweatshirt.

"Pretty girl," Sherman said. "Do you have any of her after the deed was done?"

"No."

"You didn't bring any?"

"No."

"Why?"

"Because you would masturbate to them later." Stanton noticed that Sherman had begun gently rocking back and forth. He had seen him do this but had never paid attention to it before. "Was it you?"

Sherman made a sucking sound through the gap in his front

teeth.

"Was it you, Eli?"

"No. It wasn't me." Sherman put the photo back and hung up the phone. Before leaving, he said something through the glass, but Stanton couldn't make it out.

Stanton stepped into the hallway, the door slamming shut behind him. He leaned against it and saw sweat rings under his arms. He wished he'd brought a shirt to change into. He could almost hear the madness contained just a few feet away—men who had become ghosts to their families and friends… and animals to each other. He wanted to put his hands to his ears but instead walked toward the exit.

As he left, the guard at the front entrance said, "Them two boys that cornholed him, they ended up dyin' some months later."

"How?"

"One was burned in his cell. The other had his junk bitten off or somethin' and bled out in the showers. We know your boy did it, but there ain't no good proof."

Stanton nodded and stepped outside. He had specifically asked for a room that wasn't being monitored. If Sherman had known their conversation was being listened to, he would've lied. Stanton would have to speak to him again. But he decided it could wait.

He looked around and realized the cab had left.

15

By the time Stanton landed in San Diego, it was dark. The air was different there, salty and warm, as if it had been exhaled from someone's body. He found his car in short-term parking and drove to his apartment.

A neighbor was out on her patio when Stanton got home. She was an older gal, smoking a cigarette in the dark. He saw her silhouette and the bright pinpoint of red, which would get brighter at her mouth and then darken when she lowered it.

"How are you, Suzie?"

"Doin' fine, handsome. How are you?"

Her voice was gravelly from the tobacco and alcohol she coated it with day after day.

"Not bad." He took a seat on the first step leading up to his apartment.

"Heard you workin' with the cops again."

"Who'd you hear that from?"

"Melissa stopped by tonight to see you. She told me."

"Oh."

"You miss her?"

"Yeah, I guess I do."

"I like her. She went outta her way to say hello to me." She finished the cigarette and put it out in an ashtray on a table next to her then lit another one. "When you gonna have your boys over again?"

"Next weekend. We're going to Disneyland. They say they're sick of it, but I know they always have a good time."

She blew out a puff of smoke and took a sip from a can of beer. "I ever tell you I got kids?"

"No."

"I got three. Cindy, my youngest, still lives 'round here. My two boys moved, though—I think to Vegas, but I don't know.

I ain't talked to 'em since Clinton was president. I remember that 'cause Clinton was on the TV last time I talked to 'em, lyin' through his teeth about blow jobs or somethin'."

"You know what the president of France said when he heard Clinton got a blow job in the White House?"

"What?"

"'Why else would anyone want to be president?'"

She laughed and then sat quietly, staring out into the parking lot as someone drove past, slowed, and then sped away. "What happened with you two, anyway?"

"I don't know. It was so gradual I don't think either of us noticed until it was too late. I know she didn't like living on a community college professor's salary. But there was more to it. At some point, we stopped talking to each other. After that, we didn't care if we talked or not." He rose and began walking up to his apartment. "I better hit the sack. Have a good one."

"You too, hon."

The apartment seemed cold, though he checked the thermostat and it read seventy-six degrees. He placed his badge, wallet, and keys on the kitchen table and noticed his gun hanging from his holster on the chair. He lifted the holster without touching the gun and placed it in one of the cupboards.

He went to his bathroom, undressed, and climbed into the shower. The bathroom was the place he least liked to be. While married, he would spend a lot of time there, reading books or newspapers or surfing the internet on his phone. He would hear Melissa outside, trying to gather the kids together long enough to serve breakfast and get them ready for the day. When Jon Junior was young, he would pound on the door and yell, "Dada, Dada!"

It made Stanton uncomfortable to think of those things in some apartment he had no connection to. He closed his eyes and let the hot water run over his head and down his back. The splashing drowned out the sounds of the world, and he imagined he was in the ocean, being carried away on a current to some unknown place.

He put on fresh undergarments—the garments bought from the LDS Church for members that had been endowed—and took out a protein shake from the fridge before sitting on the couch in the living room.

He flipped on the television and began going through the channels. Nothing was on except crime shows and reality television. One show was about the wives of criminals who were exploiting their husbands' notoriety for profit, and he watched it a moment before changing the channel. Two hundred channels and now he couldn't remember why he had gotten that many since he was almost never home.

His cell phone buzzed. The ID read San Diego Police. "Hello?"

"Hey, it's Jessica Turner. So I just heard from Tommy that you went to visit our mutual friend."

"I did."

"I just wanted to know how it went, I guess. Or just to call and check on you. I don't know... I guess I don't really know why I called."

"It's okay. I'm glad you called. I wanted to apologize for not getting together for dinner with you yet."

"That's okay. I get it. I was married to a cop once."

Stanton leaned his head back into the couch. "How was that?"

"Well, he wasn't much of a guy. But I was eighteen and really wanted to get out of my house. At least he did that for me."

Stanton sensed her discomfort and changed the subject. "How's your case panning out?"

She took a deep breath and exhaled. "Talked to at least ten people today. No one saw or heard anything, and they refuse to cooperate with me. What the hell is wrong with these people?"

"There was once a woman in New York that was stabbed nearly forty times in daylight. Over thirty witnesses were watching from their windows, but not a single one called the police. A couple of psychologists interviewed all of them, and it turned out they all just assumed someone else was calling the police. If there had only been one witness, they likely would have called."

"You think that's it? They think someone else will help me?"

"I don't know, maybe. I think people don't want to get involved in each other's lives."

"It's funny, though, 'cause I don't remember that when I was a kid. All the neighbors looked after all the kids so we could play at night. I went back through my old neighborhood once, and I didn't see any kids playing at night anymore."

"No, I think parents would have to not care to let them out at night here."

She hesitated and then said, "Um, so do you want to get dinner tomorrow? I'm free." A pause, and then she chuckled. "Sorry. It's just... I just moved down here, and I know it's only like two hours from where I used to live, but it feels like I moved to a new state."

"I know. It's okay. I would love to have dinner with you tomorrow."

They talked about where to eat and then Stanton hung up. He turned off the TV and went to lie down in bed. He stayed up another hour before dozing off, an image of a young blonde girl in a University of Iowa sweatshirt burned into his mind.

16

Stanton went into his office Friday morning and found Chief Harlow sitting at his desk, quietly staring out the window. He was dressed in a polo shirt and blue jeans with Italian leather shoes that gleamed from a recent shine. The photos of Jon Junior and Mathew were turned slightly off center, so Stanton knew Harlow had been looking at them. A copy of the *Herald* was spread on the desk.

Harlow pushed the paper across the desk and said, "Read this."

Stanton picked it up. On page five was a caption that read, "NEW COLD CASE UNIT FILLED WITH TROUBLED PASTS."

Next to the caption was a photo of Stanton. It had been taken when he was released from the hospital after Eli had shot him. Reporters were hounding him as he was being pushed in a wheelchair to an awaiting taxi. His face was contorted with anger, and bits of spittle were visible on the edges of his mouth. Anger was not an emotion he felt often, and he hadn't realized before how awfully it suited him. He sat down in the chair and began to read:

The San Diego Police Department has made an effort in recent years to begin solving the county's enormous backlog of unsolved homicides. Chief Harlow's latest attempt is the formation of the Cold Case Unit. In conjunction with the FBI, NCIS, LAPD, and the San Diego County District Attorney's Office, the unit is assigned cases older than one year that have no active leads. The theory is that with nothing else on their plates, the detectives can focus their absolute attention on a single unsolved homicide, and the likelihood of an arrest should increase. A noble goal, but with one problem: some of the detectives assigned to the unit should not be writing parking tickets, much less solving homicides...

Stanton read the article in its entirety as Harlow waited. It mentioned Chin Ho having legal trouble with the IRS. Nathan Sell had had an affair with a superior officer at the San Diego PD and was demoted and transferred three years ago as a result. Philip Russell was responsible for a botched home entry by the FBI in which two unarmed civilians were shot and killed, one of them sixteen years old. Russell was sent to San Diego afterward, the article claimed, as punishment. Jessica Turner had taken a leave of absence from the LAPD due to "familial stress" and issues with domestic violence. The article listed Zoloft and Prozac as medications she was currently taking. But Stanton's past took up the lion's share of the article.

It discussed the time he had spent in 5 North, the county's psychiatric unit, after the Eli shooting. It discussed his inability to see Eli for what he was and how that had led to more deaths. It talked about the fact that he had left the police force to teach and was brought in on a whim by the chief because none of the established detectives wanted the job. It talked about the fact that he didn't carry his gun with him.

The article was written by Hunter Royal.

"What do you think?" Harlow asked.

"I think it's an op-ed, but it's not in the opinion section. Hunter must know some of the higher-ups at the paper."

"That's it? That's all you have to say?"

"What would you like me to say, Mike? It's all true. He didn't make any of it up."

"So what? I'm talking to the county attorney about suing his ass. He can't tell the world what medications my detectives are on. And how the hell does he know you don't carry a sidearm?"

Stanton shrugged and placed the paper down on the desk. Harlow stood and walked toward the door. His neck was splotchy red. Stanton had only seen his neck get that way after a good shouting match, and he wondered who had been chewed out.

"If I were you, Jon, I'd start carrying your sidearm. Never

know who reads this shit."

Stanton crumpled the paper into a ball as Harlow left. He threw it in the trash bin by his desk. He took out Tami Jacobs's file again and rummaged through everything. There was a day planner he had seen but hadn't looked through in detail.

He found it near the bottom of the box, a pink planner with white ring binding. Little hearts were on the front, and the inside cover read, "Property of Tami."

The page on the date of her death was blank. He flipped through the previous month. Then he started from the beginning and read the whole thing. A few birthdays were in there, and Stanton wrote their names down, though most were only first names. One particular entry that caught his attention was Halloween, the year she was killed. It read, "Meet hottie at the Trapp."

He Googled the Trapp and found it was a bar in La Jolla. He wrote down the address and flipped through the day planner one more time to see if he had missed anything. His phone rang.

"This is Jon."

"Jon, this is Marcy from Vice."

Stanton remembered Marcy from her days as front-desk receptionist. She was legendary for how protective she was of her beloved SDPD. A rumor floated around that she once spent three hours talking a citizen out of making a complaint to IAD.

"I have a message from Captain Young. He says he's not going to be able to set up a meeting between you and Detective Hernandez at this time."

"When can he do it?"

"That's all the information I have, Detective. We'll keep you posted."

Stanton hung up and left his hand on the receiver. He tapped it three times, grabbed the photo of Tami out of the file, and then got up and ran to the elevators.

The San Diego Police Department had nine divisions splitting the city into districts. La Jolla was in the northern division. Young, though captain over Vice operations for the entire city, was from the midwest division, and that was his baby. He wouldn't care that much about one murder up north.

Vice administration was on the third floor. Stanton walked through their reception area, holding up his badge to the secretary. She was a newbie and seemed uncertain whether that was proper procedure or not, but Stanton knew confidence was everything, and he seemed certain even if she didn't. She let him pass without a word.

He got to Young's office and saw Marcy sitting at a small desk out front. He ran to the office door, and she began yelling as he opened it. No one was inside.

"What the hell are you doing?" she yelled. "You can't barge in on a captain! I'm calling—"

"Where is he?" Stanton noticed photos on her desk. Two teenage daughters. Her husband had his arms wrapped around their shoulders, and they wore softball uniforms.

"None of your business, Jon. Now you—"

"Marcy," he interrupted. He pulled out the photo of Tami. He placed it in front of her, and her eyes went to it. "She was twenty-three years old. He raped her for hours and then tortured her to death. George has information that can help me catch him. Please, where is he?"

Marcy swallowed, and the slightest trace of tears welled up in her eyes. He left the photo out a little longer than necessary and then slowly put it back.

"You can't say—"

"It stays between us."

"He's having breakfast at Bencotto. It's on Fir Street near the PCH."

"Thank you."

Stanton sped out of the parking lot and rolled down his windows. He didn't even know why he was rushing. Young would be back in the administrative offices later that day. Maybe, instinctually, Stanton wanted to catch him off guard—stop him somewhere he wasn't used to having authority and at a time he didn't want to have the conversation.

Stanton raced along the freeway, weaving in and out of traffic though it wasn't necessary. A small part of him said he missed this: the panicked chase, the feeling of his guts tightening so much he thought he might vomit.

Bencotto was chic and urban, the lower level opting for glass instead of walls. The servers were all attractive and well groomed, the bar hosting a few people getting drunk before heading in to work.

Stanton stepped inside and scanned the restaurant. Captain George Young was sitting at a table with a blonde. She was stunning, even from across the restaurant. Her artificial breasts bulged from underneath a sleek summer dress. Stanton went and stood next to the table.

At first, Young didn't recognize him, and then his brow furrowed. He threw his napkin on the table and stood up. "Outside," he said.

They went out to the parking lot, and Young looked around to make sure no one was near. His muscles rippled underneath his clothes, and Stanton guessed he'd gained at least thirty pounds since the last time they met. He knew Young had been taking steroids since he transferred to Vice almost five years before. There was some sort of predisposition in the Vice cops that lent itself easily to dangerous behaviors. They were the most on edge, the line between them and the people they were after occasionally blurring to the point of being unrecognizable.

"What the hell are you doing here?"

"Why can't I see Hernandez?"

"Are you shitting me? You came all the way out here for that?"

"He's got information I need. What's the big deal?"

"The big deal is he's under with the Sureños, and if they even fucking think he's a cop—"

"We weren't even going to meet in the city. This happens all the time. I know he meets with you for review. Just let me be there and ask a few questions at the next one."

"No way. I'm not jeopardizing a year of work so you can play detective on some cold bullshit case."

"Let me talk to him on the phone, then. I only need a few minutes."

Young stepped closer, within inches of Stanton's face, using his superior size to try to intimidate him. "I said no. When he's out and the investigation is over, come see me. Till then, stay the fuck away from my detectives."

17

Stanton drove down to Mission Beach and sat in the sand, watching the waves roll into shore and crackle and foam before being pulled back into the vast sea again. A heron dipped underneath the water and came out glistening in the noonday sun. He took off his shoes and pushed his feet farther into the sand until they were covered.

The beach always calmed him. Most locals took the ocean for granted. Eventually, they grew so accustomed to it they hardly ever came. That was why he preferred watching the tourists. They were there just to be in the presence of the ocean.

He took out his phone and called the chief. Harlow picked up on the third ring.

"What's up, Jon?"

"I have something to ask you. How badly do you want me to close this case?"

"What kinda question is that?"

"I need access to an undercover in Vice."

A long silence, and then he said, "Talk to Young. He'll get you —"

"He already said no."

"Well, then, the answer's no."

"It's one of the original detectives on the case. His report isn't complete. There's information missing, and I need to know why."

"Look, Jon, I'd love to help you. You know I would. But if I were to come down on one of my captains like this, not even to mention if he found out you went over his head, there'd be a shit storm. He'd never trust me again, and he'd keep me outta the loop on things I need to be in on."

Stanton grew angry until he admitted to himself that Harlow was right. The chief, no matter how well liked, was seen as an administrator by the rank and file. If he overrode a captain, who was right there in the field making calls, it would hurt morale, and less information would be kicked up the chain of command.

"This isn't how it's supposed to work, Mike."

"It is what it is. Hey, we'll talk more about this later. I'm in the middle of something."

A homeless man came up and asked for change. There was something desperate about him, so pitiful that it tugged at Stanton, and he pulled out a five and gave it to him. The homeless man had a little pad with him. He sketched a quick drawing of Stanton sitting in the sand. It was actually good. The man ripped the white page off the pad, and a yellow carbon copy was underneath. He gave the top copy to Stanton and walked away.

Stanton stared at the drawing and wondered when in the hell he had gotten so old.

He turned back to the ocean, about to put his phone away, and a thought hit him. Clearly, the police weren't going to help him. But maybe someone else would. Stanton Googled Maverick "Hunter" Royal and came up with bios and pieces he'd written but no phone numbers. He called Tommy and asked him to search the police records and get it for him. He was about to hang up, thinking he would get a call back in ten or fifteen minutes, but Tommy told him to wait. He had it up in thirty seconds.

"Since when can we do that?" Stanton said.

"Since this year. PD's connected to the DMV, FBI, California DOJ, and the DOC records. We can do a search from any computer here."

"Consider me impressed."

"Considered. What'd you wanna talk to this guy for, anyway? I saw that piece he did."

"Just want to tear him a new one."

"Gotcha. Here's the number. I'll text it to you."

Stanton put the number into his contacts and then dialed. Hunter answered himself, with a hint of confusion in his voice.

Stanton knew this was his personal cell number.

He and Hunter had had a good relationship before the shooting, and he frequently leaked tidbits to him that didn't impact an investigation. Perception was everything, and Hunter helped create that perception. Most people in the SDPD saw him as a pariah and refused to cooperate with him. But Stanton knew, pariah or not, he was occasionally an important part of clearing a case.

"Hunter. It's Jon Stanton."

"Johnny baby. Whaddya know, whaddya say?"

"How you been?"

"Same. How you adjusting to badge life again? Tin's not too heavy, I hope."

"No, not yet, anyway."

Hunter mumbled to someone there and Stanton could tell he had his hand over the phone.

"Hey, Johnny, I, uh, I'm sorry about that thing in the paper. You were always one of my favorites, you know that, but it was a hack job on the unit. I had to go for the jugular."

"We both got a job to do. I don't hold it against you. But throwing in the stuff about my gun was a little low."

"Yeah, as soon as I read that I regretted it. It just made for such good print."

"Well, you owe me one, then. And I want to collect."

"Whaddya need?"

"Vice detective is undercover with the Sureños. I need to know where he is."

He whistled. "Whew, dangerous stuff, Johnny boy. That's not gonna be cheap to find out."

"How much?"

"Four thousand, easy. Maybe even five."

"I'll see what I can do. His name's Francisco Hernandez. He was with Robbery-Homicide until a year ago."

"Okay, got it. Hey, when you gonna come out drinkin' with us?"

"When you start coming to church with me."

“Ha. Message received. Alright, get working on those five G’s and I’ll see what I can dig up.”

18

"You want *how much*?" Tommy looked as if he was about to either pass out or start yelling.

Tommy was technically a police officer rank two, just beneath a detective. But he had never shown any initiative for taking the next step up the ladder. After Harlow picked him as his personal assistant, Tommy never wanted to work a regular beat again. He was young and full of bravado; sometimes he was the only one in the entire force with the guts to stand up to Harlow. But he was overly loyal. If Harlow needed something done that wasn't on the up and up, Tommy would do it.

"It's necessary." Stanton sat across from Tommy in the office next to Harlow's. It was the second largest office on the floor, larger than that of the executive assistant chief under Harlow.

"The only thing that could justify that much scratch is a drug buy. No way I can approve that, Jon."

"Mike said we would get anything we need."

"Yeah, but within reason. Five grand in cash without you being able to tell me what it's for is not reasonable."

"You can take it out of my salary, over time. I just don't have that much on me."

"Out of your... are you crazy? You want to pay five G's of your own money on this stupid case?"

Stanton was reminded of how everybody viewed the homicide of Tami Jacobs. It was something they didn't want to speak about. Cases that were deemed unsolvable were often treated that way. They were a mark of failure, of insanity that showed itself and disappeared.

"I didn't mean it that way," Tommy said, regret flashing across his face. "It's just... five G's is a lot to not have a reason for."

"I'm paying someone to reveal a source. A good source that is absolutely necessary for me to do my job."

Tommy was quiet, looking Stanton in the face as though it would reveal something to him. He turned to his computer and pulled up a disbursement sheet. "Fine, you'll have it in an hour. But if this doesn't go anywhere, I can't authorize any more spending."

"Deal."

The restaurant Stanton had chosen specialized in Nepalese cuisine but still considered itself an Indian establishment for marketing purposes. It was decorated with posters of Mount Everest, cloth tapestries with small jewels sewn in, Nepalese bowls, and paintings of everyday scenes from the Himalayas. Stanton pulled Jessica's chair out as they were seated near the windows and then ordered two strawberry lassis.

"Do you come here a lot?" she asked.

"I used to. After a shift, me and my partner would come here for a late-night dinner."

"You can say his name, Jon. I'm not a child."

"I didn't mean to patronize you. I just don't like talking about him."

The lassis came, and she dipped her straw in hers and pulled it out to suck the fruit bits off the tip. "Did you read the paper? The piece about our unit?"

"Yeah."

"They made me seem like a nut job."

Stanton grinned. "It wasn't as bad as everyone's making it out, and people will forget about it in a few weeks. There's always a new story, a new person to attack."

They ordered their meal, and some naan and mango chutney was brought out for them. They ate in silence, and Stanton wished he hadn't brought up Sherman. He had found himself, over the past two years, speaking about his old partner at inappropriate times.

"I had a sister that was in Five North for about three weeks."

"Really?" Stanton said, unsure what else to say.

She nodded. "She committed suicide a little later. When she got out. They can fix 'em while they're there, but they can't do shit when they get out."

"The facility treats you like you're not human sometimes. You either do as they say or they'll restrain you and do it anyway. Luckily for me, it was all talk therapy with only a couple of meds."

"Must've been scary."

"Sometimes. I mostly just stayed in my room and kept to myself." He took a forkful of chicken. The bite was moist and went down as easily as warm butter. "I had a sister too… I hope you don't mind, but I'd like to talk about something else."

"Me too. How about we talk about Harlow?"

"What about him?"

"Everybody's dying to know how you two are so tight. We were from the application process and then went through three interviews and screening before being chosen. The rumor is he recruited you personally."

"Mike was my supervisor in Special Victims. We hit it off and stayed friends. Some people can do that. Make a quick connection that never breaks. I trust him."

"I wish I had that, someone to trust. So far, I haven't seen anyone worthy of absolute trust."

"Maybe you're searching the wrong places."

She was attempting to answer when Stanton's phone buzzed. He checked it and found a text that read, *money in ur acct good luck-Tom.*

"Who is it?"

"Tommy. He came through on something for me I wasn't sure he could come through on."

She absentmindedly played with the food on her plate a while and then said, "So this Mormon thing… I've never known a Mormon. I have a few questions, and then I won't ask about it again."

"No worries. Ask away."

"I've heard you guys think the Garden of Eden is in Missouri?"

"True."

"Isn't that kinda... silly?"

"Why? Do you think having it in Africa or Jerusalem is somehow more serious?"

"Well, no, I guess not. How about multiple wives?"

"I'm all for it."

She smiled and said, "No, be serious."

"Abandoned that practice a long time ago."

"Everyone?"

"Everyone. So I'd like to ask you something now."

"Okay."

"I noticed you only wear one earring. I thought you'd forgotten or lost the other one, but then I saw that you do it every day."

She looked down at her plate. "My sister and I would share earrings when we were kids. She'd wear one and me the other. When I used to visit her, toward the end, we started doing it again. I put one of all of my earrings in a little box that was buried with her. Now I just wear one."

Then her phone interrupted them, and she checked the ID. "Sorry, have to take this. It's the sitter."

As she rose and answered her phone, walking out to the front entrance to talk, he texted Hunter, *Deal's on. 5 is the highest I can go.*

Ten seconds later, Hunter replied, *no need got it for 2.*

19

It was nearly eleven o'clock when Stanton dropped Jessica off at her apartment. He made his way to Rancho Santa Fe to meet Hunter at his place.

Rancho Santa Fe was easily the most affluent area of the city and one of the top three most affluent places in America. The median household income was right under two hundred thousand, and for a small cottage with no yard, someone could expect to pay over a million dollars. The neighborhood was predominantly white, and in every driveway was a Mercedes or BMW or Cadillac or Lincoln. The usual indications of people living in a neighborhood were not present there—no toys left out on lawns, no neighbors barbecuing together. Whenever Stanton went through that area, it gave him a heavy, gray feeling. Becoming successful enough to live in Rancho Santa Fe was the goal of most people in the city, but the center was hollow.

He pulled into a cul-de-sac in a quiet street and parked on the curb. The home was square with a well-manicured lawn and trimmed hedges. A neon sign hung above the door:

ABANDON ALL HOPE YE WHO ENTER HERE

Stanton walked up the driveway past a BMW 7 Series and knocked on the door. No one came. He knocked again and rang the doorbell. He tried the door; it was open.

The house was immaculately clean, and a small note with a mint sat on a table by the door. Art hung on all the walls. It was neither good art nor bad, but the eclectic mix gave it a certain randomness that made it appear tacky.

The living room was a large space with three flat screens on a single wall, all tuned to the same vampire show. On the leather sofas taking up most of the room were two partially nude women, one black and one white. They were wearing bathing suit bottoms but no tops, and the stench of marijuana smoke was thick.

"I'm looking for Hunter."

"He's in the pool," one of the girls said without taking her eyes off the televisions.

The pool was large and lit with underwater lights on each end. Hunter was splashing around with a woman, both of them nude. A male was passed out in a lounge chair, a small line of cocaine laid out on a mirror on his chest.

"Johnny boy!" Hunter yelled. He stuck his tongue in the girl's mouth then said something that made her giggle before he climbed out of the pool and wrapped a white robe around himself. The initials "MHR" were stitched in gold lettering over the heart. "Hungry, thirsty, horny?"

"I'm fine, thanks. I brought the cash."

"Straight to business, huh? Well, at least come inside and watch while I get drunk."

They walked inside to the kitchen. Hunter opened the fridge and scanned up and down, clearly unfamiliar with what was in there, and reached for a bottle of cognac.

"Who put my cognac in the fridge?" he yelled to no one. He poured some into a wineglass and drank half before motioning to the living room. He plopped between the two girls and put his arms around them. "Interesting little cookie, this Francisco."

"Can we talk in private?"

"Oh, don't worry." He lightly pushed the girls' heads together. "They're empty as rocks. Ain't you, girls?"

"Asshole," one of them said.

Hunter took a drink and grinned. "They got him set up on Cleveland Ave in a little shitty apartment. The name of the apartments is the Boca Del Rey. His undercover name's Hector Garcia, and he's a foot soldier with the Sureños. They sent him in for the prostitution the gang's been running. Prostitutes are a much safer business than drugs. Most pimps are low-level guys out there by themselves. Sureños think, with their rep, they can muscle everybody out and have it to themselves. They're probably right too."

Stanton wrote everything down in his pad and then took out two thousand in cash in an envelope.

"No, no," Hunter said. "On me. For the gun thing."

"Thanks. Consider us even."

"Even Steven." He began pushing the girls' heads into his lap. "You sure you don't want to stay?"

"Positive."

Stanton sat in his car outside a while, staring at the information in his notepad. He had to move forward cautiously. If the crew Francisco was running with even suspected that he was working with the cops, much less was a cop, it would be instant death. No words would be exchanged, no explanations given—just a bullet in the back of his head when he wasn't expecting it.

He pulled away and got onto the interstate, taking his time to get to the exit nearest Lincoln Avenue. The area was primarily apartment high-rises and low-income tenements. It was segregated into three different districts: white, Mexican, and Russian. He remembered a case he'd had there. A wife had shot her husband after finding a receipt from an escort agency in his pants.

The Boca Del Rey was a square cream-colored building with a large front porch and a keypad entry. Two young Mexicans were smoking on the porch. They saw him, and Stanton could tell from the looks on their faces that they took him for police before his car even came to a stop in front of the building.

He got out and looked around. In heavily populated gang turf, scouts were everywhere. Their job was to alert the street's enforcer, the person in charge of protection from rival gangs and the police. They had grown sophisticated over the past two decades, choosing to take to sniping from rooftops rather than face-to-face combat. A lot of officers were shot because they weren't aware of what they were up against. Newbies would act tough, thinking they would win by intimidation, and set off red flags from the scouts that this officer wasn't going away.

"Smells like bacon, Holmes."

Stanton stepped onto the porch. Too late for subtlety, so he flashed his badge and crossed his arms; he couldn't afford to let them see he wasn't packing a firearm. "Someone called 9-1-1."

"Ain't no one called from here."

"Look, guys, someone called 9-1-1. Female. Said her boyfriend or someone was beating on her. Just let me talk to her and make sure she's okay, and I'll get outta here."

The men looked at each other. They mumbled something in Spanish, and Stanton made out the words *dumb bitch*.

One of the men entered a code on the door. "They in 2-C."

Stanton walked through without looking at them. It had the feel of a compound, and he'd just gotten past the sentinels. Not five miles away were a police station and a courthouse, but there was no law here. He suddenly felt foolish for not carrying his gun.

The front lobby had orange carpet and walls, and a staircase led to the second floor. The mailboxes were covered in graffiti, and most had been pried open. He wondered how the people got their mail or if they were so disconnected from the rest of society that mail didn't matter.

He took the stairs to apartment 2-C and knocked. A young woman answered.

"Are you okay?" he said.

"Who the fuck are you?"

"I'm the police. Someone called 9-1-1 and said there was a domestic disturbance here."

"Ain't no domestic disturbance."

"So you're saying you don't need any help?"

"Do I look like I need any fucking help?" she said, taking a step closer to him.

"No, you certainly don't. Sorry to take your time."

She slammed the door in his face, and he went back to the first floor. It was enough. The men out front would think she'd called, and when she denied it, they would think she was lying. The boyfriend would deny hitting her, but everyone denied that. They wouldn't think a cop made the whole thing up. Not until they checked her phone and saw she was telling the truth.

Francisco's apartment was at the end of the hallway. He made sure the two men on the porch weren't paying attention before crossing over into that hallway and hurrying across the soiled carpet. Stanton could smell cooking food, pork or beef. A Spanish television station was turned up somewhere, and he could hear it through the walls.

Stanton knocked and then stepped to the side of the door. It opened, and the tip of a .38-caliber Remington stuck out.

He twisted and grabbed the gun, spinning to his left and tearing it out of the person's hands. The man was short and bald with a thick goatee. Stanton stepped back and held the gun firmly pointed at his face.

"Inside," he said.

Francisco stepped back into the apartment, not raising his arms. They walked down the hall to the living room and stood quietly as Stanton glanced around.

"Is there anyone else here?"

"No."

"You sure?"

"Yeah."

Stanton lowered the gun and held it out for Francisco. "I'm Jon Stanton. I'm with SDPD." He took out his badge again.

Fury filled Francisco's eyes. "Do you know what you've—"

"I don't care about your hooker operation. I need your help."

"Fuck you." Francisco was animated now, his arms beginning to move, his brow furrowed in anger. He grabbed the gun and pointed it at the ground.

Stanton had met him once a long time before and remembered that he'd spoken perfect English. Currently, his speech patterns were of someone whose primary language was Spanish.

He's been under too long.

"Do you remember the Tami Jacobs case? She was killed in her apartment in La Jolla? I have it now. I have some questions about the investigation."

Francisco stepped within an inch of his face. "Fuck... you." He shoved him at the shoulders.

"I just need five minutes, and then you'll never see me again."

Francisco's right hand was clenched into a fist, and Stanton thought only a bare minimum memory of being a police officer was holding him back from smashing it into Stanton's face. No conversation would occur that night.

"I'll leave."

When he was outside again, he heard the two men on the porch, laughing at him as he got into his older-model Honda. As he drove away, he looked at the sky and saw a crescent moon hanging over the city and, on the rooftop of a building, a young boy with a rifle slung over his shoulder.

20

Saturday at Disneyland flew by in a heartbeat, and on Sunday morning, Stanton had to return his sons to their mother before heading to church. Melissa had once been Mormon but abandoned the faith before their marriage ended. Stanton's older son informed him that they played on Sundays, going to barbecues and parks and sailing with Lance's friends. Melissa objected to the boys being exposed to God. It pained Stanton that he couldn't share religion with his kids without their mother telling them it was BS, but it was something he had to learn to live with.

The gospel was important to him. Stanton read either the Bible or the Book of Mormon every night. They were his foundation. In a world he felt was crumbling around him, his faith was a shining gem that he could hold on to. A necessary gem. Regardless of whether God turned out to exist or not, He was necessary to Stanton.

After church, he went home and made a sandwich. He took it and a bottle of juice to the balcony and sat on the bare cement instead of a chair.

Sunday was a day to rest for him. He tried his best not to think about Tami Jacobs, but she wouldn't get out of his head. He would close his eyes and see her broken body staring at the ceiling as if calling for help. When he daydreamed, it was of her or people associated with her. His mind always had difficultly putting up partitions between things in his life. They would become associations, and everything would meld until all his thoughts were one compost heap of jumbled ideas and links. From this heap, he would begin to reassemble what he needed.

Before he could eat, his phone rang, a number he didn't recognize. He answered and heard Jessica speaking with somebody.

"Hello?" he said.

"Hey, Jon. We're out and about, and I was wondering what you're doing today."

"Nothing. Just relaxing."

"I made a picnic if you want to join us."

"Sure. Why don't you guys come down here? We could eat at the beach."

Stanton gave his address and then went to put the sandwich away. When he opened the fridge, he felt embarrassed at the contents: deli meat, bread, mayonnaise, ketchup, an old container of pesto sauce, and a few bottles of juice—nothing else. Melissa used to do all their grocery shopping, and going to the store made him uncomfortable.

Twenty minutes later, a silver Volvo pulled to a stop in front of his apartment. He walked down and met them. The boy was handsome, with long eyelashes, and was fully involved with his phone.

"Hey," she said. Instinctively, without a thought, she pecked him on the cheek. "Sorry. Habit."

"No worries. Who's this?"

"This is Andrew. Andrew, say hello."

"Hello," he said without looking up.

"He's a real talker, as you can see."

Stanton looked down the beach and saw surfers coming back for a lunch break. "We should eat at the beach. Has he ever surfed?"

"Once or twice."

"Hey, Andrew, do you like surfing?"

"Yeah," the boy said, finally looking up.

"Well, I happen to have a board just your size. You wanna head down with me?"

"Sure."

They went upstairs to the apartment, and Stanton changed into a bathing suit. Mathew had a few suits there, and he got one that would fit Andrew. From the apartment storage room Stanton rented for a monthly fee, they picked up two surfboards and some surf wax and headed to the beach.

The water appeared blue and clear, a soft breeze blowing over and causing ripples. Jessica set up a blanket and began preparing sandwiches out of a basket she had brought. Stanton and Andrew were closer to the water, going over the basics of paddling and keeping balanced on the board, things Andrew should already have known but didn't. When Andrew felt ready, they ran into the ocean.

The water was warm, and Stanton was glad he didn't have to wear a wetsuit. He enjoyed the feel of water against his skin and the salty taste as it splashed onto his lips. Morning was nice, when no one was out and the sun was just beginning to rise. It would sometimes reflect off the water so fiercely the entire ocean looked as if it had been dyed orange. But night surfing was the best. Occasionally, it was so quiet Stanton could hear the cries of whales farther offshore.

They paddled out far from the beach, and Stanton yelled a few instructions to Andrew before they caught their wave. Stanton lay flat for a while, letting the wave dictate where he went before hopping to his feet. He glanced at Andrew, who was still lying on his belly. Stanton motioned with his hand for the boy to rise, but Andrew shook his head.

They surfed only half an hour before Andrew said he'd had enough. Toward the end, he'd attempted to stand once and immediately fell over. As they walked back onto the beach, Andrew said he didn't like surfing.

"You have to get used to letting the ocean be in control," Stanton said. "We're used to guiding ourselves every day, but it's not like that out there. You have to give yourself up completely to the ocean. Once you do that, you'll become just an extension of it, and instead of fighting it, you'll be part of it. Some of the top surfers even say they can predict where the ocean will go, how it will move, just by feeling."

"Yeah, I guess."

They ate sandwiches and drank Perrier until the afternoon. Andrew talked about school and his friends, about his trip with his father up to Alaska to fish, and about all the other things going on in his life. His mother grinned the whole time, and Stanton knew he wasn't normally like this. The ocean had that effect on people.

When they finished and were saying goodbye near Jessica's car, she loaded Andrew in and gave Stanton a quick kiss on the lips. It was dry, but a sweetness and familiarity clung to it that Stanton had missed.

As they drove away, he stood and watched, the image of Tami Jacobs in her bed pushed out of his mind for the first time in several days.

21

Stanton went to work early on Monday. Their unit meeting was scheduled for ten o'clock, and he wanted to get some hours in before that. The floor was empty except for a few offices that had their lights on, and he found the silence relaxing as he went to his office. While he waited for his computer to boot up, he looked out at the passing traffic and was grateful for the window.

He logged in to the SDPD intranet using the password the administrator had emailed him and went to the human resources tab. He found the file for Francisco Hernandez.

Francisco's life was a story Stanton had heard before. He had grown up in a gang and had a juvenile record that he had gotten expunged. At twenty-two, he pulled himself away from his gang life and joined the police department to help clean up the degradation he must've seen in his neighborhood. He didn't graduate high school but finished his GED later in life and then, at twenty-four, got an associate's degree in criminal justice at a local city college.

His third year on the force, he was involved in a shooting. A young Mexican kid tried to shoot him when he pulled him over for speeding. Francisco managed to fire two rounds before being run over by the car. After any officer-involved shooting, the procedure was to visit the precinct psychiatrist, who would write a psychological profile and clear the officer for duty. Stanton searched for the profile but didn't find it.

He rose and went to Tommy's office. Tommy had his feet up on the desk and was talking on the phone so softly that Stanton couldn't hear what he was saying from three feet away. Stanton sat down across from him and waited.

Tommy held up his forefinger and continued to speak. He seemed to be placing an order for something, but when the conversation was done, he said, "Love you." He hung up and looked at Stanton.

"I need a favor, Tommy."

"So soon?"

Stanton threw an envelope with the five thousand in cash on the desk. "That should buy me one favor, I think."

"What happened?"

"I saved the department some scratch. Like I said, I think it buys me one favor."

"Depends what the favor is."

"I need the psych profile for a detective."

Tommy stared at him a moment and then burst out in laughter. "Can't you ever ask for a credit card to buy gas or a new gun or something like that?"

"I don't need those things. I need a psych profile."

"Why? Oh, wait. Let me guess. You can't tell me?"

"I could, but I prefer not to."

"Well, indulge me, Detective. Please."

"I want to find something I can use to convince the detective to give me the information I need."

"You mean blackmail?"

"No, I don't. Just something that can give me some insight into him."

"That's out there. Even for you. What's going on?"

Stanton looked out the window. The building across the street had a construction crew on the roof, and they were standing around in the morning sunlight, two of them hard at work and the others laughing and joking.

"I can't get this girl out of my head, Tommy. She came here looking for a new start because her life back home was so messed up. What she found instead was the grim reaper waiting in her apartment one Wednesday night. She was twenty-three, a kid, and she went through just about as much pain as a human being can go through before she died. She deserves something for that, Tommy. She deserves me getting this guy."

Tommy appeared to think about what he said and then

straightened up in his chair. "You've always had a way with words. Who's the detective?"

"Francisco Hernandez. He's in Vice."

"We could both lose our jobs for this. You know that, right?"

"Yes."

"But we're going to do it anyway, aren't we?"

"Yes."

Francisco's profile was there in less than two hours. It came in paper form with instructions from Tommy to shred the document afterward and never mention it to anyone again. It was two pages long, and Stanton knew the psychiatrist had not been paying attention. The job was just a paycheck to him, his goal to process as many cops as possible and get them out as quickly as possible.

The profile talked about issues with authority and antisocial tendencies. One section spoke about prior drug use, marijuana, but didn't go into details. In the second-to-last paragraph of the second page, Stanton found what he was looking for: "Subject transferred from the Sex Crimes Unit after two weeks due to his inability to separate current caseload with the sexual assault suffered by his younger sister, to which he was privy."

He felt a twinge of guilt in his belly, but he thought about Tami in her bloodied bed and chose the lesser of two evils. He left the building while the rest of the unit was assembling for the mandatory Monday morning meeting.

22

Stanton dropped by the evidence locker at the Central Division precinct. The evidence custodian was an older officer, one who had passed his prime and the prospect of giving a damn a long time before. He had probably already served his twenty and retired but come back to the force.

The custodian glanced casually at Stanton's credentials and got him the file he wanted. Inside was a CD, and Stanton signed for it and slipped it into the pocket of his suit coat.

He drove back to the Boca Del Rey and parked farther down the street this time. The two men from the other night had been replaced by two different men, boys, really. They couldn't have been over fifteen. And it was early enough in the morning that the scouts weren't out. They wouldn't be up until around noon.

The heat in his car was unbearable and began to cook him. He turned on the air conditioner, but the air that spewed out was warm and dusty. He rolled down the windows instead and loosened his tie. The seats reclined only so much, and he put his head back on the rest and waited.

He watched the people entering and leaving the apartment complex. Many were young kids who should have been in school, and he knew their parents were strung out somewhere, aching for their next hit.

Nearly three hours later, Francisco Hernandez stepped out of the building. He was wearing khakis riding low and a white T-shirt. He hung out and smoked a cigarette with the two boys on the patio and then went out to his SUV in the back. It was a decked-out Bronco with shining rims, fresh paint, flames across the sides, and gold trim around the bumpers.

Stanton pulled away from the curb and followed him, staying just close enough to see him. Francisco would spot a tail if he wasn't careful.

The Bronco eventually stopped at a car wash, and Francisco got out and threw the keys to one of the employees. Stanton parked around the corner and jogged to the entrance. He peeked through the glass double doors and saw Francisco flipping through a magazine. When the car was done, Francisco paid and came outside.

"I like the car," Stanton said.

Francisco stopped and turned to him. He shook his head and glanced around. "You just ain't gonna leave me alone, are you? I'm gonna have to—"

"I told you last night if you give me five minutes, you'll never have to see me again."

"And I told you, fuck you."

"I can't keep it a secret forever. I'm not going to stop, and at some point the homies are going to notice a cop following you and start asking questions. Or maybe they won't ask questions." He stepped closer to him. "Five minutes. That's all I want. Besides, they're still drying your car."

"Fine. Five minutes."

"Come with me to my car. I have something I'd like you to hear."

They walked around the corner and climbed into Stanton's Honda. Francisco got into the backseat. He ducked low enough that no one would see him. Stanton put in the CD.

The noises were muffled at first, filled with static, but then voices came through. They spoke quietly, then the sound of tape being ripped off of flesh filled the car. Next came a scream that made the speakers rattle. A young girl begged for her life. Male voices were laughing and swearing and yelling while the young girl pleaded and cried. The CD continued for over twenty minutes, but Stanton played only two when Francisco told him to turn it off.

He looked back at Francisco, whose face was ashen white. He hadn't moved the entire time, curled up on the backseat with his head below the window line.

"I had this case five years ago." Stanton faced forward as he spoke. “Three ex-cons. They got out of prison and decided to celebrate. She was fifteen. They picked her up on her way home from school and recorded while they raped and tortured her in the back of a van. When they were done, they threw her out onto the middle of the freeway in broad daylight. No one stopped. She died in the hospital from brain trauma and blood loss.” In the rearview mirror, he locked eyes with Francisco. “Tami Jacobs went through the same thing. This type of killer, a sexual sadist, is the most dangerous type of person. They can’t achieve climax without inflicting pain. They have no remorse, no guilt, and they’re usually smart. They fantasize so much about what they’re going to do to their victims that they know ahead of time what evidence they are likely to leave behind. And they don’t stop. Ever. There have been cases of them being imprisoned and the guards finding insects they keep in their cells to torture. They’re Satan.

“I’m probably not going to catch him, Francisco. Not without your help. And he’ll keep killing. If he’s as smart as I think he is, he’ll probably also leave the city and kill somewhere else. Our investigations will be disjointed. He’ll get away.”

Subtle, but Stanton could see the crack. It began in Francisco’s forehead, just a slight crease. Then his eyes softened. “What do you want to know?”

23

Stanton hit Record on the digital recorder in the front seat. He turned back to Francisco. "Kelly Ann Madison. On the day of Tami's murder, she traded shifts with Kelly. You spoke with her but never put it into your report. Why?"

Francisco moved around on the seat and stared out the window and repeatedly looked down at his hands and then out the window again. Stanton stayed quiet.

"I was told not to," Francisco said.

"By who?"

"I can't tell you that."

"Francisco, I need your help."

"I know. But I can't. But he ain't the killer you're looking for, anyway. And I ain't no snitch."

"Snitch for what?"

Francisco shook his head without looking up.

"I know it's a cop. Can you at least acknowledge that for me?"

"Yeah," he forced out, "but he didn't do her."

"But he knows who did, doesn't he?"

"I don't know, man." He scoffed. "This is bullshit, man. All turning to shit. I thought I was doing a favor, you know. Looking out for my brothers in blue, you know what I'm saying?"

"They will never know we spoke. I will deny everything and not testify in court about it."

"Can't help you, brother. I said all I can. I ain't no snitch." He opened the door and got out of the car. He walked to the driver side and rested his hands on the top of the car. "Keep digging, Detective. You'll find what you're looking for. But I can't help you."

Stanton returned to the office and collapsed into his chair. He leaned his head back and stared at the ceiling a long time. He took two Excedrin with water from an old plastic bottle. He noticed Jessica was standing in the doorway.

"Rough day?" she asked.

"Yeah." He put his feet up on the desk and crossed his hands over his stomach. "How was the meeting?"

"Didn't happen."

"Why?"

"You weren't there. Harlow said everyone or no one. They've been waiting for you to come back. Conference room in ten."

Everyone was seated by the time Stanton sat down beside Harlow near the front of the room. His head was pounding, and he was starting to see stars. He leaned back as far as he could, but the fluorescent lights penetrated his eyelids. He stood up and turned them off. Sunlight was still coming through the windows and breaking into fragments through the blinds.

"You don't mind, do you?" Stanton asked.

"That's fine," Harlow said. He quickly glanced around and made sure everyone was there. "Jon, I know you're busy—we all are—but I would really like everyone here Monday mornings if possible."

"I had to catch a witness when they weren't expecting me. I'll make sure I'm on time next week."

"Great." Harlow grinned as though he had just performed some wonderful managerial sleight of hand. "Let's get to business. Ho, what's going on?"

Chin was dressed in a Calvin Klein pinstripe suit and wore designer sunglasses pushed onto his forehead. His blue tie had little British flags on it. "Todd Grover. This was the liquor store owner that was shot in his store. The arresting officer's report was sloppy 'cause he was green. He left the PD to become manager of a nightclub downtown. We tracked him down, but he didn't remember much. Most of the witnesses have moved away or gotten locked up. I think one of them died. In the ghetto, nobody sticks around for too long, I guess. We're following up with them, though. Shouldn't be too long before we track a couple of them down."

"Good as can be done," Harlow said. "Nathan."

"Alberto Dominguez Jovan. Shot in front of twenty people in the parking lot of a strip club. 'I don't know nothing' has become 'I don't remember nothing.' Rough going for now, but there's one witness I spoke with that's holding something back. When I was at her house, I smelled burnt meth. I'm thinking get a bust and use it as leverage."

"Good thinking. Run anything you need by Tommy. Philip, whaddya got?"

"Rodrigo Carrillo. Killed during a drive-by. I've got a suspect." He waited for a reaction, and when he didn't receive one, he cleared his throat. "Gang member that—get this—dated Carrillo's girl after he was killed. They met at his funeral. I'm putting together an affidavit for a warrant to search his house. I think he's still got the firearm they used in the drive-by."

"Good work. Keep me informed. Jessica?"

"James Damien Neary. Stabbed while walking home. No leads, no witnesses panning out. So far, it's just random."

"Nothing's random," Harlow said. "Keep digging. You'll turn up something." Jessica nodded but didn't look at him. "Jon?"

Stanton thought a moment before speaking. "Tami Jacobs. Have a lead I'm following up on."

"What is it?" Harlow said.

"She may have been dating a cop that was never identified."

"Shit," Harlow said. "You sure?"

"Not yet. But a coworker said a cop used to pick her up from work. Tami talked about him a couple of times and told people they were sleeping together."

"Why wasn't that in the initial reports?"

"I don't know yet."

"Jon"—he pointed—"that information doesn't leave this room. Understood?"

"Yeah."

Harlow tapped his finger on the table, staring out the window. He appeared lost in thought a long time and then said, "Jessica, drop Neary. I'm bringing in a couple of new detectives to the unit soon, and I'll pass it to one of them. Partner up with Jon and follow this Jacobs case through."

"Sure."

"Good. All right, I'm pleased so far, guys. I'm hearing good things, and it seems like resources are being used wisely and sparingly. Keep it up. Meeting next week, we'll probably have some new faces, so treat them well. Dismissed."

Harlow rose and dialed a number on his phone. He was speaking before he was out the door. He had never before used the word *dismissed* to excuse a meeting.

"Well"—Jessica stood up—"I guess that's it for Neary. Where are we on Jacobs?"

Stanton motioned toward his office, and they walked there together. He shut the door, and she took a seat.

He perched on the edge of the desk and folded his arms. "One of the assigned detectives on the case told me that someone higher up ordered him not to include good evidence in the initial homicide report."

"Holy shit."

"Yeah."

"What're we gonna do?"

"I don't know."

"Did he tell you who it was?"

Stanton shook his head. "No. And I don't think he will."

"Any hunches?"

"One. And we should follow up on him now."

24

Stanton sat in his car outside the two-story house in Del Mar. Jessica sat next to him, reading a paperback novel and sipping a Starbucks coffee.

The street was quiet with no signs of children. The neighborhood primarily consisted of youthful couples that had inherited money or retirees ready to spend some. More than once, Stanton saw women in their forties and fifties wearing tight spandex workout pants and tank tops and climbing into massive SUVs, presumably to head to the gym and then the tanning salon.

George Young climbed out of a new Hummer and checked his mailbox. He wore a white shirt with the sleeves hemmed to show off his arms. The tip of a tattoo poked out on the right biceps. A woman in a dress opened the door and kissed him on the cheek as he walked in. It was not the woman Stanton had seen him having lunch with.

"That him?" Jessica asked.

"Yeah, that's him. You never met him?"

"No, haven't had the pleasure. Seems like a douche."

"He is a douche. He and a few other guys in Vice steal steroids from the evidence lockers. I think they pay off one of the custodians."

"Have you talked to Harlow about it?"

"Doesn't work like that. I would be more despised than them. I wouldn't find any proof, anyway."

"So you just let it go?"

"Of the seven Vice guys I knew doing it, three have been fired for unrelated things, and one is serving time in County for assault. They screw themselves. They don't need me to do it unless they're smart. Not too many of them are."

She watched the house in silence a moment. "So what's the

game plan for him?"

"I just want to see how he reacts. He's obvious. He won't be able to hide his surprise."

"You sound pretty sure of that. What if you're wrong and you just tip him off?"

"Then we're back where we started."

She exhaled. "All right. Lead the way."

They went to the porch. Stanton knocked and took a step forward, nearly to the door.

The woman answered, "Yes?"

"I'm Detective Jon Stanton. Can we speak to Captain Young, please?"

"Sure." She turned and yelled, "Honey, it's for you."

Young stepped out of the kitchen. His face turned red when he saw Stanton there, inches away from being in his home. He mumbled something to the woman and then came out onto the porch, pushing his way past Stanton and nearly shoulder-checking Jessica. "What the fuck are you doing here?"

"Why did you tell Francisco not to include the information about Tami Jacobs dating a police officer in his report?"

Anger flared on Young's face. His lips curled, and his eyes widened. Stanton put his hands behind his back and lifted his chin slightly, as if welcoming a blow.

"Are you fucking *kidding* me?" he bellowed. "You talked to him after I gave you orders not to?"

"You're not my supervisor, George. And I'm investigating this case and asked you a question."

"Fuck you." He jabbed his finger into Stanton's chest. "I'm going to Harlow." He got in Stanton's face. "If anything happens to any of my guys, I'm comin' after you."

He slammed the door behind him. Stanton looked over the yard. It was immaculate, much like the inside of the house he had seen. The woman that had answered had perfect nails and soft, smooth hands—not a housewife's hands. They hired help for the yard and house.

"Well, that was productive," Jessica said.

"It wasn't him."

"How do you know?"

"He was more worried about his undercover than the accusation. Plus, he wouldn't go to Harlow and risk being found out. It wasn't him." He looked at the Hummer. "But I think he's doing more than taking the steroids."

Stanton finished up at the office and was about to leave when he got a call from Tommy. The chief wanted to see him. He went to Harlow's office and knocked.

"Come in."

He waited by the door without sitting down. Conversations went faster when one of the participants stood. "What's going on, Mike?"

"I just got a call from George."

"Yeah?"

"Tell me you didn't accuse him of what I think you accused him of."

"I had to. But I don't think it was him."

"Why did you have to?"

"One of the detectives in the case was ordered not to include the information about Tami dating a police officer in the report. I thought it could be George. But I was wrong."

"He's a good cop."

Stanton didn't say anything.

"What?"

"How long have you known he's been dealing steroids?"

Surprise flashed across his face only a brief moment and then went away. "A while."

"It's dangerous, Mike. Other people see it and get ideas that the department doesn't care what they do."

"I'm working on it. I only found out about it a few months ago and didn't realize how deep it ran. A lot of careers could be ruined, and I don't want to do that just yet."

"Up to you. I got work to do. I'll see you tomorrow."

"Jon?"

"Yeah?"

"How'd you guess that I knew?"

"He's too open about it. Someone doing it on the sly wouldn't buy a seventy-thousand-dollar car. I figured he had somebody's permission."

"I'm going to stop them, Jon. I promise."

Stanton looked at him a long time. He had the urge to look away but didn't. "Yeah."

25

Stanton got home late. Suzie's window was open, and she was asleep in bed, snoring. He usually never thought about it, but he could've used some company right then.

His apartment seemed cold somehow, and he felt as if he were being forced to stay there. He looked at the bare walls and considered picking up some art the next day, things that would lighten the place up. He had always admired Tamara de Lempicka and found her works uplifting. He would find prints online and have them framed nicely for the walls.

He wasn't hungry but went to the fridge anyway. He stood there looking at the empty shelves for a minute before closing the door. There was a Diet Coke box on the counter, and he lifted it. Empty. His headache had returned, and sometimes caffeine and Advil together helped, but he was too tired to run to the store. He knew he hadn't done any real physical exertion and wondered what had exhausted him.

Stanton took eight hundred milligrams of ibuprofen and went to bed. He lay in the dark and stared at the ceiling. The moonlight came through his window and lit up the room with a soft blue light. He began counting the swirls of paint on the ceiling, tracing the pattern with his eyes and making out familiar shapes. Slowly, he began to drift off.

Stanton's cell phone woke him up. He didn't realize what it was until he remembered that he had thrown his phone onto the nightstand without turning it off. He fumbled with it, sleep still in his eyes, and answered without looking at the number. "Hello?"

"Jon, it's Mike. I, ah, got something."

"Where are you?"

"Home. Some uniforms just woke me. I've sent down a patrol to pick you up."

"Why? What's going on?"

Silence on the other line for a while before Harlow said, "It's Detective Hernandez, Jon. He's been killed."

The scene was chaos. At least ten patrol cars had their red-and-blues twirling in the night. Yellow police tape stretched twenty feet from the apartment complex and held back a large crowd. A few had brought chairs and drinks. A news van was parked near the curb outside the tape. A tall blonde in high heels was having makeup applied as the camera crew set up.

Stanton's driver parked a basketball court's length away to avoid the cameras and the crowd. He walked slowly, and when he neared, he saw that on the sidewalk in front of the Boca Del Rey, Chief Harlow stood with George Young. As soon as Young spotted Stanton, he darted toward him. Harlow yelled something, and two uniforms grabbed Young.

One of them shouted, "He's not worth it!"

Young was taken to a cruiser and leaned against it as several officers went to him, trying to calm him down. Stanton went under the police tape and approached Harlow.

"Sorry to call you out like this," Harlow said, "but I figured you'd want to be here."

"What happened?"

"Gangland happened, Jon. We think they got wind and popped him."

"I'd like to go inside."

"Go ahead. I gave Chin the case."

Stanton walked past the officers standing on the porch. They gave him long, cold, penetrating stares before turning away and pretending they hadn't seen him. He made his way down the hall and saw flashes from the forensic unit's industrial cameras. The apartment was packed with police officers. Any time an officer was killed, everyone on the force wanted to be there. He guessed there was a sense of "that could've been me."

Dying was also part of the job, and every officer tried diligently to prepare for it, but Stanton had yet to meet one who was ready to die for a paycheck.

Chin Ho was in the kitchen, typing something on a tablet. Stanton turned away and looked at the corner of the living room. Francisco's corpse lay lengthwise, his arm under his head, blood pooling around him from a gaping wound in his skull. Written in blood on the wall next to him was the word *PIG*.

Stanton carefully brushed past the uniforms and stood next to the body as forensic investigators finished taking their photos and vacuuming for hairs. Someone called the medical examiner's office to send body lifters to haul it away.

Stanton waited patiently for forensics to finish. Though not police officers, they had carried a sense of self-importance and condescension since the airing of *CSI*. They weren't even allowed to carry firearms, but applications to the police academy had declined in recent years, and applications to forensics schools had skyrocketed. One forensic investigator had attempted to interview a witness, and he was promptly fired and lost his state licensure. But because of a television show, people now looked to them to solve crimes.

Stanton bent down and looked at the large hole in Francisco's head. He had gunpowder burns on the skin of his face, meaning he had been shot at close range. No defensive wounds anywhere, no sign of struggle.

"Did you know him?"

Stanton turned to see Chin standing there, staring at the body as one would stare at something that puzzled but didn't interest.

"You could say that."

"I don't know why the chief gave this to me. I think it's really pissing off some of the locals."

"It's just yours tonight. Mike knows everyone's emotional, and when they're emotional, they make mistakes. They'll calm down by tomorrow, and that's when he'll call you into his office and tell you he's under pressure to keep it local."

"Huh. Smart move, I guess. So whaddya think?"

"Not typical gangland. These guys are crazy, but I don't know if they're crazy enough to kill a cop and make a big deal about it. They know a lot of theirs would be next. They'd want to keep it quiet, just make him disappear. Then again, I haven't worked gang unit. I hear they're a lot less scared of police now."

"They would want to send a message, though. You send us undercovers, and this is what happens. But check this out." He led Stanton down the hall to the bathroom. Chin turned the lights off and grabbed a portable black light from one of the forensic investigators.

Splashes of blood lit up like glow-in-the-dark stickers, all over the toilet, the wall, and the floor, thickest near the bathtub.

"Shot in here," Chin said, "but there's only droplets on the hallway carpet."

"More than one?"

"That'd be my guess. Probably three. Two to hold him, and one to pull the trigger while his head was down in the bathtub. Then they carried him to the living room and let him bleed out."

"Why not leave him here?"

"No idea. But they tried cleaning the blood with bleach."

"Everyone knows that doesn't work."

"Well, these guys think it does."

"Where's the entry?"

"No damage we can find. These guys were invited in."

Stanton shook his head. "I was careful."

"Not careful enough."

Stanton left the bathroom and watched as the body was placed in a black bag and zipped up. The lifters from the ME's office were quiet when they carried it away. They were the low men on the totem pole. Typically, they were either young, looking to apply to forensics school or to become pathologists, or they were old, having grown comfortable with the silence of the dead. Live customers were much more difficult to deal with.

The officers stood still and, out of respect, didn't speak until the body was out of the apartment.

Stanton went outside. The air was warm, but there was no breeze, and the warmth sat on him and made his skin sticky. Harlow had left. That was his rebuke. Rather than tell him about it later, he'd had him come down to show him what he had done.

But the scene didn't make sense. They had attempted to clean up blood in the bathroom but wanted to leave a message on the living room wall. A disconnect existed between what had happened in the bathroom and what had happened in the living room. Something had not gone right.

Out of the corner of his eye, Stanton saw Young speaking with another officer. Young said something, and the officer looked at Stanton and nodded.

26

The next day, Stanton went surfing before the sun was up and stayed on the beach well into late morning. Someone with a large truck was selling tacos out of the back, and he bought two breakfast tacos and a horchata and ate near the surf, letting the water foam at his ankles. He then slept, the sun warming his cheeks and neck, and rinsed in one of the public showers before heading into the office.

The entire building was quiet. No one was laughing or telling stories, and people spoke only when absolutely necessary. Officers would nod to each other in understanding when passing in the halls, to everyone except Stanton. Word had already gotten around.

He went to his office and shut the door. He turned on music as he let his thoughts drift for a while before turning to his computer. There was an email from Chin:

Hey, you were right. Taken off the case this morning.

CH

When he was through checking his emails, he listened to two voicemails on the office line. One was from Melissa, wondering if he had the number to a doctor they liked to use when they were married. It was an odd little link they shared, and it pulled at him to be reminded of it. They would both have to use the same doctor. No, one of them would change. Someone would have to. The other message was a hang-up.

He spun his chair around to look outside. No clouds were in the sky, and the sun was cooking the city. He wished desperately he could've spent the whole day at the beach.

Tommy buzzed him. The chief wanted to see him.

Harlow wasn't on the phone or even flipping through paperwork when Stanton walked in. He was sitting quietly at his desk, peering at his monitor. He faced him as Stanton sat down. "I'm not a bullshitter, Jon. You know that."

"I know."

"So I'm not going to bullshit you. This is bad. One of my detectives was killed because you didn't follow the orders of your superior. The media's gotten hold of it already. Hunter wrote an op-ed in the *Trib*."

"Yeah, I'm sure he did."

"George wants me to refer this to the DA to see if there was any criminal negligence. I don't think there was, and I'm not going to do that. But I can't have you on the unit anymore. It would taint everything we do."

"I know."

"I'm going to put you on administrative leave, with pay, until this thing blows over. Won't be long, I'm guessing. Some meth head will shoot up a party 'cause he thinks the CIA's out to get him, and people will forget about this."

Stanton rose.

"I'm sorry about this, Jon. I wish this coulda turned out different."

"Me too."

Stanton waited by the fence at Theodore Roosevelt Elementary until his son walked out. Mathew was carrying drawings he had made, and Stanton wondered who they were for.

"Hey, squirt."

"Dad!" The boy ran up and threw his arms around him.

Stanton hugged him back and kissed the top of his head, smelling his hair. He remembered a day at the hospital when Mathew had a fever of 103 and wasn't yet a year old. He remembered rocking him late into the night and the scent of his skin and hair, the fear inside him as he looked at his boy's cherubic face.

"What're you doing here?" Mathew asked.

"I just wanted to come by and see you. So what's going on?"

"I got picked for football today, and Josh threw the ball really hard, and it hit me in the face. I got a bloody nose."

"Oh no."

"Yeah, but I didn't cry. I just threw the ball back and said I was fine."

"Good for you."

Mathew pointed. "There's Mom."

Melissa was climbing out of her car. She saw Stanton and waved, a slight smile on her lips as they walked toward her. "Hey," she said.

"Hey. I just wanted to see him. Where's Jon Junior?"

"He's at day care."

"Since when do you put him in day care?"

"Just a few times a week so I can do my yoga."

"Melissa, we talked about this."

"Not now, Jon. I don't want to hear it. I have a life too. It can't all be spent at home."

Stanton looked down at Mathew, who was hugging his leg. He had moonlighted early in his career as a bodyguard, a bouncer, and even a night watchman at a warehouse so that they would never have to put their kids in day care. He had done two years in Special Victims and had seen videos of what happened when monsters were left alone with children and thought nobody was watching.

"Let's go, Matty," Melissa said.

"I want to go with Dad."

"You'll see him on the weekend. Come on."

Mathew grudgingly let go of Stanton's leg and got into the car. He smiled and waved as they pulled away.

Stanton turned toward his own car. He saw some boys in football uniforms assembled on the school's field. On the sidelines, the parents were chatting. He walked onto the field and stood away from the other parents but close enough to listen in on their conversations. It was mundane and obvious, but he ached to join them, to brag about his son's time in the forty-meter dash or how they had been practicing tackling in the backyard. But he knew that wasn't his destiny. That was now Lance's… if he wanted it.

27

Stanton went home and flopped on the couch. He thought about turning on the television—the mindless banter might distract him—but decided against it. He just lay there, listening to the sound of traffic outside and children yelling as they got home from school.

He was twirling his keys when he suddenly realized he hadn't checked the mail in a long time. He wasn't expecting anything and had no inclination to see anything anyone had sent him, but there was a purpose in it that he needed right then, like crossing something off a to-do list.

He went downstairs to the line of metal boxes. He opened his and saw that the mailman had crammed everything inside, wrinkling and folding most of his mail. He pulled out the advertisements and mailers and threw them in the trash can the complex provided next to the boxes. As he walked back to his apartment, he flipped through the rest of the mail. It was primarily bills, with one letter from the University of Utah psychology department asking him to donate as an alum. There was also a handwritten envelope addressed to him with his last name misspelled. He opened it as he climbed the stairs.

Before anything else, the signature line screamed to him, and the rest of the mail dropped out of his hand:

Sincerely,

Francisco Hernandez

Stanton sat on his couch a long time and read the letter twice before laying it on the table and going out to the balcony. He watched some children playing in the complex's playground and then went inside to read the letter again.

I'm sorry it had to come to this. This fucking department don't have room for cops like us. Assistant Chief Anderson was the one that told me not to put in that stuff about the vic and the cop.

Sincerely,

Francisco Hernandez

The return address was the Orange County address for Disneyland. Stanton folded the letter and put it back in the envelope.

Anderson had come up through Vice, an eleven-year stint when most detectives could only put in two or three. He was known in the department for his undercover work until he began to go prematurely bald, and wrinkles started to show on his face. The end came when every prostitute on the street would greet him as "Officer." He took a desk job and rose through the ranks via old-fashioned brownnosing and putting in long hours. But Stanton knew him to be a by-the-book policeman.

A story had come down about Anderson. As a patrolman in Indiana, he had promised his captain that he would be back at the precinct at a certain time to chauffeur the governor to a function. He was running late and speeding to catch up. He glanced down for a second to change the radio and hit a cow in the road. The cow bounced off the car but not before shattering the windshield and emptying its bowels over the car. Anderson, unwilling to break a promise to a superior, had driven the remaining ten miles to the precinct, cow feces flying off the car and into his face.

That was always how Stanton had pictured him, with a serious expression on a face covered in cow dung. Stanton picked up the letter and slipped it into his pocket before heading out the door toward his car.

28

Assistant Chief Rodney C. Anderson was in the men's room when Stanton checked in with his secretary. He took a seat on one of the couches and waited. In front of him, a coffee table was covered with issues of law enforcement magazines, along with *Guns and Ammo* and a hunting magazine called *The Happy Outdoorsman*. On the cover of the last was a man dressed in full camouflage hunting gear, holding up the severed head of a buck. Stanton turned the magazine over.

A few minutes later, Anderson returned. He was tall and bald, slim at the shoulders with jowls that were just beginning to appear. "I was told you need to speak to me, Detective."

"I do. Mind if we talk in your office?"

"Not at all."

His office was orderly and sparse. The only ornament indicating anyone even occupied the space was a photo of Anderson and his wife on a boat. His arm was around her, and he was smiling in a way that said he was not a man used to the expression.

Anderson took his time settling into his high-backed leather chair. He sat rigidly and folded his hands across the desk. Stanton knew instantly he was a man who had served time, a long time, in the military.

Stanton took the letter out of the envelope and placed it on the desk. Anderson picked it up and read it. Stanton was impressed when the man showed no reaction at all.

Anderson calmly placed the letter into the waste bin next to his desk. "I assume he sent that to you recently?"

"I got it today. It was postmarked yesterday, the day he was killed."

"What are you suggesting, Detective?"

"Nothing, sir. I just wanted to talk to you about it."

Anderson took a deep breath, and his hands went to his lap.

He leaned back in his chair, gazing at Stanton, but Stanton guessed anybody could've been sitting in that chair and receiving the same look. "When I started in this department," Anderson said, "it was a whole different beast. There was... predictability in it. Most of the guys came from the armed services. Uh, were you in the service?"

"No, sir."

"Helluva experience, Detective. Vietnam. You know, I used to stick my rifle up and shoot without looking at what I was shooting at. I was an eighteen-year-old kid, and what I did almost all day was shake." He stood up and walked to a cupboard in a corner. He took out a bottle of what appeared to be whiskey and poured three fingers into a glass. He looked to Stanton. "A glass?"

"No, thank you."

He returned to his desk with the drink. "Twenty-four hours a day, Detective, I shook. And I was always wet. If it wasn't raining, I was drenched in sweat. The humidity was something you can't even imagine. The weather just stuck to you. You could taste it. It had a taste." He took a long drink and placed the glass on a coaster of the American flag he pulled out of a drawer. "Anyway, that's all the past now. Most of the detectives I know up here want to get flashy positions so they can get the good jobs later, guarding dim-witted celebrities or whatever. You know, that's one of the hallmarks of a civilization in decline, when the celebrities are more revered than the day-to-day folks. Happened in Rome, happened in Gaul, happened to the French and English."

"Yes, sir."

Anderson finished his whiskey. "So what is it you want, Detective Stanton? I know the chief suspended you. Do you want to be reinstated? At a higher grade, I'm sure?"

"No, sir."

"Then what do you want?"

"I want to find who killed Tami Jacobs."

Anderson looked at him a few moments. "Why? It's one homicide. You got us by the balls on this thing, and you don't want to use it?"

"No, sir. If I may be frank, I was retired before this case. I don't care about my career. But the type of person that killed her is very rare. And very hard to catch. Given the timeline, I expect that since her death, he's killed anywhere from one to ten other girls depending on whether he is a plant or roving killer."

"What does that mean?"

"Plant killers fix themselves in one spot, like they have a home somewhere. But roving or rogue killers travel around, usually between cities and states but sometimes even between countries, and look for victims. Because law enforcement has been slow in communicating with disparate agencies, they go for years, sometimes decades, without getting caught."

"And you think that's what you got here? A rogue?"

"I don't know what I have, sir. He's extremely smart, probably trained or self-taught in forensics. There's little physical evidence left. What I do know is that, outside of a shark attack, I've never seen a victim as badly mutilated as this girl."

Anderson nodded as if he understood. "And all you want is to catch him? No fame or money?"

"No, sir. I don't even need my badge back. I just want to make sure I'm given access to a few things I may need."

Anderson looked down at his glass. "You shame me, son." He leaned forward and placed his hands on the desk. "Well, need it or not, you got your badge back. I'll clear it with the chief. What else do you need?"

"Why did you order that information be kept out of her case file?"

"Because like Detective Hernandez, I was following orders too. And there's only one person in this whole place that can give me an order I have to follow."

29

Chief Michael Harlow's house sat on top of a small hill overlooking the beach. It was upscale, more so than even a chief of police of one of the largest cities in the country could normally afford. The home was filled with two children, a wife, and a mother-in-law with a live-in nurse.

Stanton parked in front of it and sat in his car. He watched the neighbors come and go. A utility man was on a power line, repairing what looked like damage from someone throwing objects up there. A pair of kids' shoes hung over one of the lines. That used to be a signal to potential buyers driving through that drugs were being sold—a sort of Open for Business sign. But that had stopped since law enforcement picked up on it. Now they used red porch lights.

Stanton guessed this neighborhood had some rowdy children, ones that had rich parents that were never around to see exactly what their kids were doing. In many respects, though the media painted the poor as responsible for most crime, the rich committed just as much. But there were so few rich that it didn't seem significant.

He saw the family was having dinner, so he waited. Eventually, the children ran off, and Mrs. Harlow cleared the table and then began helping her mother back to the guest room upstairs. The chief sat alone at the table, sipping wine.

Stanton knocked on the window to the kitchen rather than the front door.

Harlow got up, opened the front door, and stepped outside. "What's going on, Jon?"

"I need to speak with you. In private."

"If this is about reinstating you—"

"I don't care about that. I just need to talk to you for a few minutes."

"All right. Well, come inside before one of my neighbors shoots you as a prowler."

Stanton followed Harlow to a study off the living room. Books lined oak shelves, and a puffy brown leather couch took up an entire wall.

Harlow sat down at an old desk and lit a cigar. "Well?"

"You ordered Anderson to halt progress on the Jacobs case. Then you brought me in. You had to have known I would eventually find all this out. So that means you're in trouble somehow, and you thought solving this thing could get you out of it. My best guess is that you found out the cop she was dating was Eli and you didn't want another body attributed to the San Diego PD. But why bring me in? What if I just went to IAD?"

Harlow puffed at his cigar. "I was hoping you could handle this without finding out certain aspects of it. I had a sneaking suspicion you would, but I had to risk it." He put his cigar out in the ashtray. "But you're wrong. That's not how it was."

"Then what happened?"

Harlow rose and shut the door. He came back and sat down on the couch. His shoulders slumped, and his belly puffed out of his shirt as he stared at the carpet. In a few seconds, he had gone from a man in control to a man spinning wildly through the universe. "I met her at that restaurant. I was having lunch with Tommy. I think I actually offered him his position there."

"Who'd you meet there?" Stanton knew the answer but wanted to hear it from him.

"I asked her out to dinner, and we started talking on the phone. We would talk—get this—for two or three hours sometimes. When was the last time you talked to anyone for two or three hours? I felt like a teenager again."

"Say her name, Mike."

Harlow looked at him. "You're a cruel son of a bitch sometimes, you know that? Tami Jacobs. I was having an affair with Tami Jacobs." He chuckled. "Would you believe me if I told you it actually made my marriage better? I was more attentive with Crystal. It felt like the time I would spend with her and the kids was more special. I can't explain it. But that's the way it was."

Stanton thought about the young girl in the sweatshirt, her arms thrown around her grandfather, the look of joy on her face at being able to spend a sun-filled afternoon with her family. "I can't believe you can sit there and tell me this like it's okay."

"I know it's not okay, Jon. Hell, I knew it right when I started doing it. You asked, and I'm telling you what happened."

"She was a kid. She was lost and looking for anyone to hold on to, and you used her like trash."

"Hey, who the hell do you think you are? I cared for her. You think working three days a week at that shithole paid her rent? I bought her clothes when she needed, I took her out, I got her car fixed... I did everything I was supposed to do."

"Except save her life."

A low blow, and Stanton felt the pain of his words cut deep into his boss. He regretted saying it but then thought that perhaps Harlow deserved it, that it might be the only time someone would be able to say it to him.

Harlow put his face in his hands, and they sat in silence. An antique clock ticked softly on the wall. A shower started somewhere in the house, and the groan of pipes ran through the room and then faded away.

"You're right about something, though," Harlow said. "I am in trouble, Jon. And I need your help." He stood up, walked to a space behind the desk, and knelt down. A safe key jingled and clicked, and a metal door creaked because it needed to be oiled. Harlow came back with a small box. He opened it and showed Stanton what was inside—letters. Stanton glanced through them. They each demanded different amounts of money.

"After she was killed, I got one of these in the mail with a photo of me and her checking in to a hotel. You gotta see, this was right after Eli. I mean *right* after. The media was all over us, looking for anything they could use to show that we were all sick fucks like him. I couldn't let this get out."

The idea of the chief of police manipulating a murder investigation to cover himself... "You have to turn yourself in."

Harlow paled. "Are you kidding me?"

"Having your detectives selling steroids and you taking a cut is one thing. This is something else."

"Taking a—"

"I'm not blind, Mike."

"No, you're not. I'm sorry. These are things that just... Not even Crystal knows these things about me."

Stanton looked him in the eyes. "You need to turn yourself in and resign."

"Now hold on a second. We go back a long ways, you and me. This ain't just a Boy Scout solution to turn myself in, and everything's going to be fine. I'll be thrown off the force. I'll lose my pension. You know the forfeiture laws as good as me. All this"—he waved his hand around the room—"they'll take it all and sell it at some fucking IRS auction. I got a family relying on me."

Stanton rose. "You let them down a long time ago. Turn yourself in, Mike. Or I will." He got out to the hallway before Harlow was on his feet.

"You're not such a fucking saint! You got a good detective, a detective with a family, murdered for nothing."

"I didn't get him killed, Mike. You did."

Stanton left the house and went to his car. He laid his head on the steering wheel. He remembered something his grandfather had told him: "No one is what they want you to see. No one."

30

Stanton couldn't sleep. He would toss to one side of the bed then the other and stare at the floor for what he thought were long periods of time. Then he would look at the clock and realize only a few minutes had passed. At two in the morning, he stopped trying. After throwing on shorts and sandals, he walked down to the beach.

The ocean was more primal at night. The water appeared like dark tar, devoid of any color and swallowing everything in its path except for the glowing of the moon. Most predators in the sea hunted at night, and there were no ships or sailboats or yachts. But there were occasionally surfers, the crazier ones that had little in their life outside their time on the ocean.

Stanton remembered he had been one of them briefly as a youth. A shack was on the beach about five miles from where he was sitting. The landlord was an old hippie who used to rent the space to surfers in exchange for free weed whenever he wanted. Sometimes there would be more than twenty people sleeping in a single room and only three or four blankets and cots between them. Many of the people were homeless, their only possessions their boards and a few trinkets from their previous lives, when they had parents and schools and plans laid out before them.

Stanton fit in with them. None of them were looking for friendship. They knew each others' names, and that was enough. They would share a meal when they could score some money, but that was the extent of their bond. Eventually, no matter how long they'd been there, everyone would drop away one by one and be replaced by a new face.

Despite his parents' pleas to come home, he'd stayed in that shack for over nine months after high school. He met a girl there, a pretty brunette with hazel eyes and a smile that made him think of the patients he had seen when visiting his father's hospital as a kid. An empty and meaningless smile, full of genuine joy at nothing at all. He worked part-time pumping gas and surfed every morning and night. One day he woke up and the girl was gone. He asked around about her, but no one could give him a definitive answer. Everyone just assumed she had found something better. He had cash in his wallet, which he'd hidden near the oven, and she knew where it was. When he had checked, all the money was still there.

The night was warm, almost hot. He lay back on the sand, stared at the moon, and thought about that girl. He wondered what she was doing then, wondered whether she ever thought about him or what their life might've been like if she had stayed. He wondered whether she thought about their clumsy attempts at lovemaking and if it ever made her smile.

With her face and soft caresses swirling in his thoughts, he closed his eyes and drifted off to sleep.

A crash woke him. Wood splintered, and a lock fell onto concrete. The noise was in the distance, but it was loud.

Stanton sat up, disoriented. He stretched and checked his cell phone: 7:14 a.m. He turned to look in the direction the sound had come from and saw three police cruisers and a SWAT van outside his apartment complex.

He was about to head over to find out what was going on when he saw an officer in full SWAT gear step onto his balcony. The officer signaled to a commander standing on the sidewalk below and shook his head. The commander spoke into a small walkie-talkie attached to his collar.

Stanton fell to his stomach on the sand and watched. His guts felt icy cold.

A few minutes later, he rose and, staying low, ran along the beach until he was out of sight of his apartment. He worked his way through a maze of dilapidated buildings, crossed the parking lot of a burger joint, and didn't stop until he was near a grocery store almost five blocks away.

He dialed a number on his phone as he entered the store. The fluorescent lights made his head ache. Inside, the place was almost empty, just a few cashiers standing around.

"Hello?"

"Jessica, it's Jon Stanton."

"Jon! Where the hell are you?"

"I just saw the SWAT guys tear my place apart. What's going on?"

"There's a warrant out for you. I just got off the phone with George Young asking if I knew where you were."

Stanton stopped near the produce section. "Warrant for what?"

"For homicide. They're saying you killed Francisco."

Stanton was silent long enough that Jessica asked if he was still there.

"Yeah, I'm here. Do you know how to access the CCJS database?"

"Yeah."

"Can you look up the probable cause statement for me?" When she didn't respond, he asked, "You don't really think I did this, do you?"

"Of course not. But I could be an accessory after the fact."

"No, that wouldn't be the charge. It would be assisting a fugitive from justice. But I understand. I should go."

"No, wait. Hold on a second... Okay, I have it up."

"Could you read it to me?"

"On or about May the second, at approximately thirteen hundred hours, an officer from the San Diego Police Department observed the suspect, Jonathan Nephi Stanton, at the Boca Del Rey apartments on 4521 South Winchester Boulevard. The suspect entered the apartment of the victim, Francisco Hector Hernandez. The officer heard shots fired and called for backup. Upon entering the apartment, the officer observed the suspect escape through a sliding glass door located in the front room.

The victim was found in the front room with several gunshot wounds to the head and torso. Medical arrived at approximately thirteen hundred twenty hours and pronounced the victim deceased."

"Who's listed as the officer on the affidavit?"

"Detective George B. Young."

"Okay. Okay, I need some time to think. Jessica, if I call you, are you going to help me?"

"Yes."

"Okay, I'll call you later today. I just need some time to process this."

"You can't do this alone. Meet me somewhere so we can talk."

"Where?"

"I don't know. Where do you think?"

"Barbeque Pit in La Jolla. You know it?"

"I'll find it."

"Let's meet at lunch. It'll be packed."

"Okay. And Jon?"

"Yeah."

"I... I don't think you did this."

"Thanks."

Stanton hung up and walked down the aisles until he reached the deli. He bought a Diet Coke and left the store. A security guard glanced at him before turning back to a magazine he was reading.

31

Harlow watched Jessica Turner hang up the phone. He and Assistant Chief Anderson sat across from her desk. A tech was at a laptop on the other side with a wire running from her cell phone to the laptop and then to a tracking device on the floor.

"Anything?" Harlow asked.

"Still working," the tech said.

Harlow exhaled loudly. He tapped his fingertips together a while and then looked over the office to occupy his mind. The photos were a nice touch, but there were too many of them. How many pictures of their children did people really need? His eyes moved to Jessica, who was biting the tip of her thumbnail, staring absently at the desktop. "Detective Turner, something the matter?"

"It's just hard for me to believe... I just can't picture him doing that."

"I know. I've known Jon Stanton a lot longer than you. He used to sleep in this shitty apartment I had back before he was married. We'd stay up talking and drinking scotch. Well, I would drink scotch. He would drink milk or some other bullshit drink. He's a friend of mine, but nothing anyone does surprises me anymore."

"But why would he do it? He has no incentive. There's no reason for him to—"

"You're thinking like a civilian, Detective. You've seen the monsters just like I have. The blackness that's in people, it doesn't need an explanation."

"I know, but—"

"Somebody, a high-ranking, decorated captain, saw him do it. With his own eyes. George was following him that day on a hunch, and the hunch paid off. You can question it all you want later. For now, we need to find him. Understood?"

"Yes, sir."

"Hey!" the tech shouted. "I got something."

"I got something, *sir*," Anderson corrected him.

The tech rolled his eyes. "I work for the city, not the police. You're not my bosses, so have a doughnut and chill out."

"Enough," Harlow said. "Whaddya got?"

"I can only narrow it down to a couple blocks, but it looks like he called from less than a mile from his apartment. There's some other complexes there, a tanning salon, a smoke shop, a grocery store, and a warehouse."

"Rodney," Harlow said, "get units out there right away. I want people searching every fucking inch of those two blocks."

"Got it." Anderson rose to leave.

"Detective Turner, I need you to get Chin and head to that restaurant. I'll get some plainclothes over there to help with the takedown. I think it's going to go fine, but just in case, make sure you have your sidearm. And don't take any chances. He makes a move, you shoot."

32

Knowing his car was off-limits, Stanton took a cab down to the Barbeque Pit. The restaurant was a few miles from the grocery store, but it was the first place that had popped into his head when Jessica suggested they meet. The ride cost him seventeen dollars. Money was suddenly a great concern. He had a couple of credit cards and several thousand dollars in his checking account with about two hundred in cash. He was grateful he had the habit of always taking his wallet with him whenever he left the apartment; otherwise, he wasn't sure what he would have done.

He sat down on the curb near the restaurant and watched the entrance. It was busy at lunch, and the crowd varied from businessmen in suits to stoner surfers in wet shorts and sandals. No patrol cars were around, but there wouldn't be. What he was looking for was much more subtle.

Plainclothes officers tried their best to fit in, but if you knew what you were looking for, they could be spotted every time. Their attempt to seem natural was the giveaway. They would read a phone or newspaper or magazine too intently. A long line would cause just a little too much impatience. Stanton watched for that but didn't see anything except a hungry crowd coming in and out of the dilapidated building.

He stood up and brushed the sand off his pants before going into the restaurant. It was dim inside, but the scents of cooking meat and frying potatoes made his stomach growl. Jessica sat in the corner with her back to the door. She was sipping strawberry lemonade and gazing outside the window at the ocean.

Stanton sat down across from her. "Hi," he said, unsure exactly what to say.

"Hi."

"Thanks for coming here. I'm sorry I got you involved in this, but I don't really have anyone else. Everyone I knew in the department has transferred around."

"It's okay."

Stanton could sense hesitation in her and had noticed a minor grimace when she first saw him. He knew that she thought he had crossed an invisible line that he could never uncross, that he was a murderer.

"Look at me," he said. She raised her eyes to his. "I swear to you, on the life of my children, I did not kill that man."

"Then why are they saying you did?"

"The chief was having an affair with Tami Jacobs. That's why that information wasn't in the initial reports. She was supposed to be with him that night. I told him he had to turn himself in, and if he didn't, I would go to IAD. Francisco being killed by the gang was probably just an opportunity that he exploited."

"Why don't you go to IAD now? We could—"

"I'm sure he's already thought of that. Someone's probably been promised a promotion or intimidated or just bribed. I knew the corruption ran deep, but I couldn't guess how deep."

The waiter came over, and Stanton said he wasn't hungry but would take a Diet Coke.

"I saw inklings of it before I retired. Some drugs missing here and there, reports altered to establish probable cause when there wasn't any, but this... I couldn't imagine Mike would do this."

Jessica stared at him a long while. She pulled a pen out of her purse and wrote a single word on her napkin: *Run.*

Stanton scanned the restaurant. Standing in the doorway of the kitchen, Chin Ho mumbled something into a collar mic.

Stanton jumped up and sprinted for the door. A waiter attempted to pass in front of him, and he accidently slammed into him, catapulting a tray full of drinks and food into the air. He pushed his way past a couple at the entrance and made it outside. He dashed for a convenience store across the street.

Halfway there, he felt an impact as if a truck had hit him. He was blinded by a flash of white.

When his vision stabilized, he saw the blue of the sky and felt bright sunlight on his face. He was lying on his back. A large officer in shorts and a tank top sat on top of him, trying to twist him around to slap on a pair of handcuffs.

Stanton curled his arm and grabbed the man's elbow. He thrust his hips up, pushing the officer off him. As he turned his body into the man's elbow, he spun him onto his back, maneuvering so he was the one on top. He hugged the officer tightly, running his hands along the man's lower back until he found the butt of a handgun. He pulled it out and stuck the muzzle into the officer's ribs.

"Easy," Stanton said.

The officer held up his hands in surrender, and Stanton surged to his feet and sprinted away. A group of diners exiting the restaurant saw the gun and ducked back inside. In front of the convenience store, a young man was getting out of a Toyota.

Stanton shoved him out of the way and hopped into the car. "Sorry." He slammed the door and locked it as the man started yelling and pounding on the windows. Stanton peeled out of the parking lot, tires screeching, and got onto Ocean View Drive. He gunned toward the intersection but had to slam on the brakes and turn right as another car veered away and hit the curb.

It was a straight shot onto the highway, and he hit ninety miles per hour through another intersection, blowing a stop sign. No cars were behind him but sirens blared in the distance. They hadn't been prepared for how quickly it went down. They wanted to get some sort of confession, and the cruisers had probably been parked around the block.

The highway was packed. Stanton got into the express lane and then moved back to the right-hand side of the road. He got off at an exit near a gas station and then pulled into a residential neighborhood. He turned the car off. He could think of only one person to call.

Melissa answered on the second ring. She was at home, and the kids were in school. He told her he needed to talk, and she agreed that he could come over. As he pulled away from the curb, a thought crossed his mind: he knew in his gut that the takedown was flawed. For whatever reason, whoever had set it up wanted it to fail.

33

Deputy Attorney General Paul Harris sat across from Harlow and ordered a sparkling water. The restaurant, named *Maribelle* after the owner's grandmother, was airy and smelled pleasant from the food cooking in the open kitchen. A chest-high glass partition separated the chefs from the crowd, and everyone watched as they prepared American-Thai fusion dishes.

Harris was thin and bald, and Harlow had always been amazed how shiny he made his head. There was an art in it, and Harlow wondered whether he did it purposely.

"The AG's on board," Harris said. "Judge Baylor too. Believe it or not, we just need the warden to sign off."

Harlow wasn't surprised. Each entity in the criminal justice system was an independent cell unaware of and apathetic to what the others were doing. The local police, the state Department of Justice, the city courts, the FBI, the federal Department of Justice, the state courts, the appellate courts, and the Department of Corrections all had their own interests and goals. Getting them all to align, as they had with Harlow's request, had required an enormous number of political favors, almost more than Harlow could muster. But as the son of a former senator, he still had a few strings to pull.

"I just want it done and over with, Paul. No more motions and writs and campaign contributions and all that other bullshit. Just get the damned warden to sign the piece of paper and hand him over."

"Patience never was one of your virtues."

"Fuck patience," Harlow said. "Patience is for people who sit around and watch opportunities fly by them. That ain't me."

Harris took a sip of his water "No, that certainly isn't. Let me ask you, though, why do you need him out so badly? You got the cream of the crop in Cold Case. Throw every man you got on it, and I bet something breaks."

"Shit. This is why prosecutors should have to be cops first. Do you know how rare it is to make a collar on a cold case, Paul? Almost impossible. Unless the perp walks in and says, 'Oh, hey, sorry about that asshole I busted a cap in three years ago,' it's not getting solved."

The waitress was skinny and brown, and Harlow stared at her legs while Harris ordered. When it was his turn, he told her he wanted steak and eggs and a beer then asked when her shift was over. She smiled awkwardly and walked away.

Harris grinned. "I don't think she likes you."

"Please," Harlow said, "that was just playful banter."

Harris shook his head. "We've gotten old, Mike. I remember when I would go to a bar, get drunk, pick someone up, and head back to my apartment. Then I would go out again and drink some more. Now I'm lucky if I can keep my eyes open past ten."

"It's all in the mind. If you want to be younger, you gotta act younger."

"How's that?"

"You ever thought of maybe looking outside your matrimonial bonds?"

"Cheat on Lauren? No way. Not my style."

"I'm just saying, it's an option for guys like us. We paid our dues. It's probably time we got a little interest back."

"Yeah, well… I don't know."

"Don't wait too long, my friend. You only got one life."

Harris finished his water. "This girl, Tami Jacobs, you sure this wasn't revenge or domestic violence or something? Are you absolutely certain it's a psychopath?"

"One hundred percent. You haven't seen the photos of what he did to her."

"Are you willing to risk your career on it? If something goes wrong with this, it's on your head. The AG, the judge, the feds, everyone will point the finger at you and say that you told them it was necessary to prevent more deaths."

"I know," said Harlow. "I've thought about that. But I need…

we need to catch this monster. He's not going to stop."

Harris shrugged and looked over at the waitress, who was bent over, picking up a slip of paper that had fallen on the floor. "All right. But if you muck this up, it's your funeral, not mine."

34

Harlow ate the rest of his meal and chatted about mundane things. When they were done, he paid and went out to his black Mercedes MLS. Putting on his sunglasses, he pulled out of the restaurant parking lot.

Down the road, near the interstate, he saw a couple of thugs harassing a woman. One of them stepped in front of her and began to talk as another came up behind her and grabbed her ass. She jumped back and tried to slap him, but he caught her arm and blew her a kiss. She attempted to pull away, but the man wouldn't let go.

Harlow stopped his car in the middle of the road. The driver behind him slammed on his brakes and blared the horn. Harlow flashed his badge, making sure that as he pulled it out, the other car got a good view of his sidearm too.

He walked over to the men. "Let her go, assholes."

"Fuck you."

He raised his badge. "Let her go."

The second man ran off and disappeared into the crowd, and the woman scurried away. The first man held on a moment longer before letting go.

Harlow stepped in front of him. "I'm not going to arrest you. What I am going to do is take all the drugs you got on you, and I'm going to throw them away. Then I'm going to take that wad of cash I see lumping your pocket and I'm going to keep it. And then I'm going to let you go."

Fear flashed across the man's face, his eyes widening. If he were arrested, he would bail out in an hour. If his money and drugs disappeared, he would have to answer to someone. And that someone would not believe that a police officer threw the drugs away and took the cash without arresting him.

"Whatchyu want?"

"I just spent a hundred thirty bucks on lunch. I want you to pay for it."

The man reached into his pocket and pulled out some cash. He counted out six twenties and handed them over. Harlow kept his hand out. The man saw he didn't have any tens and gave over another twenty. Harlow smiled and went back to his car.

Seeing the line of cars behind him, Harlow climbed into his Mercedes and got onto the interstate. It was too bad the woman hadn't stuck around, he thought. He could've given her a ride home and gotten a date for later tonight. After all, who would turn down someone that had just saved them?

He listened to talk radio on the way back to the office. When he got there, he pushed his sunglasses up onto his head and looked over his car to make sure there were no fresh scratches or dings, a habit he had developed when he bought his first luxury car, a BMW, two years before. He remembered his shock when he'd found that people would purposely ding his car with their doors. When he was satisfied nothing was amiss, he went into the building and up to the fifth floor.

Before he even sat down at his desk, his phone buzzed. "Yeah?"

"Chief, can I get a few minutes?" Ho asked.

"Chin, you're two doors down. You don't have to call me. Just come over."

A few minutes later, Ho walked into his office. Harlow motioned for him to sit down. He offered him a bottled water, but Ho turned it down. Ho wasn't looking him in the eyes, and Harlow could tell he was trying to figure out how best to phrase something.

"I wanted to talk about the arrest, Chief."

"What about it?"

"It could be nothing."

"If it was nothing, you wouldn't be sitting here. What is it?"

"Jessica was having a good conversation. Jon didn't seem nervous at all. And then out of nowhere, he started looking around the restaurant and spotted me. Then he took off."

"That was my fault. I shouldn't have stationed you inside. And I should've wired her."

"Well, maybe. But I think there was something else, too. Jessica wrote on her napkin. She threw it away, so I didn't get a look at it, but now that I think about it, I think she tipped him."

"That's a big accusation. You sure about this?"

"No, not at all. She may have been doodling for all I know. But it's an odd coincidence that he ran right after she started doodling."

"I don't want to cast doubt on people just yet. Lemme talk to her and see what she says."

He nodded. "You're the boss. Just to be safe, I don't think we should have her on the task force looking for him."

"I'll take it under advisement."

Harlow waited until Ho left the office and then put his feet up on his desk. He tried not to feel moments like this, moments of glee and superiority, but it was difficult not to in this situation. Everything had gone well. He had placed Ho inside and knew Stanton wasn't stupid enough not to spot him. The plainclothes and cruisers were placed far enough away that he could escape, but it wouldn't be obvious; it would seem like a tactical error. Stanton was almost no good to him caught. But a fugitive from justice? When he was eventually caught, who would believe anything he said?

Outside the office, Tommy was supervising maintenance as they drilled plaques near the front lobby and hung large, glossy photos of the unit members. Chin, Jessica, Nathan, and Philip were all up. Two new detectives, Henry Foringer and Alberto Cabellero, were also up. One empty plaque was up on the end.

"Tommy, take that empty plaque down."

"It's already drilled. We'll have another detective here soon, and then I can just—"

"Just do as I say."

Tommy shrugged. "Your call."

35

Melissa answered the door in jeans and a T-shirt that was torn a few places in the back. Stanton could tell it had been done on purpose at the store, and it took him aback a little. She had been plain and adorable when married to him. Now, she was somehow different. Her nails were long and her skin fake-tanned. She had new piercings in her ears, and her hair had blond highlights.

She led him into the living room and then went to get two drinks. He sat on the leather sofa. Some toys were out on the living room floor and he stared at them a long time. It was always an odd feeling for him to be in someone else's home, as though he was seeing a side of them they didn't allow others to see. But the familiarity of the toys and the photos of his two sons up on the mantel gave it a sense of home that confused him and made him uncomfortable. He wondered whether coming here was a mistake.

Melissa returned with two orange juices and placed one on a coaster in front of him. The coffee table was an old, worn-out wicker stand that looked handwoven. He took a sip of his orange juice, and they sat quietly a while, the wind blowing through some trees in the backyard. The sliding glass door was open, but the screen was closed. He could see several tall trees and a doghouse.

"I didn't know you got a dog."

"Lance bought it for the boys. All it seems to do is poop and bark, but the boys love it."

"What kind of dog is it?"

"I don't know, some purebred he paid three thousand dollars for."

"I was planning on buying a dog for them sometime soon. I'm glad they have it." He put his juice down. It was bitter and had a taste of mint. He figured it must be some sort of import, like the coffee table.

"Lance'll be home in a couple of hours, and I can't have you here. It wouldn't look right. So what is it you want, Jon?"

Stanton opened his mouth, and it seemed as if the words were being pulled from the air. He told her about Harlow and the blackmail, about Jessica, about Hernandez, about Young. He had always found it easy to speak to her and was glad that hadn't changed. But something was different, something very subtle, but it was there—just a slightly lower inflection in her voice, just a few more glances away as he spoke. She was caring about him less and less.

When he was done, she crossed her legs and played with her hair, something he had seen her do when she was thinking. He had always found it adorable but now thought it insignificant, like watching the idiosyncrasies of a stranger.

"I'll talk to Michael," she finally said. "He listens to me. Or he'll at least listen to Lance."

"Not on this. He's played his hand. I have too much information on him, and he'll do everything he can to discredit me and keep me away."

"Then why did you come to me?"

"Honestly, I just wanted someone to know. It may not seem like much to you, but it means a lot that you believe me."

"I can tell when you're lying, and you're not lying right now."

He rose to leave. "If anything happens to me... well, I don't actually know how to finish that sentence."

"You don't have to."

As he walked out the front door, he turned to her. "I'm sorry. For everything. I really wish things could've turned out different between us."

"I wish it would have turned out differently too. But that's life, I guess. You think you're doing okay, and something falls on your head out of the sky."

Stanton climbed into his car and felt warm tears streaming down his cheeks.

36

Darkness had already fallen when Stanton pulled out of the Walmart parking lot. He didn't want to drive during the day. No doubt a BOLO call had gone out for him with his car's make and model. He thought about trading the car in. There were a few places he knew that would take his car, no questions asked, and replace it with another one—granted, one of less value and reliability.

He drove down the boulevard and watched the moon reflecting off the choppy water of the Pacific. A yacht was out past the pier, slowly drifting with the waves, and he wished he were on that yacht right then, enjoying the ocean breeze.

After nearly two hours, he came to a stop in front of the Boca Del Rey apartments. Two young Hispanic males were on the porch again though they were different from any others he'd seen. He walked over to them, and they stared and sucked on spliffs loaded with weed and tobacco.

Stanton held up his badge and brushed past them without saying anything.

He stepped inside, and as the door shut behind him, one of them said, "One less pig you gotta worry about."

The building was quiet that night, and a thick odor of marijuana hung in the air. Stanton remembered it was the first of the month. Welfare checks were distributed today. Many were cashed at all-night check-cashing businesses, and the money was promptly spent on drugs and liquor.

Police tape covered Francisco's apartment door, and someone had tagged gang signs all over it with black and red spray paint. He took out the Swiss Army knife attached to his key chain and slit the tape along the edge of the door. A padlock hung from the door, but the wood was so weak he just put his shoulder to it and gave it one good push. It cracked open immediately.

The living room was hot and stale from lack of circulation. A dark black stain adorned the carpet where Francisco's body had lain, like a wound that wouldn't quite heal. Dirty footprints covered the kitchen linoleum, and all the furniture had been taken from the apartment, probably by people in the building once they heard somebody had passed away.

Stanton went to the kitchen sink and turned on the cold water. He put his hand under the stream and felt the bubbles on his palm before taking a long drink. He turned the water off and returned to the living room. He peered through the blinds outside and didn't see anyone. It wasn't a good view, just cars and a withered tree sticking out of the ground like a massive weed. Headlights shone toward him and then away as the vehicle U-turned in the street. He stepped back and stood in the living room a long time before moving.

Stanton went down the hall. A linen closet was in the hallway and he opened it. A couple of dirty sheets had been thrown on the floor, and the top shelf was broken and leaning to one side. He closed the door and went into the bedroom.

The bed was still there, a king with a stained mattress and chipped headboard. He checked under the bed and opened the closets. Nothing. The view out of the window showed the back of the building, an open space covered in dirt and weeds and with an overflowing dumpster. A yellow streetlight gave the area a warm glow but appeared like the lights in a university basement.

Something crashed, and he froze. Instinctively, he reached for his firearm but felt nothing except the cloth of his shirt. It went quiet again, and then another crash. It was coming from upstairs. He listened intently as people began yelling in Spanish.

He exhaled, unaware that he had been holding his breath, and made his way to the bathroom. He stood outside the door and peered in before flicking on the light. He had bought latex gloves at the store, and he pulled them out of his pocket and put them on.

He stepped inside and shut the door. It was quiet there, and he couldn't hear the yelling any longer. He looked around the mirror and ran his hand along the edge of the sink and over the faucet. He bent down and scanned from one corner of the tile to the other then studied the bathtub and toilet.

Chin Ho and the forensics team believed two or even three assailants had killed Francisco in the bathroom then dragged him into the living room. Stanton knew it wouldn't take three. A single person could be strong enough, especially when determined. But they had scarcely considered why he would've been killed in the bathroom and then placed somewhere else. Their best guess was that the killers wanted to avoid a mess in the living room and instead opted to kill him in the bathtub. But the killers clearly didn't care about leaving evidence or a mess behind. There was something else.

What is it you want me to find in here?

Stanton lifted the cover off the toilet tank and fished around before examining the pipes behind the toilet, trying each one to see whether it was loose. He opened the cabinets below the sink. They were empty except for an old soap wrapper and a carton of baking soda. He pulled on the pipe leading to the faucet, but it was tightly wound and didn't budge.

Forensics had combed the bathroom, but he knew that once they had discovered the blood, it was a routine check from there. A grid search would have followed, checking all the traps and drains. Forensic units were never really invested in a case, and once they developed a plausible theory of what had occurred, they went on autopilot.

He ran his hands up and down the sides of the mirror and over the door, its hinges, the shower curtain, and the small window over the tub. But nothing was there. As he leaned against the counter and wiped at the sweat that had formed on his brow, the air conditioner clicked on. He glanced over at the vent tucked behind the toilet and watched a piece of lint flutter above it a moment before being blown away.

Stanton knelt down and reached behind the toilet. Even from

the floor, it was difficult to reach. He lay on his side, stuck one arm back there, and pulled off the vent guard. Cool air came rushing out, and he held his hand over it and felt the pressure against his fingers. The right side was stronger than the left.

He reached into the weaker side of the vent and ran his fingers in a circle. They touched something. It felt smooth and had a sharp edge. He squeezed lightly and paper crinkled. His fingers wrapped around it, and he slowly brought it up and out of the vent. It was a scrap of lined white paper neatly folded into a small rectangle. He carefully opened it. His heart jumped into his throat as he read:

> wElCoME to ThE gAmE DeTEcTIvE StAntON
> MoNtEgo AVEnue abErdeen driVe

37

Stanton waited several rings before someone picked up.

"Hello?"

"Jessica, it's Jon."

A pause. "Jon, where are you?"

"I'm here, in town. I need your help."

"You need to—"

"You tipped me off because you believe me. If you believe me, then you have to trust me. I need your help, and I can prove I didn't kill Francisco."

"Where are you calling from?"

"Pay phone at the 7-Eleven down the block."

"Okay. Come up. I'll leave the door unlocked."

A few minutes later, Stanton walked into her apartment and announced his presence. She was getting dressed and said she would be out in a minute. He sat down on the couch and leaned his head back, staring at the ceiling. Before long, she stepped out of the bedroom in pinstriped suit pants and a sleeveless red blouse. He noticed she was wearing her holster and firearm under her jacket. He knew the firearm display was for him, just in case.

Stanton laid the paper he'd found down on the coffee table. "I found this."

She picked it up and read it. "What does it mean?"

"I don't know. I Googled the two address terms. There's only one place in the state where streets named Montego and Aberdeen intersect. It's near the Salton Sea. But what I need from you is to check with Eddie in forensics and see if he checked the vent in the bathroom at Francisco Hernandez's apartment."

Her eyes widened. "You think it was placed there after the scene was processed?"

"I don't know," he said. "But it would be incredibly incompetent for Eddie not to look in the vent, and I wouldn't describe

Eddie as incompetent."

"Okay. Hang on." She pulled out her cell phone and dialed the police switchboard before putting it on speakerphone. She asked for Eddie Bowler and was put on hold for two minutes before a gruff voice answered.

"Yeah?"

"Eddie, this is Jessica Turner, in Cold Case."

"Yeah, whaddya need?"

"You were the one that processed the Francisco Hernandez scene, right?"

"Yeah."

"Do you remember checking the vent in the bathroom for any foreign material? Specifically a small sheet of paper."

"I'm sure I did."

"Would you mind checking?" There was a brief silence. "I know it's a pain in the ass, and I'm sorry. But this is really important to the chief, and he's on me about it."

"Yeah, all right. Sit tight."

Stanton looked out the large windows and down onto the street. A city bus passed by, blowing out plumes of black exhaust.

"Okay," Bowler mumbled, "Hernandez, Hernandez... hey, that was the detective that was iced. The one undercover."

"That's him."

"Huh. Okay, hang on... all right, we did a grid search and... yes, I checked the vent for over twenty inches and didn't find anything. It tilted at an angle, and no one could've gotten anything in farther than that."

"That's all I needed to know. Thanks, Eddie."

"Yup."

She hung up and sat down in a wicker chair with a blue seat cushion. "I guess that means it was put there after we left. How would they know you would come back?"

"I don't know. If they knew that, they had to have known I wouldn't be the one assigned to the case. So they would just somehow have to guess that I would come back and search the bathroom."

"You thinking another cop?"

"Maybe. Honestly, I don't know what to think. I'm feeling burned out."

"Jon, I do believe you. But I don't want to lose my career by helping you."

"I understand. I wasn't suggesting that I stay here. I just need to go somewhere and sleep for a while." He rose to leave. "I'm going to the Salton Sea. I'll call you afterward. Take the note into latent prints and have them run it."

"Do you need me to do anything else?"

"I don't think there is anything you can do. But thanks. You can't imagine how nice it is to have someone on your side when everyone else is against you."

"Yeah, I can."

38

Chief Harlow was not used to waiting. He sat on a metal bench at the Pelican Bay State Prison and checked his watch. They had kept him there over an hour and a half. Punishment, he knew, from the warden. The chief had scheduled a visit by his own calendar rather than the prison's, and two guards had to be pulled away and stuck in the visiting corridor.

He strove to always be honest with himself, no matter what. It was difficult enough to be honest with others, but to look at himself without judgment and without filtering was nearly impossible. That was something he had needed to work on constantly for years, from sunup to sundown. He felt he had a grasp of himself now, of what he felt and why he felt it. That helped calm him in tough situations.

But for some reason, he was fuming. He couldn't think about anything but running up to the warden's office and chewing him out. But he had no authority there. At best, the warden would yell back. At worst, he would have him escorted off the property or arrested and stuck in a cell for a few hours. Wardens and judges were the last true tyrants left in America.

The door opened, and a guard led Eli Sherman in. He placed the prisoner on the metal stool in front of Harlow, and Sherman picked up the phone as Harlow did the same.

"I heard they got you as temporary chief now."

"Position turned permanent."

"Oh yeah? What happened to Rufino Ortiz? I thought he was next in line."

"He retired based on some problems he was having."

"Problems?" Sherman chuckled. "Wow, you *are* a politician. I heard he got busted with coke. I knew Rufino. Really well. Never once saw him with coke in all the years I knew him."

Harlow took out some gum and put a piece in his mouth, not

taking his eyes off Sherman. "Yeah, well, I guess we don't really know people."

"No, guess not. So first Jon and now you. You guys miss me down there or something?"

"I have a proposition for you."

"And what's that?"

"Tami Jacobs. Twenty-three, blonde, found in her—"

"I remember the case. What about it?"

"I need your help on it."

Sherman grinned. "You took me off that case and gave it to a couple of ass-kissers that just came up from the gang unit."

"I know. I remember. But you got farther than anyone."

"Then why'd you take me off?"

"I have my reasons."

Sherman was quiet a moment and then said, "You know what, Mike? I never trusted you. From the first second I saw you, I thought you were a snake that would kill his own mother if it made him a few bucks."

"Up yours, Eli. Don't forget which one of us is on this side of the glass."

"Yeah, I know. In a just world, you'd be back here with me."

"In a just world, Jon's bullet would have been a few more inches to the right, and you'd be in a grave instead of a cell." Harlow leaned forward on his elbows. "And let me ask you something; Why the hell would you try to kill your partner? He would've worked something out with you."

"He would have arrested me and testified against me at my trial. There's no gray area for him. Now cut the shit. What do you want?"

"I want that case solved. As quickly as possible. You think you can handle it?"

Sherman's eyes lit up, and a smile came over his lips. He leaned back and spread his legs, allowing himself to slouch comfortably. "What makes you think I haven't already?"

"You would've told me."

"Would I? You gave the biggest case of my career to two

dumbasses who'd never worked a homicide. You really think I'd hand over everything I had to them?"

"No," Harlow admitted, "you wouldn't."

"You know what's interesting about you, Mike? Do you know why you just said that?"

Harlow bit the inside of his cheek. "Because I wouldn't."

"Yeah, I know you wouldn't. I know it, and it creeps you out that me and you think the same. You wanna hear something crazy? Everybody in here thinks like that. It's a type of mentality. I don't even know where it comes from. Parents, maybe. Maybe they're just born with it, though. Like the way you think is just part of your package with your guts and brains."

"I didn't come here for a philosophy lesson. You gonna help me or not?"

"Can't. Not from in here."

"You wouldn't be in there. You help me, you'll be out of custody. You'll have to wear chains and a GPS monitor at all times, and you'll have a federal marshal with you twenty-four seven, but you'll be allowed to be outside the prison."

"And?"

"That's not enough for you?"

"You knew it wouldn't be. What else did you get?"

"Your sentence is life without parole. You help me get who did this, it becomes life with parole."

"How?"

"Your attorney's gonna file a Post-Conviction Remedies Act petition, and the Court of Appeals is going to grant it. One of the justices—not in public, of course—but one of the justices has already agreed."

"Just 'cause I have the possibility doesn't mean anything. Charles Manson has parole hearings, but they won't let him out. They'll never let me out of here, either."

"That's all I got, Eli. That's the extent of my connections. You can help me or not, but I can't give you anything else. And when have you ever heard of a serial killer getting the possibility of parole? It's a huge deal."

"I'm not a serial killer. I only got two kills. FBI defines it as three kills. But it doesn't mean shit. They won't let me out."

"Fine." Harlow stood "Then I'll find another way. Have fun with your butt buddies in here."

"I didn't say no."

"Then what?"

"Put it in writing."

"Are you fucking stupid? We're talking about an appellate judge making a finding before being presented the case. I can't put that in writing. No, my friend, we're just going to have to trust each other on this one."

Sherman smiled. "Well, I guess I ain't got nothing else."

"*Ain't*? Since when did you start talking like trailer trash?"

"You are what you're around."

"Lord help us if that's true. So, you still haven't given me an answer."

"Okay. You got yourself a deal."

39

There was perhaps no more eerie place on earth for Jon Stanton than the Salton Sea. In the nineteenth century, the only reason Californians had to be near the Salton Sea was for the salt-mining operations. But the area proved too harsh an environment and went into decline.

An effort in the 1950s to rejuvenate the area had gained momentum, and celebrities from that era could be seen in old photographs, hanging out in boats and sipping wine or beer with groups of friends. But the rejuvenation never stuck, and the expected real-estate boom never materialized. Fish were introduced into the lake, but the heavier-than-expected rains and overwhelming salinity of the water wiped out the introduced species quickly. The rejuvenation resulted only in shores full of dead fish and half-finished homes staring out over the water like corpses.

Corpses were what Stanton remembered about the area from his childhood. Small fish had lined the shore in piles, their eyes dried out. Once, he found an entire beach of seashells and began happily collecting them, enjoying the crunch underneath his feet. Then his father had told him they were not seashells but the bones of dead fish and animals.

The Salton Sea was nearly abandoned. The nearby towns were known more for their massive production of methamphetamine than any tourist attraction.

Stanton took the interstate down and regretted not trading in his car. Every police cruiser he saw on the road was a potential threat, and his heart would race until the cruiser turned away or sped past him. The intersection of Montego and Aberdeen was near the shore. He looked farther down the road to the south and saw an abandoned warehouse. He cruised down and parked in front of the building.

All the windows were broken out or painted black. The wood and paint were falling off in large chunks, and the dirt surrounding the building was littered with trash. Stanton stepped out of his car, and the powerful odor of sea salt filled his nostrils. Piles of dog feces spotted the surrounding ground, telling him that packs of feral dogs roamed the area, scavenging garbage cans and eating the carcasses of dead fish and game that died near the lake.

Stanton found a door marked *Employee Entrance*. He looked around and realized he was completely alone. Maybe it had been a mistake to come, but he knew he couldn't leave. He had nowhere else to go.

He tried the doorknob—it turned—and opened the door. He went inside.

The interior was a large space with no wall divisions, and old machinery had been left to rust and fall apart on the factory floor. Stanton could see a few nests, what the homeless called the makeshift sleeping places they made with whatever soft material they could find. Mostly newspapers and blankets. Blankets were valuable, and he knew no one would leave them willingly. They would be back for them, or they were still here.

He turned toward the front of the warehouse and walked into an open doorway to the office spaces. The first office was small, almost the size of a bathroom, and he quickly scanned it before stepping out and going to the next. He opened a filing cabinet and checked the drawers, but the only thing there was rat feces. Next he came to what he thought would have been a break room with an empty water jug and an old fridge lying on the floor. The carpet had been torn out, revealing wood sticky with large patches of glue.

A calendar with a shoeprint on it lay next to the fridge. He kicked it open with his foot, revealing a woman in string bikini bottoms and no top. The refrigerator was empty except for mold.

In the third office, he found an abandoned pair of shoes that had been worn away to the point that the soles were falling off.

In the fourth was a dull kitchen knife with the handle missing. But it was all innocuous. Nothing was there.

He went out to the factory floor and wandered among the large machines. Once, they had been powered and producing goods that traveled halfway around the world. They had been taken care of, cleaned and polished and maintained. They were currently on the brink of falling to dust.

A small stairwell was near the back, leading to a platform overlooking the floor. Behind it was another office. Stanton climbed the stairs and stood on the platform looking over the factory floor. He imagined the workers that must've been here, the laughter, the sadness, the hours upon hours of mindless labor that must've dulled their souls. He turned to the office door behind him. It was labeled *Supervisor* and was thick, with a smooth steel knob that hadn't decayed like the rest of the factory.

Stanton tried the door and found it locked. He tried kicking it open, but the lock was too strong and the door too thick. Next to the door were a few windows. He broke one with his elbow and then cleared out the jagged edges carefully. He lifted himself up on the sill and climbed in. A few pieces of glass he hadn't gotten to stuck out, and they scraped and cut his knees and hands. A tiny stream of blood flowed from one palm, and he instinctively sucked on it and then wrapped it tightly in his shirt. He stood frozen, applying pressure to his hand, listening to the sounds of a dead building.

Another nest was in the office, with two old blankets. They had webs and rat droppings on them. He figured the nests were too old and too dirty to be in use. Even the homeless had abandoned this place long before.

A large desk was pushed against a wall, and behind it was another door, a closet. He walked to it and tried the knob; it was open. The door creaked, and dust kicked up as it scraped along the floor.

Though it was dark inside, he could make out an outline perfectly, soft curves leading to a disheveled top. It had been pushed far back into the closet, behind a dark trench coat and next to a box full of paper clips and documents and notepads. But the outline was unmistakable.

It was a body.

40

When Stanton got outside into the sunlight, he shut the factory door behind him. He snorted through his nostrils in a futile attempt to force the building's air from his lungs.

With little light and no context, Stanton had still been able to see a pattern: the animal-like ferocity of the attack, the torn and ragged flesh, breasts bitten or ripped away from the body. No doubt existed in his mind that it was the work of Tami Jacobs's killer.

He called Jessica and told her what he had found. He asked her not to call it in for two hours to give him time with the body. She told him she would wait one.

He took a brisk walk to the shore. Laid out in front of him was a blanket of small bones, and he could see why, through his childhood eyes, he'd thought they were seashells. He cleared a space with his foot and sat down. Bones he had missed crunched underneath him as he stretched out his legs and then curled them back against his body. The scene had caught him off guard, like the photos of Tami. As a detective in the thick of his career, he had distanced himself from horror. *Desensitized* was the word his father had used to describe it when Jon had told him how he felt. But that wasn't accurate. He was still sensitive to it but was able to push it down deep inside, where it couldn't get out—at least not right away. That was how he could function and push himself forward when he needed to.

Still, he was glad that that one was dead. The live ones had been much harder to deal with—the interviews at hospitals with broken and bleeding women or young girls. The guilt and misplaced blame they felt, along with the anger welling up inside him, tore his insides apart. He never wanted any of that to touch Melissa or the boys, so he kept it bottled up as tightly as possible, unacknowledged even by him. But it was too large a part of his life to repress. Soon, he had to repress everything and withdrew into himself. That was when he and Melissa didn't talk anymore.

He stood up and watched the small waves lap the shore for a while before heading to his car to get his flashlight.

Back into the building, he stood over the body for several minutes before he flicked on his light. In a normal scene, he would look for certain things on his mental checklist: ligature marks, synthetic and hair fibers, blood spatter, footprints, fingerprints. He would take photographs, video during three walk-throughs followed by diagramming. Later would come a rape kit administered by a nurse, and a serological analysis. But there was no time for any of that now. According to his watch, he had only thirty-seven minutes before Jessica called it in.

Holding the flashlight between his teeth, he snapped on a pair of gloves. He took a deep breath and turned his attention to the body. She was in her early twenties and blonde. Stanton moved the light closer to her face, and her mouth fell open. She gasped.

He jumped back, the flashlight falling and hitting the floor. His heart pounded in his ears. When he composed himself, he felt for a pulse. No beat. Her skin was cold and her body rigid.

When someone passed, bacteria in the intestinal tract would begin to eat the organs, releasing gas as a byproduct. That was what caused corpses to bloat. The gas would sporadically be passed through the mouth and nose, causing a gasping sound. Occasionally, if it activated the vocal cords, it could produce vocal noises. In the Middle Ages, they often mistook this phenomenon as vampirism, and the corpse would be staked, decapitated, and burned.

Stanton stepped away from the body and leaned against the wall. Sweat rolled down his face, and he wiped it with the back of his forearm.

When he was ready, he turned back to the body. He didn't want to disturb anything for the forensic unit, so he tried to run his hands carefully over the inside of the closet. He closely examined the body, the box, and the trench coat. Apart from those, the closet was empty.

He searched the office, the desk, and the blankets left on one side of the room. He checked the corners of the room and found nothing. As he was about to turn back toward the body, he heard a noise on the factory floor. It sounded as though someone had dropped something then run.

He stepped out onto the platform. The floor was quiet. Stanton walked down the stairs as silently as possible and then ducked low, looking underneath the machines. On the far end nearest the door was a shadow. The shadow moved.

Without a firearm, he felt helpless. He crouched low and ran behind one of the machines. Peering around the corner, he saw that the shadow was planted in one spot and didn't move. The main entrance was on the other side of the building, but it was bolted and chained. The employee entrance was the only way in or out.

Stanton quietly went from one machine to the next, keeping his head low so he could watch the shadow. As he was stepping to another machine, he heard a sneeze and then someone mumbling.

The person didn't respond to his movements at all, and Stanton managed to get behind him. He snuck around the machine and glanced at a man huddled on the floor. In one swift movement, Stanton sprinted toward him and threw his body weight against the man, slamming him to the floor.

The man fought back, bashing his fist into Stanton's jaw and trying to grab his neck, but he couldn't get a good grip. He flipped onto his stomach to push himself up, and Stanton wrapped his forearm around the man's neck and pressed his other arm to the back of his head, creating a scissor choke.

The man screamed, and Stanton pressed harder, hard enough that the man's body began to go limp. When the man had lost strength and was about to pass out, Stanton flipped him over and sat on his chest, using his knees to pin his arms to the floor. The man was coughing, and Stanton let him finish before speaking.

"Who are you?"

"I ain't nobody, man."

Stanton noticed his clothing was torn and ragged. "What are you doing here?"

"I live here, man. I live here. Get off me. I ain't done nothin'."

"Tell me who you are."

The man stank of marijuana and body odor. His breath reeked of alcohol, and his teeth were yellowed and blackened. Stanton ran his hands over the man's clothing but found no weapon. He stood up.

The man huffed for breath but didn't get up. "You the detective. You the detective, yeah?"

"Yes."

"Star, er, Stage something."

"Stanton."

"Yeah, man. I got a message for you."

"From who?"

"Don't know. Dude paid me a hundred bucks and said to wait here for you."

"Who was it?"

"I don't know, man. I told you. Just some white dude. He gave me a C-note and said, 'Tell Stanton there's gonna be another one in two weeks.' That's what he said. Two weeks."

"What else did he say?"

"Didn't say nothin' else. Just, 'Tell him there's gonna be another one in two weeks.'"

Stanton helped the man to his feet. "What did he look like?"

"White dude, man—I don't know."

"Did he say anything else? It's very important you tell me."

"Nah, man. That's all the dude said."

Stanton glanced back at the supervisor's office. "Do you know anything about who she is?"

He looked genuinely confused. "Who?"

"Here." Stanton pulled out a hundred-dollar bill. He gave it to him and then asked if he could remember anything else.

"Nah, man. That's it."

"Did you see him bring anything into that office back there?"

"Nah, when he gave me the money, I left. I ain't seen nothin' after that."

"Well, the police are going to be here soon. I think you should go somewhere else for a while, if you got some place."

"Someplace else costs money."

Stanton looked in his wallet. He pulled out a couple hundred bucks, all the money he had left. His bank accounts, because of the warrant, were no doubt frozen. Still, he thought this man needed it more. He gave him half the money. "Take care of yourself."

"I will, man. Thank you."

Stanton checked his watch. Jessica should've called it in over ten minutes ago.

He ran out and jumped into his car. As he made his way into Salton City, he saw two police cruisers heading toward the factory.

41

Hunter Royal watched himself in the mirror over the bed as he climaxed. The young brunette bent over in front of him, groaning with pleasure. Their bodies glistened with sweat under the red lighting. He collapsed next to her on the bed and studied his reflection. His body was hairless from waxing, and it looked good—not model good, but good. But he'd always had a problem with his nipples. He thought they were too big, considering his slender chest. He planned to pay a visit to his plastic surgeon in Beverly Hills to get them done, but it was a matter of timing. He would need to be bandaged for at least two weeks, and he was hitting the pool right now at least four times a week. Maybe in the cooler months.

"Are you spending the night?" the girl asked.

"No. I got work to do early tomorrow."

She pulled a joint out of the nightstand and lit it. The smoke was sweet, and it quickly overtook the scents of sweat and sex. They passed it back and forth for a few minutes before he rose and found his boxers and jeans.

"You could go to work from here tomorrow," she said, "if you wanted."

"Nah, you know I like sleeping in my own bed." When he had put on his shirt and sandals, he leaned down and kissed her, running his tongue over her lips. "I'll call you."

"No you won't."

"No, I won't. You call me."

He left the house and stood on the front porch a while, enjoying the evening air. The garden next to the porch was well tended and the lawn freshly mowed. The sun was climbing down and painting the sky a light pink.

Though nineteen, the girl still lived at home. Her parents were out of town. Hunter got a big kick out of sex in her parent's bed. Maybe he would send a note to her father a little later, letting him know. He only wished he could see the guy's face as he read it.

Hunter walked down to his car. As he was about to insert his key into the lock, he felt pressure on his arms. His neck snapped back as someone grabbed him from behind. He tried to shout, but his airway was blocked. He was lifted off his feet, dragged down the sidewalk to a car, and thrown in the back.

"What the fuck!" he shouted.

Two men climbed into the backseat with him. One stuck a gun into his side, and Hunter froze. Warm urine trickled down his leg.

"Listen, guys. I'm rich. I can get—"

"Shut up, you piece of shit. I don't want your money."

In the passenger seat, Mike Harlow leaned back, absently tapping a ring against his teeth.

"Mike? Are you shitting me? You can't—" One of the men sitting next to Royal elbowed him in the face, causing his nose to crack and start bleeding. "Fuck!"

"I need something from you," Harlow said. "We're both gonna get something out of it, so it's a good deal. But I need a yes or no now."

"This how you ask all your friends for favors?"

"You're not my friend, you parasite, and don't you forget it."

Hunter pressed his fingers to his nose. The blood was gushing now, so he tilted his head back, letting it go down his throat rather than his shirt.

"Don't tilt your head back," Harlow said. "It'll make you vomit if you get too much blood."

Hunter straightened up. "Whaddya want?"

"Before we talk deal, how's that little filly in there?"

"She's fine."

"How old is she?"

"Nineteen."

Harlow threw a piece of paper onto his lap and flipped on the interior light. It was a copy of the girl's high school ID.

"Shit," Hunter said.

"That's right, asshole. She's sixteen. You're smarter than that. You should always check ID. Although she may have a fake one she would've showed you. Under the law, doesn't make a difference. How messed up is that?"

"Whaddya want, Mike?"

"Now that you're in more of a dealing mood, we can talk. Eli Sherman. I got him released into my custody."

"Why?"

"He's helping with a cold case."

"How'd you manage that?"

"That's not your concern. Here's what your concern is—you can't write about it. Don't snoop around, don't ask questions, don't call any of your boys. You leave this alone. I don't want the public to know about this."

"I'm not the only reporter in town."

"No, but for some reason I think you're the only one that would find out. You got the deepest contacts, and I've seen how you operate. You wait until the crowd's gone and then come over and ask your questions and get what you want. You're a perverted little scumbag weasel, but you're a good reporter."

Despite the blood pouring over his hand, Hunter felt a small gleam of pride. Legitimacy was something he had coveted since his days writing five-hundred-word op-eds for a porno magazine in Los Angeles.

"So I don't report on it, and you don't arrest me?"

"And when I catch the cocksucker I want to catch, you can break the story and get exclusive interviews with me and Eli. I won't give it to any other reporters."

"Shit, count me in."

He grinned. "You know, Hunter, that's what I've always liked about you. You know when you're outmatched. Now get outta my car. And no more teenagers."

Hunter was thrown out and fell to the pavement. He stood up and flipped Harlow off as the car sped away.

42

Harlow walked out to his parking spot at the San Diego PD headquarters. He leaned against his car for a few minutes and stared at the full moon. It was incredible, he thought, that that rock was what Caesar and Napoleon and George Washington and Al Capone—and all the other people he had read about growing up—looked up to and saw in the sky. The same moon. It gave him some comfort that there was continuity in his species. He was not religious; bowing and praising someone or something else had never appealed to him. Life to him was random chance that could've happened on a million different worlds but ended up happening on earth. But the moon that he looked at was the same moon his ancestors had seen. Life moved on.

He didn't feel like going home to his wife. That relationship had ended years before. They were now roommates, sharing the same space because it was more convenient than going through the hassle of a divorce and custody battle. They had sat down at the kitchen table and talked it through, rationally. Less rational people wouldn't have been able to do it, and he was pleased when she was receptive.

They had agreed they would stay together but live separate lives. They belonged to different gyms, they had different circles of friends, they went on separate vacations, and above all, they slept in different bedrooms. It had been working fine for quite some time until Harlow saw her on a date with another man. They had also agreed that they would see other people, but there was a world of difference between theory and practice. When he actually saw it, he longed for her, and rage filled him. The man had been lucky Harlow was at the restaurant with other officers. He knew that for sure.

It had been confusing lately, though. They had begun eating dinner as a family, for the kids. They had started talking again, reconnecting. She had even asked him where he'd been when he had come home late one night. Another conversation was needed, and the dinners would have to end if it was going to work.

Harlow climbed in and began driving. He decided he didn't feel like taking the freeway just yet. He drove down a residential neighborhood and saw the lights on in a large white house. A couple sat watching television in the living room, and Harlow remembered it was Friday night. He had missed the Friday night fights, and he didn't have a date for the night. It would be warmed up leftovers and pornography. But he would hit the gym in the morning and see what he could find there. Sometimes, it took him only a couple of hours of faking exercise to strike up just the right conversation with just the right person. Once, he had even banged an older aerobics instructor in his car in the gym parking lot.

He parked the car at the curb and observed the couple. The male had his arm around a young blonde, and they were watching a movie. Her face wasn't visible from this angle, but he could see her sockless feet up on the coffee table. They were smooth and milky white with brightly colored toenails.

A squeal and then red-and-blues filled his car with light. A patrolman had pulled up behind him. The officer stepped out of the car with a flashlight and came to the driver's-side window. He tapped on the glass with his knuckles, and Harlow rolled the window down.

"License, registration, and proof of insurance, please."

"You're new to the force, aren't you, Officer"—he glanced at the name tag—"Rasmussen?"

"License, registration, and proof of insurance, please. Now."

"Sure."

Harlow handed him the documents, and the officer went back to his cruiser. It was a Dodge Charger, one of the two dozen Harlow had commissioned for the traffic squad. The old model Fords the city and county used to buy simply couldn't keep up with the newer vehicles coming out. More than one suspect vehicle had gotten away because the older cars were too slow and the choppers were busy. Harlow had gone to the mayor and gotten the extra funds he needed in less than three hours.

The officer was gone at least ten minutes. Harlow guessed it took him two to run his name, and the rest of the time was spent figuring out a way to apologize without coming off as a sycophant. Apologize too much, and you sound as if you're apologizing for doing your job. Apologize too little, and you offend the boss. A tough spot for a patrolman to be in, and Harlow enjoyed watching.

The officer came back. He handed the documents back to Harlow and said, "Everything looks fine. Have a good night."

Harlow watched the patrolman walk back to his car and then pull away. *Well done.* He'd appeared not to know what he had done and could later claim ignorance, but he didn't follow up with any questions or citations. Harlow had been pulled over several times as both assistant chief and chief, and no one had ever played it quite so well. He would have to remember that officer's name.

He turned back toward the couple on the couch, but they had closed the blinds. Harlow sighed and pulled away from the curb.

The city was quiet as he drove, but it was a false quiet, like someone inhaling a deep breath before shouting. Friday and Saturday nights were when madness took to the streets and the clubs and the bars. California had more madness than anywhere else in the country. Something about the people or the climate attracted it from all over the nation. And he saw it then—in the movements of the pimps avoiding him, in the nakedness of the prostitutes standing on the corners and propositioning him, and in the eyes of the killers looking at him.

He came to a red light, and a car full of girls rolled to a stop next to him. They giggled, and he smiled at them, but they turned away. He motioned for them to roll down their window, but they didn't respond. As they pulled away, he caught himself in the rearview and saw the gray in his hair and the wrinkles around his eyes. It took someone honking behind him to get the car moving again.

When he got to his driveway, another car was already there. He parked behind it and ran into the house. If there was a man in his house with his wife, there was going to be hell to pay.

He opened the front door and strode to the kitchen, where he saw Melissa Stanton and his wife sitting at the table. They both looked at him silently a moment before his wife excused herself and left the room.

"What are you doing in my house?" Harlow asked.

"Making friends. Crystal's actually delightful. I don't know why you didn't ever bring her around."

"None of your fucking business, and I asked you a question."

"You really think you could do this to me and nothing would happen?"

"Do what?"

"He's the father of my children, Mike. You think I'd let my kids go through life thinking their father's a murderer? Getting comments and stares their whole lives, not being invited to birthday parties and baseball games?"

"Not my problem."

"Oh, but it is your problem." She got up and stepped over to him. "Because you're going to fix this."

Harlow chuckled. "I've always admired your balls. Now please, get outta my house."

"I know where the skeletons are buried. I will destroy you even if it destroys me in the process."

"You don't know shit," he said, trying to hide his uncertainty.

"Oh yeah? You don't actually think Jon never told me anything you told him, do you? Do you remember smoking a fat joint and drinking Cristal in a hot tub in Vegas? You told him what you did, and then you started crying like a baby. He followed up on it, the young man in New Hampshire, just to see if it actually happened. And now I know where that young man is. I have his phone number. And he is really anxious to know who you are."

He couldn't think of what to say. He stood silently and

watched her.

"Fix it. Right away. If he's not cleared by tomorrow, I'm calling the FBI."

"I can't do it by tomorrow."

"Not my problem," she said, imitating his voice. "And just in case you want to get crazy, I told Lance everything. And he told his staffer. Anything happens to me, and they will burn you."

As she left the house, Harlow slumped down onto the linoleum. He put his face in his hands and thought about what to do, but nothing came. Calculations were always running in his head, guesswork regarding the next move and the next advantage. But his mind was blank, and he couldn't formulate even the most basic thoughts.

He picked up the phone and dialed Tommy's number.

43

Stanton stopped at a mechanic's shop and parked in front, next to a minivan. The shop looked like an abandoned gas station, and the interior was dingy and stank of grease. He asked the cashier at the front for Louis and then sat on a fake leather couch and flipped through an issue of *Time*.

"Johnny!"

Stanton smiled and stood up as Louis hugged him and slapped his back. He'd gained weight and was now at least fifty pounds heavier than he'd been when Stanton last saw him, and he was tipping the scales even then.

"How are ya, Louis?"

"Good, man. What's up wit' you?"

"Nothing much. Same old, same old."

"Yeah? How's Melissa and your boys?"

"We're divorcing."

"No shit? Ah, I'm sorry, brother. What happened? You two seemed like you was perfect."

"Just isn't in the cards sometimes."

"Ah, shit, man. I'm sorry. Look, my Juanita's got this cousin, man, Angelica—yo, she is hot. Big tits, beautiful smile, man."

Stanton grinned. "Maybe some other time."

"All right, man, but you hit me up if you get lonely."

"I will."

"So what's up? What you need?"

"I need to get rid of my car and get a new one."

"Yeah? There's a dealer that's a friend'a mine that's got some —"

"No, not like that."

Louis looked at him a second and then said, "Oh, no shit? A'ight. Well, it ain't gonna be pretty."

"I know."

"Hang out a sec. Lemme see what I got."

He went out to the back of the building and then stuck his head through a door and motioned for Stanton to follow him. Behind the building was a massive field packed with cars. Many of them were out of service and being used for spare parts, but a few could still function.

"I got a Beamer over there, ninety-six. It's a'ight but gots some problems with the catalytic converter. I got a old Taurus too. It's that red one right there."

"I'll take the Taurus."

"You sure, man? The Beamer's a nice ride."

"No, the Taurus is fine."

They did an even trade—no paperwork, no questions—and Stanton drove out of the parking lot with a 2001 Ford Taurus registered to someone halfway around the country who didn't know his name was being used to register cars in Southern California. As he pulled away, he saw Louis's team begin work on his Honda. Even though they had Stanton's permission and he would have gladly signed over the title, they would change the VIN, the tires, and any other parts with serial numbers, then repaint and sell it on Craigslist or Autotrader. Louis was known for making cars disappear. He had helped Stanton another time when no one else would, and Stanton would never forget it.

Stanton drove for nearly four hours and ended up just outside Santa Barbara. He found a motel near a liquor store and a small convenience store. The lobby held two old chairs and a rug with cigarette burns, and the cashier sat behind a desk with a large sign reading *No Checks*.

He rented a room on the third floor and made his way up the stairs. The room was small, and the bed was hidden away in the wall in what appeared to be a large closet. The furniture consisted of one 1960s couch, a small coffee table, and a nineteen-inch color television. He pulled the bed down and smelled that the sheets had not been changed since the last occupant. He sat down on the couch and dialed Jessica's number.

"Hey, Jon."

"Hey. Any word?"

"Nothing much. Imperial County's taking point, and they made a big fuss that we came down too. They think it's going to get a lot of media attention, and they want to be the ones in front of the cameras."

"Doesn't matter. They don't want to be the ones doing the work."

"Yeah, I have no doubt. But nothing's really happened yet. Someone called and left a message for the chief about it, but he hasn't called back. How are you doing?"

"As good as can be, I guess."

"Do you have a plan?"

"You sound worried about me."

"Well, yeah, it's just... I've put up with a lot of bullshit in my life, but this is something I can't really deal with. I'm thinking of quitting."

"You shouldn't do that. There need to be good cops to counter people like Mike."

"I just can't believe what he's doing to you. And that he's probably going to get away with it. I just get this kinda sick feeling whenever I see my badge."

"People like him... somewhere down the line, something will happen. It always does."

She exhaled loudly, and Stanton heard some glasses clink.

"I guess," she said.

"Look, don't quit. That's not the right move, and that's not what I want. Stick with it just a little longer."

"Jon, do you think the chief killed Hernandez? Is he that crazy?"

"I don't know. If he had done it, I don't think he would've been as brazen as leaving his body out and blaming another cop. I think it was gangland. But something else is going on. Something's overlapping with whatever happened to Tami Jacobs, but I don't know what it is. I'm getting closer to it, but it's just not there yet."

"I... just be careful."

"I will."

Stanton hung up and put his feet on the coffee table. Down the hall, he could hear a couple arguing.

44

Stanton jolted awake. He had slept on the couch, and his lower back and neck screamed with pain. Rolling his neck, he sat up and grabbed his cell phone off the table. The alarm had gone off, though he didn't remember setting it.

For a moment, he thought about taking a shower and changing clothes. Then he remembered where he was and what he was doing. There were no other clothes, and a shower, usually relaxing, would not bring him any comfort.

He went to the lone window in the room, overlooking the street. An old truck coated in rust, with a cracked windshield, sat on the curb, parking tickets piling up underneath the wipers. Across the street, a Hispanic man rode a bicycle down the sidewalk and said a few words to some friends sitting on their porch and drinking beer.

He wasn't used to the inability to act. Normally, he would be hassling the medical examiner's office or the forensics unit or the state toxicology lab to move quicker and put his case on priority status though it probably didn't merit expediting. He had always had an ability to motivate people to do things for him, and he wasn't sure he even did it consciously.

But there were no techs or medical examiners or lab assistants to hassle now. He was an outcast, no more respected than the person he was chasing.

Last night, in the lonely hours before morning, he had thought about turning himself in and hiring a good lawyer. Maybe it was better to fight this in court than out on the streets? But he knew that wasn't true. He had seen many people, innocent people, suffer through a court system that neither cared for nor respected them. The court system, no matter how good his lawyer, would not vindicate him.

As he contemplated what to do next, his phone buzzed—

Jessica.

"Hey," he said.

"You need to get down here, now."

"Where?"

"The admin offices. Harlow called me this morning. The charges against you have been dropped, and the warrant's been recalled."

"How?"

"George Young recanted, and the DA dropped the case. He said that he had actually seen someone else and, when he did a photo lineup, realized it wasn't you. They dropped the case, Jon!"

Stanton kept his excitement in check. With the chief, there were always other angles and ones usually not seen or considered. "What else did Mike say?"

"He said he knew that I had kept in contact with you, but that he wasn't upset. He just wanted you to come in and talk with him. I checked the statewide just now. It's for real. The case is dismissed."

"Give me an hour and I'll call you back."

"Okay. Hurry up."

Stanton hung up the phone and immediately called Melissa. She answered on the second ring.

"What did you do?" he said by way of greeting.

"What're you talking about?"

"Cases don't get dropped like that. Did you see him?"

"Maybe."

"Mel, I didn't want you involved in this."

"Well, you know what, Jon? I am involved. Like it or not, you're the father of my kids, and everything you do affects us."

"I know. I'm sorry. I didn't mean to upset you. I really appreciate whatever it is you did."

"I didn't do it for you. I did it for them."

She hung up. Stanton looked out the window. Sunlight reflected off a BMW driving by. Harlow would be prepared. He would have ammunition and an agenda. Stanton wondered whether he'd just gotten kicked out of the frying pan and into the fire.

Stanton walked into the San Diego Police Headquarters and Administrative Offices. The place seemed odd, like a relative's house he was no longer welcome in. The security personnel eyed him but said nothing. A few uniforms attempted to stare him down, and one shoulder-checked him, but Stanton ignored them. He was far too relieved to hold any animosity, even toward Harlow. After all, the man was corrupt and wicked, but he had just been looking out for himself and his family. Stanton, despite himself, forgave him.

He made his way to the Cold Case Unit and had to be let in.

Harlow was at his desk, going through some paperwork. He looked up but didn't motion for Stanton to sit.

"Shut the door, please."

Stanton closed the heavy door and sat down in one of the chairs. He crossed his legs and folded his hands, deciding he would not be the first to speak.

"So," the chief said, "heard any good gossip lately?"

Stanton grinned. "I heard the chief of police is an SOB."

"Yeah, well, I guess he is."

"Did you get George to lie, or did he volunteer?"

"He wanted to do something. He blamed you for Francisco's death. But it was my idea. I had the warrant drawn up and got the DA to get on board. I can't even begin to say I'm sorry. I panicked. You said you were going to IAD, and I thought about what would happen. Do you have any idea what they would do to me? I would go to prison for some of the shit we've pulled. The number of people I've put in there, the enemies I've made, I'd be dead in a week."

"Did you kill him?"

"Who, Francisco? Hell no. How could you even ask me that? That just happened and fell into our lap. No, we're gonna catch the sons'a bitches that did that. It was just an opportunity, and I seized it. I'm sorry, Jon."

"Let's just move on."

"I'm glad to hear you say that. I want you back in the unit, working the Tami Jacobs case. I don't know if Jessica told you, but there's been another homicide that matches the pattern."

"She mentioned it."

"Imperial County's got it, but they don't know what to do with it. There's still some saber rattling, but they'll eventually give it up to us."

Stanton hesitated. "Are you going to IAD?"

"Jon, come on."

"You're lost, Mike. The line between us and them doesn't apply to you. You don't have the right to run this organization anymore. I know you've probably already greased a bunch of palms at IAD. But I know you haven't at the feds. They hate your guts and would arrest you as soon as you offered it. I'm asking you. Please, resign. Don't make me go to them."

"Why would I resign? I got money coming in, I got power, I can do whatever the fuck I want. Who would give that up?"

"You have police officers selling drugs. And it's not just steroids, is it? It's gone too far. If you don't turn yourself in, I will have no choice but to go to the FBI."

"You do what you gotta do. But I ain't going anywhere."

Stanton nodded and stood. "Fine. I'll come back. I need the resources here. But after this case is closed, I'm done for good."

"Fine."

Stanton walked out of the office and down the hall. He waited until he was alone in the elevator to turn off the digital recorder in his pocket.

45

Eli Sherman lay on his bunk in his cell. There was never enough room, and today he felt as if there weren't even enough for him to think properly. The cell was nine feet by eight feet, and he shared it with another inmate. The only furnishings were a steel toilet, a steel sink, a bunk bed, a small mirror, and a stand with a television. Despite the surroundings, the cell was immaculately clean. Sherman insisted that his cellie clean whenever he couldn't get the chance.

His cellie, Tucker Matheson, was a decent man. An African American raised in Louisiana, he had a Southern drawl and deep-set eyes that always seemed to be bloodshot. His wife had taken the kids and moved in with another man while they were still married. The other man lived for six hours with his new family before Tucker beat him to death in a fistfight. Charged with murder, Tucker had pled to voluntary manslaughter. He was on the eighth year of a twelve-year sentence.

Sherman guessed it was later in the evening, but it was hard to tell. No clocks were in there, and they had to guess the time by the television shows that were playing. He jumped off the top bunk and glanced at Tucker, who was asleep.

Sherman stripped down to his boxers and stood in front of the mirror. He had grown old in two years. His hair, once jet-black, was now peppered gray. Wrinkles surrounded his eyes, and the skin on his neck appeared looser. The numerous tattoos he had received while inside he wore like badges of honor. The most prominent were the ones he had on his knuckles, spelling *hell* on both hands.

Though the prison noise had died down, it wasn't quiet. Quiet never came to this place, even in the dead of night. That was the first thing he learned about prison on his first day. The second thing was that it always smelled. The cleaning crew would come by twice a week, and they routinely cycled the stale air, but it never helped. At all times there was the stench of sweat, piss, and feces, the stink of hundreds of human beings crammed together so tightly the walls themselves absorbed their smell.

"Heard you was leaving?"

Sherman looked at Tucker but saw his eyes weren't open. "Yeah."

"You coming back?"

"Not planning on it."

"Don't seem right, you kill them girls and get to go free."

"Whoever said the world was right?" Sherman quipped.

Tucker twisted his neck until it popped. "You gonna get them urges again, Eli? The bad thoughts."

"The bad thoughts come and go. It's a fight, that's for sure."

"I ain't never got bad thoughts. I killed the motherfucker 'cause he deserved it. Don't seem right, you gettin' to go free and me bein' here."

"No, it doesn't."

46

Stanton went back to his office around six, just after everybody else had gone home. He went through the Jacobs file again. He stared for a long time at the photos, but there was no doubt. Either the same person had killed both girls or someone with intimate knowledge of the first killing had carried out the second.

Chin Ho stepped into Stanton's office. He stood awkwardly at the door a full ten seconds before speaking. "I guess there's not much I could say."

"You did your job, Chin. Besides, I don't hold grudges. They shorten your lifespan."

He fidgeted with the doorknob. "Thanks."

"You're welcome."

"So did you hear about Eli?"

"What about him?"

"He's out. He's being transported down here tonight to help with the Jacobs and Dallas murders."

"Dallas?"

"Oh yeah. Hold on a sec." He hurried over to his office and then came back, sat down, and threw a copy of a file onto the desk. "Pamela Maren Dallas. The girl in the closet at the Salton Sea."

"How'd you ID her?"

"Dental records. She's got some next of kin, too, a mother and stepfather. They haven't been notified yet. Harlow's assigned the case officially to you and Jessica. Unofficially, Eli's helping."

Stanton leaned back in his chair. "That's a bad idea."

"Why? Seemed all *Silence of the Lambs* to me. Kind of takes one to catch one." Perhaps seeing that Stanton grew uncomfortable at that, Chin quickly said, "Harlow only wants him out a few weeks. After that, if there's no developments, he goes back in the can."

"Thanks for the file, Chin."

"No problem." He cleared his throat. "You're going to get treated like shit from some of the people here, Jon. I don't know what the hell happened with George and that whole thing, but I just wanted you to know I think what you're doing, catching this bastard… I think it's noble."

After Chin left, Stanton flipped over the file. On the first page was the familiar glossy stare of the dead. Next came a few photos of the scene—not nearly as many as there should've been—and then one of the body laid out on a metal autopsy table. Despite the chalk-white skin and the purple bruising, her beauty still shone through.

According to the autopsy report, the ME detected early signs of liver failure from alcohol abuse. Aside from her height, weight, and some other statistics, no other information was in there, nothing about her life. It was the type of report that could have been written for a drug murder where victimology was not a factor. Salton City was not used to this kind of monster.

At twenty-one, Pamela still lived with her parents, and their home was in Orange County. She had been dead at least three or four days. Her parents should have called it in by now.

Stanton called Jessica and gave her the address to the parents' home. She didn't hesitate or complain that it was after hours. She just agreed to meet him there.

Stanton drove down the interstate in the waning sunlight, wishing he'd waited another day or two before trading in his car. He thought about going back, but he knew it was already altered and on the market. And it wouldn't be fair to Louis, even if the guy was a crook.

He saw a sign for Disneyland, and pain pulled at his guts. He missed his boys. There was no doubt they had heard their father was a fugitive, and he wanted to speak to them, to explain what had happened. But that wasn't possible. Melissa would do everything she could to keep them out of the darker side of his life. In her thinking, the less they knew, the better. But Stanton didn't believe that was the right approach. They had a right to know. Altering facts never did anyone any good.

The house was run-down but in a middle-class neighborhood. The lawn was torn up from being worked on, and some engine parts were strewn over the driveway. A 1968 Mustang sat in the garage, and an older man in a T-shirt and jeans was working on getting a dent out of its back bumper.

Jessica was already parked down the street. She got out and began walking toward him as he stepped out of his car. He waited for her in the driveway.

The man saw them and asked, "Can I help you?"

Stanton reached for his badge and remembered he didn't have it. Jessica pulled out hers and flashed it.

"Are you Mr. Harold Dallas?" Stanton asked, noticing that Jessica was staring toward the house.

"Yes."

"Do you have a daughter named Pamela? Born on June third of ninety-one?"

The man's face flushed. "What the hell did she do now?"

"Mr. Dallas, may we come inside and speak with you?"

"Yeah, I guess."

They followed him into the house. It smelled of cooking fat and meat, and a television was blaring somewhere. Harold led them to the living room.

Harold continued to stand but leaned against the fireplace mantel. "So, what'd she do?"

Stanton waited for Jessica to say something, but she stood quietly, gazing at a magazine on the coffee table.

"Harold, your daughter is dead. Her body was found near the Salton Sea, and she was identified from dental records."

Harold showed no reaction other than clenching his jaw, the muscles underneath his skin bulging and then relaxing. A long silence fell that seemed to go on forever.

Jessica cleared her throat. "She was murdered, Mr. Dallas. Under normal circumstances, we would just notify you, but these aren't normal circumstances. We need to find who did this quickly. Your daughter was not the first victim. If you could answer—"

"Stop!" He was shaking and ashen white. He was from a different century, one in which men did not cry even in the most deserving of circumstances. "Just stop for a minute." He straightened his back. "I need to tell her mother. Please wait here."

Harold left the room. A few minutes later, he came back and sat in a recliner next to the couch.

"Is she okay?" Jessica asked.

"No. But she will be." He looked at the floor. "Pammie's not my daughter. Her real daddy was killed in Iraq. I'm her stepfather, but she thought of me more as her grandfather."

"I don't know what to say, Mr. Dallas. I wish we didn't have to be here telling you this."

"But you are, so let's get on with it. What do you need to know?"

"Was Pam having any personal problems lately?" Stanton asked.

"Her and her mama's been fighting a lot lately. Over drugs. We… ah… one time we found her overdosed in our bathroom. She was a heroin addict, and she called us from rehab before that. She seemed to be doin' fine, so we brought her home, but that was a mistake. She shot that poison in her neck 'cause she couldn't get it in her arms no more. Since then, we been kinda expecting news like this." He sighed and shook his head. "Oh, Lord. My poor girl. I raised six children o' my own. They all doin' fine. Could do nothin' for Pammie, though."

"I'm very sorry for your loss," Jessica said. It sounded flat and unconvincing, but Harold didn't seem to notice. "She was probably killed three to five days ago. Did you see her around that time or notice she was gone?"

"No. She would come and go as she pleased. She was in Las Vegas for over a month one time and didn't even call us. I ain't seen her for at least a couple o' weeks. I know her mama ain't seen her for even longer than that."

"Did she call or email or anything?"

"No."

"Could you get us a list of her friends?" Stanton asked. "Particularly her male friends. And any boyfriends you may know about. If you know her daily schedule or routine, that would help too."

"I'll see what we can put together for you. Her mama would be the one to know. I'll get it from her when she's ready."

Jessica pulled out her card and placed it on top of a magazine. "If you think of anything else that may be helpful, please let us know."

Stanton asked, "Does she have a room here I could take a look at?"

Harold pointed at the staircase. "Yeah, upstairs to the right."

Stanton turned to Jessica. "I'll be out in a sec." As he went up the stairs, he looked at the photos hanging on the wall. They were family portraits taken at beaches and campgrounds and on fishing boats. None of them included Pamela.

To the right on the second floor were two doors. One led to a small bathroom with stockings slung over the shower rod. Feminine products and makeup were by the sink and on top of the toilet tank, and an empty waste bin sat next to the shower.

The other door led to a bedroom. The carpet was brown, and the wallpaper and bedspread were polka-dotted, red and blue and yellow. Something a child might choose. The ceiling slanted at an odd angle, and he could tell it wasn't originally meant to be a bedroom but storage. The two windows were different sizes.

Stanton opened the top drawer of the nightstand. It was filled with change, a belt, an old paperback novel, a few ID cards, and receipts. The second drawer contained a small black three-ring binder. Names and phone numbers were scribbled on every page. He pulled out his cell phone and snapped photos before putting the binder back in the drawer.

A closet was on the other side of the room, and he slid open the right side. It was cluttered and filled with clothing and shoes from top to bottom. Boxes were stacked on the floor, and he opened some of them. They held socks and underwear and jewelry. He checked a pink box with white trim and found a couple of wigs, some high heels, a few pieces of lingerie, and some makeup. He took photos of its contents.

The room held no photos, keepsakes, or memorabilia. It was like a hotel room, and Stanton suddenly felt sorry for Pamela Dallas, not just for her death but for the life that had led her to this soulless room.

He left and shut the door behind him.

47

After speaking to Jessica for a few minutes, Stanton headed to his car. He turned the key, then it hit him that he wasn't sure where home was. The SWAT team was not known to be gentle, and his apartment could be unlivable right then. But he had nowhere else.

He drove to his complex. The sun was setting, so he walked to the beach. He sat in the sand and watched the last surfers and bathers pack up for home. A young couple lay on towels near him, whispering softly, their hands exploring each other's skin and their lips locked in a kiss. When the sun was swallowed by the ocean and the moon began to shine in the sky, gray-black clouds gently drifting across it, Stanton rose and went to his apartment.

Suzie was out on her balcony, sipping hard lemonade and smoking Marlboros. "Where ya been, hon?"

"You wouldn't believe me if I told you."

"All manner a cops came to my house askin' about ya."

"Yeah, I'm sorry about that."

"That's okay. I told 'em to self-fornicate. That's what I said too. I didn't want to be crass."

"I'm sure they appreciated that."

She inhaled a long drag. "You know, I was married to a cop back in the day."

"Really?"

"Yeah." She tapped her ashes onto a plate on a side table. "Some damn-near twenty years ago. His name was Archie Haines. He was a bear. Won all sorts of state championships in wrestling when he was young. Archie told me, he said, that every cop gets their house searched by other cops. That they all get suspected of somethin' sometime."

"That's probably true."

She inhaled the smoke from her last puff deeply into her lungs and then put the cigarette out, before she rose to go inside. “Well, if you ever wanna talk about it, you know where I am.”

He walked up the stairs to his apartment and opened the door. The entire space was trashed and looked as if someone had thrown a massive party. The coffee table was kicked over, the couch was torn apart, and one of the cupboard doors was off its hinges. The television was on the floor, its screen a spiderweb of cracks. He had been suspected of cop killing, and they had not spared him any discourtesy.

The bedroom was a little better; the bed had not been demolished at least. He kicked off his shoes and lay down. He was asleep before he could remember to get out of his clothes.

When morning came, he awoke with a migraine. He hadn’t slept that long since he could remember, but it was a restless sleep, filled with nightmares of the dead watching him, calling to him. He saw the killer as a shadow cast on a wall. Stanton told him to hang on, to fight the demons as hard as he could. That Stanton was coming and that he would stop him. The shadow replied that he was trying to stop but couldn’t.

Stanton knew it was true. Many psychologists believed the notes killers sent to police were taunting, showing their superiority and disgust for the people and organization they considered beneath themselves. In some cases, this was true, but not in this case. There was no condescension or hatred in the communications he sent Stanton. In fact, they were helpful and led to more evidence. He wanted desperately to stop but needed Stanton to do it for him. A part of him was still human.

After a shower, he checked the fridge and found it empty. He left his apartment and stopped at a Subway to grab an egg-and-cheese sandwich and some orange juice. He ate in the car while he drove to the office.

As Stanton was about to get on the elevator, George Young

stepped off. He looked into Stanton's eyes a long while and then walked away without saying a word. Stanton got onto the elevator and noted that a few uniforms waited for the next one.

He settled into his office and flipped on his computer. He heard Harlow in the conference room, speaking with somebody. His phone buzzed, and Tommy asked him to come in.

Stanton went to the conference room but stood in the doorway. Harlow, Tommy, and two federal marshals stood at the front. He noticed the breakfast spread and Jessica sitting with her arms folded, listening to Harlow speak. He noticed all this, but only one thing stuck out: Eli Sherman sitting with his back to him.

"Jon," Harlow said, "sit down, please. We have a few things to go over."

Stanton chose a seat at the end of the table.

Sherman glanced at him and winked.

"Jon," Harlow said, "I know this must be hard for you, but Eli has some insight that we may need."

"He doesn't have anything. And I'm quitting. You can deal with this on your own." Stanton rose to leave.

"Wait," Harlow said. "Just wait. Eli was the original detective assigned to the case. He spoke with some people that weren't put in the initial report. He can help with this, Jon."

Stanton was about to ask why that information had been buried but knew Harlow wouldn't tell him with federal marshals and Jessica present. He sat down.

"You can quit if you want," Harlow said, "but I don't think you want to. I think you want to catch this bastard more than anyone here. I know seeing Eli is unsettling, but I think he can help us save some lives." Harlow turned to Jessica. "So, what've we got?"

Jessica put her hands on the table and said, "We spoke to the family yesterday. There's definitely drug abuse with the second vic, and we're following up on that. Family hadn't heard from her in weeks, but apparently that was normal. We're working on getting a list of boyfriends and friends."

"Okay. And what about the note to Jon?"

"I submitted it to latent prints, and there was nothing there. I checked the paper stock, but it's a common brand, something you'd pick up in a supermarket."

"Jon, was there an envelope or anything?"

"No. I found it at the Hernandez scene, stuffed into an air vent. It was folded a few times but no envelope."

"How the hell did forensics miss a note in a vent?" Harlow asked.

"It was put there after we left."

"How would he know about Hernandez? You think he's responsible?"

"Maybe. Or maybe he had knowledge of it from somewhere else and came to the scene after we were gone. Or maybe he was there with us."

Harlow watched him. "Are you telling me you think this cocksucker is a cop?"

"I don't know," Stanton replied. "It could be someone close to cops, like reporters or ME staff, forensics… It would make sense, though. They knew I'd be back at the scene. And when I got there, the police tape wasn't cut. It was fresh, and it was the official stuff, nothing you'd buy at the Army-Navy store or online. So he either left with the rest of us or had some new tape."

Harlow sighed. He looked at Sherman, who was grinning. "Tommy, tell me we followed protocol and had a sign-in sheet at the scene?"

"We did, Chief."

"Make copies and get that to everybody. I want every person there looked at but not confronted. We need to keep this low-key. Capeesh?"

"There is one more thing," Stanton said. He told them about the homeless man and the message.

Everyone sat in silence, the undeniable truth hanging in the air. He was going to kill again, and another family would need to be notified.

"All right. Tommy, follow up on that with Jon. See if we can find this homeless guy."

"Sure thing."

"That's it for now. I cannot stress this enough, people. No talking about this in public to anyone outside this room. All right, excused."

"You didn't ask me anything," Sherman said.

"Okay, what do you have to add?"

"I would put Missing Persons on notice for blondes in their early twenties with large breasts. Anything they get should be kicked up here for review."

"Well, shit on me, but that's actually a good idea. I might not regret bringing you down here after all. Tommy, get on that too. Anybody have anything else? All right, we're done."

Stanton went back to his office and rummaged in his drawer for some ibuprofen. He found two in a cellophane wrapper and took them out, swallowing them without water.

Jessica came in, shut the door, and leaned against it. "You okay?"

"Fine," he said.

"I don't know what's going on. I don't know why Eli is here. I don't know why the charges against you were suddenly dropped. But I don't think I can take this anymore. I've put in for a transfer."

"To where?"

"Vice."

"Are you kidding me? You want to work for the LAPD version of George Young?"

"It's not about him. It's about how quickly I can get out. They're always looking for female officers to work as decoys in prostitution stings. Thought that would be interesting for a while."

"It's not, trust me. And it's a mistake for you to leave. A few years here, and you can write your own ticket to anywhere you want to go."

"That's just it. I don't know if I want to go anywhere. It feels like I'm moving through quicksand. We deal with the worst parts of people and none of the good. And the faces…"

Tears formed in her eyes, and she stopped a moment to compose herself before continuing.

"And the faces of people looking at me from the grave, begging me to help them, and knowing that I can't. This girl, Pamela. She was in Madrigals in high school and then enrolled in college and majored in dance before dropping out. I did that, Jon. I did that same thing."

"Don't do this to yourself."

"I just don't get it. I don't get why I'm standing here and she was stuffed into a closet like garbage. And even when she died, nobody gave a shit. Not really. We see it as a challenge, but we don't care about her, either."

"You care about her, Jessica."

"Do I?"

"Look, just finish this case before you put in your papers. That'll give you time to think. Once the case is done, and you still want to go, then you should."

She nodded. "Okay. I'll finish this case with you. Then I'm done."

48

A trip was arranged for Eli Sherman to go to the Salton Sea and walk around the scene of Pamela Dallas's death. Stanton found it grotesque, but he didn't have a choice.

The federal marshals followed Sherman and Stanton inside the abandoned factory. Stanton went to the stairs leading to the managerial office without waiting, but Sherman followed, the rattle of leg chains echoing in the factory.

Though he had been given civilian clothes, Sherman's double-locked handcuffs and the thick chains running from his ankles to his wrists still showed. An ankle monitor with a blinking red light was locked around his right leg. If the light at any point went green, meaning Sherman was out of range of the city center by more than twenty miles, the built-in GPS device sent coordinates to the SDPD SWAT team and the federal marshals. They had orders to shoot first if that situation ever occurred.

"Must be insulting seeing me out like this," Eli said.

Stanton opened the door to the office. "Haven't really thought about it."

"Bullsh—" He stopped himself and thought a second before saying, "I don't believe it."

"Trying to stop swearing?"

"I know you hate it."

Stanton turned to him. "Since when do you care what I hate?"

"Just trying to be courteous."

Stanton turned toward the office. He glanced back and didn't want to admit to himself that he was comforted to see the marshals right outside.

"What's the matter, Johnny? Don't want to be alone with me?"

Stanton turned and stood face-to-face with him. "You won't be here long."

"How do you know?"

"Because I know you don't have anything to add to this case. Mike's got twenty detectives that were better with evidence than you. He doesn't need you walking around a crime scene."

"Then why bring me?"

"He thinks that you know who the killer is. Once he realizes that you don't know anything, you'll be heading back."

Sherman moved in close, their faces nearly touching, and whispered, "Don't bet on it."

"Hey," one of the marshals shouted, "get away from him!"

Sherman stepped back and leaned against a wall.

Stanton turned to the scene. Muddy boot prints were on the carpet that weren't there before. He guessed they would also find fingerprints and fibers that hadn't been there. The local cops, probably thinking that this was bigger than their office and would be someone else's problem, clearly didn't care about contaminating the scene.

"There's another note," Sherman said. "He wouldn't give you just one."

Stanton glanced at him and then turned his attention back to the room. He ran his eyes over the entire space, taking in every corner and stain and chip of paint that had fallen to the carpet. He knelt down and scanned the floor in a circular pattern, beginning in the center and working his way outward until he hit the walls. He sat at the desk and went through the drawers. The ceiling was exposed, and he studied each beam carefully. At the far end, nearest the closet, one of the water pipes was slightly off center.

He climbed onto the desk and pushed at the pipe. It came loose immediately and spilled putrid water down his shirt and onto the desk and floor. Ignoring the water, Stanton pulled the pipe down and looked inside. A clear plastic bag was taped to the side. He pulled it out, and inside was a folded piece of paper.

"Well, well," Sherman said, "looks like you are a cop after all. Tell me something, though; How many people were through here and missed that?"

Stanton shook his head. "Maybe the locals would have, but our forensics are too good to miss it. It was put here after we'd already gone through."

"What's it say?"

"You don't need to worry about it."

"Tsk-tsk. Don't make me go to the boss."

Stanton hopped down and walked past Sherman onto the factory floor. He called Jessica and asked her to meet him back at the office. She suggested dropping the note off at latent prints, and he agreed. He wasn't expecting to find anything, but one never knew.

When he was alone in his car, he slapped on some latex gloves and took out the note.

Detective Stanton,

What do you think? She's much better than the first, no? A tigress in the bed, too. You wouldn't believe how much loving this little bitch could give. I've kept a few pieces for myself, hope you don't mind, but I didn't think she would be needing them. Maybe I'll send a few to her parents?

See you in a couple of weeks.

Sincerely,
Quaker

Stanton drove back to the office. He went to latent prints on the second floor and submitted the note after having a copy made. He didn't find Jessica in her office or the conference room on the fifth floor, so he tried the cafeteria downstairs and saw her sitting at a table by herself, eating a salad and drinking a Diet Coke.

"Hey"—he threw the copy of the note in front of her—"read this."

She read the note carefully and placed it back on the table. "Where'd you find it?"

"Stuffed in a pipe at the scene."

"He's trying to piss you off."

"Maybe. Something's off, though. Most killers like this hold in their urges as much as possible until they can't and they have to go out and hunt. That's why some go for weeks or even months without killing. Then their urges take over, and they have to kill more frequently. But they're also sloppier 'cause they haven't had months to fantasize and plan every detail. For how meticulous and careful he is, two weeks is too short a time frame. At two weeks apart, he'd be a crazed animal, killing in broad daylight with witnesses. It doesn't make any sense."

"Since when do any of these assholes make sense?"

"Good point."

She took a bite of her salad. "How was it, being there with Eli?"

"Awful. And it breaks my concentration."

"I won't be in the same room with him anymore. He told me I had nice tits in the conference room, and the chief said I wouldn't have to work with him."

"He won't be with us long, I'm sure of it."

She shrugged. "Hope so. So what do you make of the name?"

"I thought about that. Maybe he has some roots with the Quakers?"

"Could just be trying to throw us off. I once had a case where someone left a note talking about other victims and it turned out to be the vic's husband that had just killed her for the life insurance."

"I don't think that's it. He's leading me to something, but I don't know what it is."

"Can I be honest with you, Jon?"

"Of course."

"I've never seen a detective analyze every little thing like you do. These people are crazy and evil. There is nothing else there. Their actions are random. I think we just need to work the evidence, and sooner or later, he'll screw up, or some neighbor will turn him in, and we'll have him."

"Do you like abstract art?"

"Abstract art?"

"Yeah, Jackson Pollock, Rothko, stuff like that?"

"Not really."

"Why?" Stanton asked.

"I think a five-year-old could splash paint on a canvas. Doesn't mean anything."

"That's exactly what I used to think when I was younger. I don't believe that anymore, and I love abstract art now. You know why? Because nothing is random. Nothing. Our unconscious is the bulk of our minds. It's what motivates and controls us far more than what we see as our conscious mind. In fact, the more random you try to make an expression of yourself, the more the unconscious comes through. Guys like Pollock, their paintings may seem like throwing paint on a canvas, but that paint represents something buried deep inside them that even they may not want to admit is there.

"It's the same with the monsters. The more they try to throw us off, the more they reveal. They can't help it. Everything we need to find him is right in front of us. We just have to make the right connections."

Stanton's phone buzzed with a text from Tommy. Pamela Dallas's stepfather had just dropped off a list addressed to him and Jessica.

"Come on," he said. "We need to get upstairs."

49

They sat at the conference-room table and looked over the list. Four names, and only one was male. Scribbled next to each name was the relationship the person had with Pamela: two friends, one cousin, and one ex-boyfriend.

"Dropped it off himself." Tommy looked over Stanton's shoulder at the list. "Coulda just called or emailed."

"He's from a different time. This was something he wanted to do himself."

"Yeah, I guess. My grandpa still refuses to use a computer. Says technology is throwing off the balance of nature and causing the world to go crazy."

"Well," Stanton said, "I think I should hit the ex-boyfriend. Do you want to hit the two friends and the cousin?"

Jessica looked over the list one more time, memorizing the names. "I think I should talk to the ex. If it is him, it may piss him off if you come at him."

"Okay. I'll hit the friends and the cousin. Let me know as soon as you're done with him."

Jessica rose and left the room. Stanton leaned back in the chair and put his hands behind his head, trying to force himself to relax.

"You sleeping all right?" Tommy asked.

"Good enough. Why?"

"You look like shit."

"Thanks."

He sat down in a chair next to Stanton. "How you holding up?"

"I've been better."

Tommy glanced around. "I know what the chief did, Jon. It made me sick when he told me. You didn't deserve that—no cop does. As far as I'm concerned, he crossed the line."

"But you didn't do anything to fix it, did you?"

"I... no. No, I didn't. Truth is, I'm a coward. I think you need to be to do what I do. I'm basically his assistant. I've never sought a promotion or to branch out or anything like that. I just do what I'm told. But I'll tell you, there's freedom in that. I don't have to think, just act."

Stanton rose. "That's slavery, Tommy. Freedom at the end of a leash isn't freedom. Thanks for the list."

No one answered their phones at first, so Stanton had to leave messages. While he waited for return calls, he tried to busy himself by reading the newest issue of *Scientific American* and going through some profiles of known sex offenders who had been released from prison around the time of Tami's death. He wasn't sure what he hoped to see, but he studied every face, every expression. He wished that something would scream at him or at least give him an uneasy feeling. He needed something to follow up on, some goal to be working toward rather than treading water and wasting time.

As the day wore on and people began leaving work, the calls came in. Pamela's cousin was the first to call. She worked at the makeup counter at the local mall and hadn't seen Pam for at least a year. They had exchanged a few messages on Facebook but nothing substantive. She didn't know anything personal about Pam or who she might've been dating. The thing the cousin knew for sure was that Pamela was a drug addict, that her family had spent their savings to get her into the best treatment facility in the state—in Palm Springs—and that Pamela had convinced one of the other patients to steal a car and take off with her. One time, she was certain, Pamela had prostituted herself for a thousand dollars.

The conversation was chilling, not because of anything she said but because of how normal she and her family were. There was a disconnect somewhere between the life Pamela should have had and the life she'd actually lived.

Stanton talked with the friends next, but they were even less help than the cousin. Both of them spoke in the unintelligible whirlwind speech of addicts, and Stanton guessed one of them, if not both, was Pamela's dealer. Many addicts believed their dealers were actually their friends.

When he hung up the phone and realized he had no one else to call, a heavy melancholy came over him. He hoped Jessica had fared better. Pamela's family had given up and abandoned her; she had no friends and no one that really cared about her. He prayed that he would not be another in a long line of people that had failed her.

Tommy poked his head in the doorway. "Hey, they found him."

Stanton's heart jumped. "Who?"

"The homeless guy at the factory. They've got him at Salton City. Jessica's heading down there right now."

50

Jessica hurried into the Imperial County Sheriff's Department with an iPad under her arm. She was greeted by a uniformed officer with a handlebar mustache and tattoos on his forearms. She was at the Salton City branch rather than the main branch. A small building joined to the fire station, it reminded her of the small-town caricatures of police departments she would see on old television shows like *The Andy Griffith Show* and *Perry Mason*. The back of the space even had a drunk tank with an old man sleeping on a bunk.

"What do you need?" the uniform asked.

"I'm Jessica Turner with SDPD. I called earlier about interviewing a Mr. Hood."

"Sign in here, and leave your firearm with me."

She signed the sheet and handed her .38 Special over the desk. The uniform stuffed it into a small box behind him and gave her a laminated badge that read *Guest*. He led her to the back and opened a door leading down a corridor to another metal door that he unlocked.

In a small room with a desk and three chairs sat an older man wearing an orange beanie though it was over ninety degrees outside. He had bruising around his eye and a scuff mark on his cheek.

"Hi, Darrell. My name's Jessica. I've driven up from San Diego to see you." He didn't respond, and she sat down across from him. "I'm just here to show you some pictures. Would that be okay?"

He shrugged.

She took out her iPad, placed it on the table facing him, and flipped it on. A screenshot of eight photographs came up. "I want you to tell me if you see the man that you told Jon Stanton about, the man that told you he had a message for Jon. If at any time you get tired or want to stop for a little bit, you tell me, okay?"

He nodded.

She began flipping from page to page, eight at a time.

They sat for over an hour, looking through seven hundred photos, but he didn't recognize anyone. She stepped outside and called the SDPD dispatch.

"Dispatch."

"This is Jessica Turner, CCU, number 28546. I need a sketch artist down at the Imperial County Sheriff's Office, Salton City Department, as quickly as possible."

"We're gonna need authorization from a captain and a request form faxed over."

She hung up and called Tommy. He said he would have a sketch artist there in half an hour.

Jessica went back into the room and asked Darrell if he needed anything. He said he'd like a Sunkist orange drink, so she went to the vending machine.

When she returned, she sat down and scanned the room for cameras or audio recorders. She didn't see any. "Darrell, I know that somebody hit you, and I would like you to tell me who it was."

"Don't matter."

"It matters to me. Would you please tell me?"

"Cops round here, they ain't too friendly. Don't want no homeless in their town. Whole town's goin' to hell 'cause a tweekers, and they tryin' to run us out for sleepin' in their parks."

"Was it one of the cops here that hit you?"

"I don't want no trouble." He popped open the Sunkist and took a long drink. "I'll take a sandwich if you got one, though. Ain't eaten since yesterday."

She went back to the vending machines. She bought a ham-and-cheese sandwich, chips, and a slice of chocolate cake. While he ate, she checked her emails.

"So why you need to find this dude?" he asked around a

mouthful of food.

"He's done some very bad things. He's an evil person, Darrell, and you could be saving some lives by helping us find him."

He nodded. "Lotta bad people in this city. Why's he so special?"

"He's a rare type of person, one that we need to find right away."

The sketch artist arrived twenty minutes later. He was tall and slim with wire-frame glasses and Converse sneakers. He looked annoyed and didn't say hello. "They have sketch artists here," he said as he sat down and placed his pad on the table.

"I wanted the best I could get."

He rolled his eyes and turned to Darrell. "What can you tell me about what he looked like?"

Darrell began describing the man, and the artist made a rough outline. Next, he pulled a thin album from underneath his pad. Inside were stock photos of various people. He began pointing at them and asking if the suspect's nose looked more like one photo or another, if his eyes were one shape or another shape.

Within half an hour, and after only a handful of erasures, he was done. He handed the pad to Jessica.

"Shit," she said.

"What?"

"I know who this is."

51

Stanton, Jessica, Chin Ho, Harlow, and Tommy sat around the conference room table, and each looked at the composite drawing. It had already been uploaded into the ViCAP database, and a search was running to match facial features with mug shots. Sherman had not been transported from the local jail that morning, on Harlow's orders.

"It's him," Harlow said. "No doubt about it. Jon?"

"There's definitely a resemblance, but I don't know. He doesn't meet the profile. He's successful, comes from a good family, is highly educated. I think the person we're looking for is a heavy drinker, going from job to job, never succeeding at anything... but there's rage in him. I can see it whenever I talk to him. I just don't know."

Ho said, "We pulled his rap. Nothing on there, but just to be sure, we did a check for expungements too. He has a sexual battery charge from eight years back. The case was dismissed for lack of evidence, and he got the charging documents expunged and sealed."

"Jessica, what's your take?"

"He's a slimeball. The first time he met me, he asked if there was any amount of money he could pay me to have sex with him. He offered me ten thousand dollars."

"Wow," Tommy said, "for ten grand, he could have sex with me."

There was some awkward, subdued laughter, more a relief from tension than a response to humor.

"Well," Harlow said, "unless we got something better, we're following up on this. There'll be two teams on him, but I don't want any of you involved in the actual takedown."

"Chief," Ho said, "maybe we should surveil him first? We've got enough for an arrest warrant but not enough for a jury. We need more."

"You don't think he'll crack?"

"No."

Harlow pointed at Stanton. "I once saw him break open the toughest son of a bitch I've ever seen, a three-hundred-pound Hell's Angel that killed his girlfriend's sister by smashing her head in with a hammer. Refused to talk, even to tell us his name. Jon came into the interrogation room and put the hammer on the table and just leaned back in the chair and waited. He waited for seventeen hours and didn't say a thing. The guy broke down and started talking. He couldn't take any more."

"I'd still like to tag him for a while."

"There's no guarantee, Mike," Stanton said. "He's clever. He might not talk."

"There's only one way to find out. I want him picked up. He's got money and friends. If he gets a whiff that we're onto him, he might be in Guatemala by the time we get our act together. I'll email Judge Hilder and get the arrest warrant and warrant for his house. You guys get ready to make him talk. Anything else? No? All right, let's make it happen."

As everyone filed out, Stanton picked up the composite drawing. Add about twenty pounds with a bigger forehead, and there wasn't a doubt: it was Hunter Royal.

52

Stanton sat in the backseat of a black Mustang with tinted windows. Jessica was next to him, and a plainclothes officer from SWAT was in the driver's seat. They were parked at a meter downtown in front of a strip club called The Bush.

The lights of the city flickered around them. Evening was when the real residents came out, the ones that never left, never transferred jobs, never vacationed. They were the blood of the city, keeping it open and functioning. During the day, they cleaned its streets, threw out its trash, served its food, mopped its floors, and fixed its broken parts. But at night, they were at clubs, feeding on the youthful energy and bodies of young women and men that had been abandoned by life and thrown into a pit of vipers.

Stanton counted twenty-six prostitutes. Among them were nine young men dressed in jeans and tight shirts. The rest were women wearing little more than underwear. They stood on corners in groups, waiting for cars to pull to a stop. After a brief conversation through the passenger-side window, they would get into the car and go to some hidden alley or parking lot. The smart ones had a motel room around the corner rented for the night, splitting their revenue with the motel owner or desk clerk.

He could see the progression of the career. On the last corner, farthest from the street lamps and the most out of the way for passersby in cars, were the newest and youngest ones. Their faces and bodies were flawless, and they worked with an exuberance based on the perception that this was a temporary job to earn some cash and move on to what they really wanted to do.

On the other end of the block, taking up the prime location to make it easy for johns to pull up and pull away, were the experienced ones, the ones that realized there was no leaving this life and had given up. Their faces were scarred and worn and their bodies sagging and unkempt. In between the two other groups were the ones just beginning to realize what they had done to their lives.

"Angel One, I don't have the target. Over."

The driver picked up the sleek black walkie-talkie. "Copy. Witness on scene says he's in the back, getting a private lap dance. Over."

"Copy that." A few minutes of silence. "Negative, Angel One. Two lap dances, neither is the target. Rest of the rooms are empty. Over."

"Copy that. Hang tight." The driver turned to Stanton. "Can you go in there and point him out?"

"He knows me too well. If he sees me in a strip club, he'll know something's up. We want to take him as quietly as possible."

The driver exhaled, as if in protest of being asked to do something ridiculous. "Angel Two, be advised I'm staking the first floor. Check the bathrooms and the bar on the second floor. There may be some private rooms up there that weren't in the blueprints submitted to City Hall. If you can't ID him, let me know. Over."

"Roger that."

"All right"—he pulled his jacket on—"you guys wait here."

Stanton watched as the driver left and went into the club. The man was not used to undercover work, and it showed. He glanced around too much, looked at people just slightly too long. SWAT was a hammer and was not used to the razor-blade work required in an undercover operation.

"I worked prostitution for a while," Jessica said. "Did I ever tell you that?"

"No."

"I was a uniform fresh out of the academy in Los Angeles, and they needed new faces. New female faces. I was stuck pretending to pose as a prostitute at a Motel 6 near a Mexican bar. The bar would get people drunk, and the bartender would set them up with the hookers across the street at the motel."

"Did you enjoy it?"

"No."

"Then why do you want to go back to that?"

"Because there were no victims, not in any real sense. Nobody got hurt. Even the johns usually just got a fine." She looked out the window at the people passing on the sidewalk. "There was one time, though, where there was a young girl on the corner with me. She was maybe fourteen. I gave the arrest signal to get her off the street, but they didn't catch it. Some trucker stopped and picked her up before I could alert anybody, and no one saw her again. I like to think she was just dropped off somewhere else, but I don't think so. I talked to the other girls later, and they said she disappeared."

"What was her name?"

She shrugged. "I don't even remember. How awful is that?" She pulled out a piece of nicotine gum and unwrapped it. "Sometimes I don't think it's even worth it, Jon. The darkness is so thick. It's like a blanket that covers us up and won't let us out. And it just seems to get worse instead of better. I remember when I was growing up, I had so many good people to look up to. Neighbors, teachers, local cops and firemen... I think now I could count how many good people I know on one hand."

"They're out there. They just don't get as much attention as they used to."

"Not sure I believe that."

Stanton was watching the front entrance and saw a man in jeans and a black sports coat leave. He turned and said something to the bouncer, and they both laughed. It was Hunter.

"Wait here," Stanton said. He jumped out of the car and caught up with Hunter as he was walking through the parking lot next to the strip club. "Hey, Hunter."

"Jon? What the hell are you doing here?"

"I needed to talk to you."

"Now? Why didn't you just call me?"

"No, not over the phone."

There was only the slightest hesitation, a single moment in which Stanton's mouth opened but no words came out. It was enough.

"Shit!" Hunter sprinted between two cars, out of the parking lot, and into the street.

Stanton ran after him, shouting toward the Mustang for Jessica to call it in. Hunter turned into an alley where a chain-link fence was behind a dumpster. He climbed the fence and tore a cuff on his pants as he hopped over. He dashed for the intersection.

Stanton hopped the fence and felt burning in his hands as he scraped the top on the way over. He saw Hunter run through the intersection against a red light. Cars screeched and metal groaned as one car rear-ended another that had to slam on its brakes. Horns were still blaring when Stanton got there. He maneuvered past the mess, got to the sidewalk on the other side, and spotted Hunter running into an apartment high-rise.

Heading that way, Stanton instantly recognized the building. It was low-income housing, and the cheap red carpet and tacky wallpaper of the hallways screamed government contractors. He'd been there several times previously on various calls.

A set of stairs was at the end of the hall past the elevators, and Hunter was bounding up two at a time. Stanton got there just as he was rounding a corner to the second floor. Stanton reached the top of the stairs to the second floor and looked down the hallway to his right and then his left. It was empty.

He closed his eyes and listened, but all he could hear was his own heavy breathing. Then, almost as softly as the patter of mice, he detected the quiet sound of shoes on carpet. Stanton sprinted down the hall and found a utility closet. He opened it, and Hunter bashed him in the face with a janitor's mop bucket.

Stanton heard a crunch in his nose as blood instantly began to pour. He stumbled back as Hunter tackled him. He felt Hunter's hands searching him for his gun, and it gave Stanton just enough leverage to twist him off and onto his back. Stanton climbed on top of him, cradling him with his thighs, and smashed his fists into the man's face until both were coated in blood, small droplets raining over Hunter's face and clothing.

Hunter went limp, his breathing labored and gurgled with blood. Stanton collapsed next to him, his lungs on fire and his shoulders aching and stiff.

Several minutes passed before Hunter stirred, appearing stunned and unfocused. His hand went to his face, and he attempted to stop the bleeding by applying pressure to a gap in his teeth. "You mocked oup my ucking peeth!"

"Why did you run from me?" Stanton asked, his chest tightening from the exertion and making it difficult to breathe.

Hunter turned over and spat out some blood. "You know why I ran. Johnny, I'm leaving. You're not taking me in."

"You're not going anywhere."

Hunter climbed on top of him with a yell and pressed his forearm into Stanton's throat. He was heavier than Stanton by at least fifty pounds, and Stanton, out of breath and weak, couldn't get him off. The world began to go black, and little sparkles of color appeared in his vision.

Stanton heard the sound of a hammer cocking. He looked over to see Jessica pointing her firearm at Hunter's face. She steadied her arm and naturally fell into the Weaver stance. Hunter put his hands up, and Stanton choked and spat as air rushed back inside him.

53

Hunter sat in an interrogation room for the second time in his life. Though the first time had been years ago and in a different state, both rooms looked the same—gray and empty of any semblance of normality. A desk, two chairs, and a pad of paper with no pens or pencils. A camera was mounted in a corner and covered with a tinted hard-plastic shell. A two-way mirror was in front of him, and he stared at his reflection.

The paramedics had done a good job cleaning and bandaging his face. His teeth had stopped bleeding. He knew protocol said they were supposed to take him to an ER whenever there was "substantial bodily injury," but that phrase meant different things in different jurisdictions.

Life has a sick sense of humor.

The day before at this time, he'd been having sex in his hot tub with a model he'd met at a Hollywood party. There were no A-listers there but some actors that had passed their prime and were now in sitcoms or made-for-TV movies. He had done cocaine in the basement with at least ten other people and drunk Bacardi and Cokes.

Now, he was beaten and bruised and staring into a mirror, wondering where his youth had gone. He was forty-two years old and still a boy, clinging to everything he had dreamed about when he was a kid.

Stanton came in and shut the door softly before sitting down across from him. "How's your teeth?"

"Only one fell out, but a couple of 'em are loose."

"I'm sorry about that, Hunter."

"You want to know the fucked up thing? I think you actually are."

Stanton gave him a courtesy grin. "The homeless man at the Salton Sea, Darrell, identified you."

"I figured. He was so high when I spoke to him, I didn't think he would remember me."

"How many more are there?"

"How many more what?"

"Victims, Hunter. How many more girls am I gonna find?"

Hunter's eyes went wide. "Whoa. Wait a second. You think *I* killed those girls?"

"What should I think?"

"Johnny, you know me. I'm not into that S and M stuff. I like my sex nice and sweet. I could never do that. Tami Jacobs—check my calendar and with my secretary—I wasn't even in the country when that happened. All I did was tell Darrell to give you that message and paid him a hundred bucks."

"The note I got was signed *Quaker*. You went to the University of Pennsylvania. I think that's the mascot, isn't it?"

He was silent a long time. "That piece of shit. He's trying to set me up."

"Who?"

He glanced at the camera. "I want a deal."

"A deal for what? If all you did was pay someone to tell me something, you won't get an accomplice or conspiracy charge. Maybe obstruction of justice at worst. I won't go forward on assaulting a police officer or fleeing. A good lawyer'll take care of it in a month."

"I take it you have an arrest warrant for me?"

"Yeah."

"And a search warrant for my house?"

"Yeah."

"I want a deal on what's going to be found in—"

The door opened, and Harlow walked in. He placed a CD case on the table and stared at Hunter.

"What's that?" Stanton asked.

"Tell him, Hunter."

Hunter kept his eyes low, staring at the table.

"Should I tell him?" Harlow tapped the case. "Okay. Well, Jon, these are homemade DVDs. Short films starring a new up-and-coming actor—Maverick Hunter Royal. Tell him who your actresses are, Hunter. No? Cat got your tongue? Okay, I'll tell him. The actresses are young girls. We're talking—what, Hunter?—seven- and eight-year-olds?"

"That's all overseas, man. Never here. You got no jurisdiction."

"Oh, but get this, my friend. Some of the DVDs are labeled. Mostly Singapore and Thailand, but a few in Pakistan, of all places. Rape of a child is punishable by death in Pakistan. Did you know that, Hunter?"

"It was never rape. They were prostitutes at brothels. You can find them everywhere over there."

"It's rape because a child can't consent under the law." Harlow put his hands on the table and leaned in closely. "You're a child rapist, you piece of shit. And you can't bribe your way out of this."

"I want a deal."

"A deal means you got something I want. What do you have that I want?"

He looked at Stanton. "The guy that killed those girls. I have his address."

Stanton and Harlow went down to the cafeteria. It was after hours, so Harlow had to ask the front-entrance staff to open the kitchen for them. They made grilled cheese sandwiches in the microwave and got two bottles of water. It was dark, so they turned on half the lights and sat across from each other. They ate in silence.

Harlow checked his watch. "They should be done by now."

They headed back upstairs to the third floor. Technically, as part of the administrative offices, the interrogation room was not used in investigations and was just a training room for rookie detectives. But Harlow wanted this one close by.

They sat on a sofa by the receptionist's desk with two uniforms guarding the door to a conference room down the hall. After twenty minutes, the door opened, and a fat man in a gray pinstripe suit stepped out. He walked toward them, sweat glistening on his forehead and neck, and took the chair next to the sofa.

"Shit, Marty. Whaddya do, sleep in your suit?" Harlow said.

"Just always on call," he said. He turned to Stanton. "How are ya, Jon?"

"I'm good. You?"

"Good, good. Crime's a growth industry, so there's always good business for lawyers."

"All right, Marty," Harlow said, "what's the deal?"

He leaned forward and grunted as if he'd just done a push-up. "My client says he knows the actual, physical address of the man you're looking for."

"How'd he get it?"

"The man contacted him, said he was a fan of his work or something. He sent my client—ah, this is all off the record and excluded from court as plea-bargain negotiations, by the way."

"There's no one from the DA's office here, but all right. It's all off the record," Harlow said.

"He sent my client a letter about the victim at the Salton Sea. Said he would give him more information if he passed along a message to a homeless man that had set up camp there."

"Why didn't Hunter just come to us?" Stanton asked.

"That, I can't say. My guess is he just wanted to follow a good story. Maybe he was a little scared too, that if he didn't do what the letter said, the man would never contact him again."

"This smells like bullshit, Marty," Harlow said.

"Hey, I'm just the messenger. Take it or leave it."

"How'd he get the address?"

"He traced the letter back to its source. It was sent from a forwarding address in Las Vegas, but—again, off the record—if you can hand out some cash at the post office, you can find out anything privileged."

"What city is the address in?"

"Can't say that without a deal, Mike."

"Marty, damn it. Just tell me the city. I'm not asking for the whole thing."

"No, we want the DA here and a deal in writing."

"What kind of deal?"

He shrugged, as though he was thinking. "Well... no extradition of course. And a charge of one gross misdemeanor for unlawful sexual contact with a minor. One of the girls on the discs is American, and my client has no doubt you'll discover it as you go through them. Also, you'd have to dump all the child porn charges. Just that one charge, no jail."

Harlow glanced at Stanton. "Marty, he rapes girls."

"The guy you're looking for kills them. Take your pick."

Harlow shook his head then turned to Stanton. "Whaddya think?"

"The misdemeanor won't put him on the sex offender registry."

"I know. Is it worth it?"

Stanton ran his tongue along his dry, cracked lips and realized he was dehydrated. "No. Hunter's not the more dangerous, but he'll have a lot more victims."

Marty shrugged. "Up to you guys. Otherwise, we'll just take our chances."

"Hold on," Harlow said. "One felony, no jail or prison, but he has to register. Tell him that's the best we can do. I know the DA real well, and he won't go less than that no matter how many killers Hunter knows about."

Marty appeared to think about it a moment then nodded. "That's doable. Get the DA down here, and I'll convince my client to take it."

54

By the time Stanton got home, it was nearly one in the morning. Hunter's alibi had checked out. His secretary, who ran to the police station with his official calendar once Hunter's attorney called her, placed him in Singapore the week of Tami Jacobs's death. Stanton checked the airlines and the hotel. The hotel had records going back only a year, but the airline had him checking in and out when he'd said he had. Hunter's bank also had credit card transactions from Singapore at the time.

The district attorney had sent an ADA to negotiate the deal and draw up the plea bargain contract. They would be there a couple of hours, hashing out the details of Hunter's guilty plea. When they were done, a uniform would call Harlow and let him know they had the address.

Stanton kicked off his shoes, took off his clothes, and changed into sweats. He was too wired to sleep, so he flopped onto his couch and turned on the television. An interesting fantasy series was on, and he watched an entire episode before getting up to go to the bathroom.

When he came out, he checked his fridge before remembering there was no food. He ordered a pizza from a twenty-four-hour joint—extra cheese and tomatoes.

As he sat down, he was struck by how much he missed his boys. It was too late to call them. He wondered whether, when they got older, they would even remember him.

His own father had been distant, and Stanton felt as though the man couldn't have cared less what he was doing. His grandfather had raised his father that way.

His grandfather was a man with tightly held Victorian values. His father had told him stories about how, at the dinner table, everyone had to give him absolute silence. His grandmother once tried to ask about everyone's day, and his grandfather had quickly shut her down and let her know that the dinner table was no place for conversation, especially from a woman.

Someone knocked on his door. Stanton went into the kitchen and pulled his gun from a cupboard. He held it behind him while he answered the door.

Jessica stood there holding a pizza and a six-pack of Diet Coke. "Hey."

"Hey."

"Can I come in?"

"Sure."

She walked in, sat on the couch, and placed the pizza on the coffee table next to his pizza. "I couldn't sleep. I was just going to come over but I didn't want to come empty-handed. Looks like you already ate."

"I was just starting. Let me get some plates."

He placed the gun on the counter and pulled out two plates and glasses and sat down next to her.

He and Jessica ate and chatted about their kids and careers. When they were done, they watched a DVR recording of *The Tonight Show*. Jessica laid her head on his shoulder, and he wrapped an arm around her.

Stanton was woken by the sound of his shower.

He got up, went to his balcony, and sat cross-legged. He said a long, meditative prayer and then went inside, catching her as she was walking into the kitchen.

"Afraid all I got is cold pizza."

"It's all right," she said, putting her earring in. "I was just gonna grab some coffee before heading in."

When she left, he changed and headed to the beach for a morning of surfing. The waves were light and the water choppy. By seven, there were too many families and teenagers on the beach to foster a spiritual experience on the ocean. Occasionally, though, when there was no one and nothing but the sea, the morning mist, and the sun, he would have deep experiences with God—deeper even than those he had in church. He finished early and headed back to his apartment.

As he got in, he checked his phone. A text from Tommy: *got address get ur ass down here.*

55

The conference room was packed, and the noise of ten different conversations numbed Stanton as he walked in. Every seat was taken, and extra chairs had been brought in and placed around the room. A map was up on the screen connected to Tommy's laptop. It was a satellite view of a house and neighborhood.

Imperial County had faxed Stanton a copy of the autopsy report. It read like Tami Jacobs's with one exception: semen had been found. The sample had been rushed to the state lab, and Stanton had been assured there was enough for a DNA comparison should he have a suspect.

Stanton saw the pattern immediately: the monster was growing arrogant. He had been so careful with Tami not to leave evidence behind other than fecal matter. Not even pubic hair had been found, which meant he probably shaved it before the attack. But with Pamela, it was different. He didn't care if he left DNA behind. He was getting more careless but also more dangerous.

Stanton sat down in a corner next to Chin Ho and read through the autopsy reports again. He leaned over to Ho and said, "Where's Eli?"

"Shipped back to Pelican Bay. Didn't need him anymore."

"Okay, everyone," Harlow bellowed, "listen up. We got a white male, forty-one years old. Brady Louis Rattigan. Lives with his mother in this house. His mother is wheelchair bound and has high blood pressure. When we go in, we're goin' in hot, but avoid any heroics. The last thing I need is this douchebag's mom croaking from a heart attack." Quiet laughter came from the group. "I'd show you a photo, but we don't have one. No driver's license, no ID card, no bank accounts. All he's got is a social security card with a name and birthday. This guy's living completely off the grid for obvious reasons.

"Now, we're having surveillance until we get something good, and you all got your assignments. Four shifts in six-hour increments. AC Anderson is gonna go over the details, but I want to be kept in the loop on everything. Rodney?"

Anderson stood and began going over the logistics of the operation. Harlow motioned for Stanton to follow him, and they went to his office.

"Shut the door." Harlow sat down at his desk.

"Where's Hunter?"

"County lockup. He'll probably get bail today, though, little shit. I kinda wish his alibi didn't check. Anyway, why I asked you here, I need something done that's delicate."

"What is it?"

"The window we got right now isn't for surveillance. Don't get me wrong, the bastard can't take a shit without one of my detectives being there to smell it, but that's not why we got surveillance going. This one's smart. I'm not expecting to find anything."

"What do you have planned?"

"We checked out his mother, too. Cancer, two strokes this year, and dementia. I'm willing to bet she sleeps most of the day. I need someone to go in there."

"You got a warrant already?"

"No, actually. We don't. I can't list what we're looking for in the warrant with any particularity. 'Stuff showing he killed some girls' doesn't hack it."

"What authority do we have to be in there, then?"

"None."

After an awkward silence, Stanton folded his arms. He thought about it a few moments and said, "No, we're doing this clean. I want it to stick."

"It will stick. No one's going to know."

"Someone always knows. I'm not doing it."

"I wouldn't normally ask you, but like I said, it's delicate. I need someone that's going to be careful, and that's you."

He shook his head. "No way."

"Well, then, Detective, your involvement in this case is over. We'll talk about some new assignments on Monday."

"Mike, you can go self-fornicate." He walked out, gathered a few things from his office, and left.

56

Zoe Kelly had finished her shift at the mall and was counting out the register when Brian Newman walked by. He pointed at his watch, and she mouthed, "I know," and continued counting.

She'd suffered through a long day. One customer went to the manager because she was enraged that a blouse that she claimed was in her size wouldn't fit. Another yelled at her because they couldn't issue a refund without a receipt.

But that was finished. She just needed to count out the stupid registers, and she was done until Monday.

When the money balanced, she walked around the displays in the windows and made sure everything was okay. A kid had spilled some frozen yogurt on the pants of one of the mannequins. She tried to scrub it out with a wet cloth, but it ended up a dark stain instead of white splotches.

She unlocked the glass double doors and yelled to Brian. He came inside the store, and she locked the doors again.

"What's taking so long?" he asked.

"I'm almost done. Some little asshole put frozen yogurt on our mannequin and I need to change its pants."

"Just let the morning shift do it."

"I can't. They'll get mad and tell Rebecca."

"Well, hurry up, then. We're supposed to be at Jason's at nine."

"I'm trying, Brian. Why are you being such a dick?"

"I'm not. But we told them we'd be there, and they're gonna wait for us before going."

"I'm so sick of clubs, anyway. Why don't we just go on a date?"

"Like what?"

"I dunno, like dinner and a movie."

"Fuck that." He checked his watch again. "Just hurry up. I wanna get drunk."

"You're such an asshole."

He laughed then grabbed her by the waist and kissed her neck.

She swatted at his arm. "Let go of me!"

"Make me." He ran his tongue up her neck.

"Cut it out."

"Let's go in the back room."

"No."

"Come on. It'll be quick."

"No, they have cameras. Now go wait outside. I'll be done in a second."

He groaned. She unlocked the doors again, and he slouched out and sat on a bench. Zoe put the new pants on the mannequin and then did a quick walk-through of the rest of the store before turning off the lights and flipping on the alarm. The mall was almost empty, but a few of the shops still had people inside. She went next door to Forever 21 and saw her friend Candice folding some shirts.

"Aren't you done yet?" Zoe asked.

"No." Candice threw a glare at a couple that was still browsing. "These guys won't leave. I've told 'em we're closing."

"Just tell them to get out."

"I did that once and got in trouble. I have to wait until they leave, but I can't even count out the register 'cause they might buy something."

"That sucks."

"I know. But what can you do, I guess. Hey, I saw Brian. What are you guys doing?"

"We're supposed to go to Jason's house and then to Desert Ice."

"Again?"

"Yeah, we're there, like, every week. I'm getting bored."

"Well, my brother said any time you get sick of Brian to give him a call."

"Yeah, I dunno, maybe. I need some time to think, ya know? Anyway, I guess I better go."

"See ya. Don't get too drunk."

"I won't."

She went over and sat next to Brian. She thought about Candice's brother. He was a buff Latino and had a good job as a club promoter. Brian lived at his mom's house and mostly played video games when they were together. She was so sick of *Call of Duty* that she would get a queasy feeling in her stomach whenever it came on.

Then, Brian put his arm around her, and she remembered why she was dating him. She rested her head on his shoulder a second, and he kissed her.

"I have to get my stuff out of my car," she said.

"I'm parked by the food court. Come over there when you're done."

He kissed her again, and she got up and made her way through the mall. She stopped for a couple of minutes and said hi to her friend at GNC and then went out into the parking lot.

The air was warm, and the moon was out. The lamps in the parking lot lit up all the stalls with a warm glow. She took out her cell phone as she walked toward her Prius. She'd gotten one text from her mom, asking her when she'd be home, and one from her friend Angie, asking if she wanted to come over because her parents were out of town. She replied to Angie that she might later and asked if it was okay if Brian came, too.

A van was next to her car, and it was parked so close that she could barely fit to get to her driver's door. She opened her purse and started rummaging for her keys.

The passenger door of the van opened. She registered a flash of white then felt warm pavement against her face.

57

Detective Marcos Garcia sat with his feet up on his desk. The Missing Persons Unit was split into two sections, and he had recently been promoted to what was considered the less stressful section: adults. The juvenile section, he believed, was the most painful unit of the police department, next to Special Victims. An average of twenty-three missing persons reports were filed in the county every week. With both units combined, they had only nine detectives working them.

Many people, especially the families of the missing, were shocked to learn that so few resources were dedicated to this unit. But they didn't understand, and he sure as hell wasn't going to explain to them, that seven out of ten missing persons were never found and had no workable leads. In reality, only a handful of real, feasible cases per month came in. The rest had no leads, no evidence, and no hope.

His phone buzzed, and the receptionist told him someone was there to see him. He told her to have them make an appointment, but the receptionist said it was a mother who needed to file a report on her daughter.

"Send her back," he said.

He took his feet off the desk and straightened his tie. Though most detectives at that point in their careers were phoning it in, he believed in his work and thought that the way he treated the families mattered. People could sense when someone was really going to work for them or not.

An older brunette—Garcia guessed she was in her early fifties—came to the door. She'd had some plastic surgery, her breasts definitely but probably her face also. Her eyes were swollen and red, and she wore no makeup. She sat down across from him without being asked and passed him a photograph. "This is my daughter Zoe. She went missing last night."

"Did you speak with her last night, Ms...?"

"Mrs. Mrs. Diane Kelly. Yes, I spoke to her. She was at work at the mall, and we were texting back and forth. She was supposed to go to some dance club with her boyfriend. She went out to the car to get some clothes and makeup, and she never came back. He called me."

Garcia began typing into a document. "What's her boyfriend's name?"

"Brian Newman." She took out a sheet of paper covered in names with phone numbers and addresses next to them. "These are her friends, and his number's on there too."

"How old is your daughter?"

"Nineteen."

"You sure she's missing, Mrs. Kelly? A lot of times, nineteen-year-olds stay out too late and—"

"I'm positive. That's not her. We talk. She tells me everything, and she always lets me know where she is. This isn't like her at all. And her car is still at the mall. It's Fashion Valley Mall. I went and saw it. Her keys were on the ground next to it. Something's happened."

"What kind of car does she have?"

"A green Prius. It's parked right out in front of Macy's."

"Mrs. Kelly... Diane. Ah, may I call you Diane?"

"Yes."

"Diane, I'm going to ask you some questions now, and they're going to make you uncomfortable. But I promise you they are necessary. And if Zoe is missing, they are going to help us find her, okay?"

"Okay."

"Does Zoe have a drug problem that you know of?"

"No, she doesn't use drugs. She drinks sometimes, I know that. She comes home smelling like alcohol. But we talk about it, and if she's been drinking, she doesn't drive. We have a deal that if she's been drinking and needs to drive home, she has to call me, and I have to not get angry or punish her. She's very good about that."

"Okay. Now, is Zoe promiscuous?"

"What kind of question is that? No, she's not promiscuous. She's nineteen. I don't think she even really knows what sex is."

"Okay, again, I'm not trying to be invasive or hurtful. I just need to rule out a few things. Now where was the last place anyone saw her?"

"Inside the mall. Brian was the last to see her."

"Well, I'm going to give Brian a call and speak to him. Then I'll draft a report, and we'll wait forty-eight hours, and if she doesn't turn up, we'll file the report and then put out a—"

"Forty-eight hours? She's missing. We can't wait that long."

"I understand your frustration, Diane. But that's the law. We have to wait—"

"That's bullshit! My daughter is missing. Find her."

"We will, but I can't file a report for forty-eight hours."

She began crying, and Garcia pushed a box of tissues toward her.

She took two of them and dabbed at her eyes. "Please, just find her."

Garcia drove down to Fashion Valley Mall. He was not required to take any action on a missing persons case for forty-eight hours. A lot of cases were people that had fled and wanted a break or, more likely, people with mental illnesses that had gotten lost and would eventually wander back. The forty-eight-hour waiting period, though painful for the families, was necessary so that the detectives could spend their time working actual crimes.

But something about Zoe Kelly's case didn't sit right with him. He had spoken to Brian and didn't get a good feeling. The guy was too flippant about it, too calm. He asked too many questions, and they all involved him: "What do *I* have to do if she doesn't turn up? What will *I* have to fill out if she's missing?" He showed little concern for her. Though the boyfriend wasn't yet a suspect, Garcia decided to keep his mind open and take a look at the car while it was still in the mall parking lot.

His air conditioner didn't work well, and it spewed warm, dusty air in his face. He turned it off and rolled down all the windows as he got onto the interstate. It was a scorching day, and the sunglasses sitting on the passenger seat were too hot to put on. He squinted as sunlight reflected off the windows and metal emblems of the cars in front of him.

He got off the exit and drove down a palm-tree-lined road to the mall. He had to circle around to find the Macy's. He slowly went up and down the rows of cars. On the third one over, parked between a motorcycle and a truck, was a green Prius with the license plate number he had pulled from the DMV.

He pulled up behind it and got out. The car was new, and the interior looked clean and polished. Hanging from the rearview mirror was a picture of Zoe and some of her friends hugging on the beach. A CD case lay on the passenger seat, and on the backseat were a pair of sunglasses and white flip-flops next to a makeup bag and some clothing.

Garcia checked the doors and trunk. He realized he should've asked her mother for a copy of the key or for her to meet him there.

He looked underneath the car and didn't see anything. As he was about to stand, he noticed a small discoloration on the pavement. He bent down and looked at it a minute longer before going back to his car and retrieving a cotton swab from a little container he kept in the glove box. He dabbed at the stain with the swab. Though it was dry from the heat, he could see particles of black entwined in the cotton. It could have been blood. It also could have been tomato or prune juice.

He went back to his car and looked at the photo of the girl again. He had been debating whether to send an email, and it was still unclear to him whether he should. He opened his car's built-in laptop and reread the email Assistant Chief Anderson had sent to the Missing Persons Unit:

Report any and all missing women with approximate ages from twenty to twenty-nine, blonde hair, and slim figures with large breasts directly to the homicide unit.

Garcia typed up the email and sent it.

58

Stanton saw Tami Jacobs. She was lying on her bed, tears streaming down her face as she begged for her life. Blood was everywhere. It wasn't the fruit punch appearance, like in the movies. Blood, fresh blood from a body, was almost black. The walls and bed and floor were coated in black, and they were closing in on him. But he couldn't think because she was screaming.

And he saw Pamela Dallas. She was crying and choking but couldn't speak. Finally, through the tears, one word came out: *Help*.

Stanton jumped awake with a gasp. Cold sweat stuck to him, and his sheets were soaked. He took off his undergarments and got into the shower. He let the water run over his head and cover his ears so that he heard nothing but the rushing droplets hitting his flesh. The bathroom filled with steam.

He stayed in the shower until the water ran cold, and then he got out and changed. He knew there would be no sleeping again, so he decided to go for a walk in the moonlight. He slipped on shorts and sandals and headed outside. After he had already locked the door, he unlocked it, went back inside, collected his holstered firearm, and tucked it into his shorts.

The heat came off the pavement and mingled with the salty ocean air. It smelled like New Orleans. Stanton had lived there almost a year. A vacation after the completion of his doctorate had turned into an indefinite stay. Something about that city couldn't be found elsewhere in the States. It was magical and deadly and depraved in equal doses.

He wasn't sure why he had left New Orleans. But something had told him he had to leave, to get out, and to never return.

As he walked along the beach, he came to a convenience store and went inside. The lighting hurt his eyes, and the bright tile of the floor was aggravating. He saw a man behind the counter reading a *Hustler*. He bought a Sprite and some Tums and left for the safety of the beach.

He sat and buried his feet under the sand. The moon was a bright crescent in the sky, and he stared at it a long time. In the distance, he could hear a whale, or at least what he thought was a whale, and it delighted him for a reason he couldn't name.

He took out his phone and dialed Melissa's number. She picked up on the fourth ring.

"Jon, what are you doing? Do you know what time it is?"

"Yeah, sorry. I figured you might be up."

"No, I took an Ambien. Hold on a sec." He heard sheets rustling and then footsteps. "What's going on?"

"Nothing. I just wanted to talk to you. How are the boys?"

"They're good. They miss you."

"Are you sure?"

"Yes, I'm sure. You're too hard on yourself, Jon. They love you. They just don't understand what's going on."

"How's Lance?"

"You don't want to hear about him."

He watched the ocean a moment. "No, I don't. I don't know why I said that."

"Because you want to accuse me of something, but you don't want to say it. So just say it. I already know you're thinking it."

"I never would've brought someone else in to raise our kids."

"I was lonely. You wouldn't understand because you like being alone. I thought for a long time that's how you handled pain, but I think maybe it makes you stronger somehow."

"Maybe, but I've never liked it. I understand why you did what you did. I just needed to say it."

"I know. I'm not mad." She hesitated. "I miss you."

"I don't know what to say to that."

"Tell me you miss me too."

"You know I do."

"I... I talked to Lance the other day about the wedding. I think I need some more time."

Stanton felt a surge of joy at the thought of their marriage falling through and then felt a tinge of guilt for it. He wanted her to be happy, even if it was with someone else.

"How much time?"

"I told him I want to put it off until next year. He seemed upset, but he said he understood. Why do you think I did that?"

"We've shared a lot of time, Mel. I think eventually you'll move on, but now might not be the time."

"What about you? Will you move on?"

He glanced up at the moon. "No, you were my first love, and you'll always be my first love."

"I hate how you do that. How you always know just what to say to make me feel like shit."

"I didn't mean to."

She sighed. "I know. I better get back to bed. Lance already doesn't like you."

He grinned. "He's a tool."

"Jon," she said with a giggle, "he is not."

"Yes he is. Look up what *tool* means, and you'll see."

She chuckled and he remembered that he loved her laugh.

"Good night, Jon."

Stanton put his phone on the sand and waited a long time, as long as the phone call had lasted, until he closed his eyes.

Hearing her voice and talking about something other than the dead made him feel light and happy, but it didn't last. The images came right back. Tami and Pamela had burned themselves into his mind, and that was all he saw: their pleading faces as they were torn apart. He wondered whether, in that last moment, they cried for fathers that had left them long ago. They had lived alone and died alone, discarded by everyone that should have cared about them.

But he wasn't going to be one of them.

He texted Harlow: *I'll do it.*

Though he wasn't expecting it, a text came right back: *I knew you would.*

59

On the flight back to Pelican Bay State Prison, Eli Sherman thought about the last time he had been on a plane.

Almost ten years before, he had been dating a girl who loved to travel, and though he lived on a detective's meager salary, she was independently wealthy because of an inheritance from an uncle she talked about incessantly. Sherman had always suspected they had been lovers in her youth.

He remembered sitting next to her on the plane, and a child was across the aisle. The boy was perhaps ten and reading a book when his father knocked the book out of his hand and said something about not being a "faggot." The child leaned back and stared at a spot on the chair in front of him and didn't move, not when his little brother kicked him and not when the stewardess brought out drinks and peanuts.

Sitting in the four-passenger plane, shackled from ankles to wrist, Sherman wondered what had happened to that little boy, what he had grown up to become. A father could either make or break a child like that. He hoped that the boy had been made stronger for it.

The marshal sitting next to him jabbed a finger in his ribs. "Excited to get back, you piece of shit?"

Sherman stared out the window at the horizon. He had been cut out of the loop and would not be given anything Harlow had promised. He had suspected as much and was not surprised. The trip was worthwhile, anyway. Even shackled, he found that being out in the sunlight and the ability to walk without walls made a man feel free.

The plane landed after scarcely an hour in the sky, and he was placed in a Department of Corrections van and taken back to the prison.

The prison seemed smaller and grayer, and the sounds were

louder than he remembered. Filled with wailing, laughing, crying, and maniacal conversations that made no sense. Seemingly out of the ether, Sherman's mood changed. His persona had to go back up. His chest puffed out, and his chin tilted upward. It was all an act, as was everyone else's—hardened criminals all acting as though they were harder than they were—and only for each other's benefit.

He was led back to his cell, but no one was there. Sherman sat on the bottom bunk and stared at the floor, waiting for someone. To pass the time, he flicked on the television and watched cable news. Something about a military strike in the Middle East. He'd followed the Iraq War closely—thousands upon thousands of people dead. How was it that politicians could get away with killing so well and he was sitting in here?

An hour passed, and he noticed someone standing by the cell—a female guard. She was overweight by at least sixty pounds, and her hair was long and brunette. She had a pug's face.

"I missed you," she said.

"I missed you, too."

"I kinda thought that maybe you wouldn't be back."

He rose and walked to the cell door. "And how would I manage that?"

"I don't know. You're smart. I didn't think you would let them bring you back."

She reached into his cell and stuck her hand down his pants. She glanced around and made sure no else was on the floor before kissing him through the bars, their tongues rolling over each other. He stretched out his arm to put a hand between her legs and caress her.

"I need something from you," he said.

She breathed heavily. "What is it?"

"I need you to send a letter for me."

"Okay." Her eyes closed, and her head tilted back.

"And then I need you to bring me something."

"What?"

"A new belt."

"For what?"

"I'm going to trade it for something."

"What are you trading it for?" she asked breathlessly.

"I'll tell you when I have it."

He bit down hard into her lip and tasted blood.

60

She felt dampness at first, like being wrapped in a wet towel. Then there was the sensation of the hard floor against her back, and thick dust in the air made her nostrils itch.

Zoe's eyes fluttered open. The light hurt, and she squinted until her eyes adjusted. The first thing she saw was an unfinished ceiling: water pipes and electrical cords between thick wooden panels and fiberglass. The right side of her head pounded, and she instinctively reached her hand up and found the stickiness of dried blood behind her ear.

She looked around, her neck stiff. Darkness mostly, but light came through a door at the top of a set of stairs, and she sat quietly and stared at the light. She remembered the mall and closing the registers... going to her car... and then waking up here. As she tried to sit up, she felt pain in her feet and saw they had been tied together securely with a length of plastic. She tried to pull it off, but it was wrapped so tightly she couldn't get her fingers underneath the straps. She worked at it for a long time before giving up and crawling to a wall. She pulled herself up using a built-in shelf.

A children's bike, red with white trim, stood in the corner. It was covered in dust, and the tires were flat. Behind that was a shelf packed with all manner of things: glass jars filled with nails and screws, tools, old books, broken photo frames. The space appeared to be for garbage more than storage.

She ran her fingers along the edge of the wall, and a splinter broke off a shelf, embedding in her thumb. She put her thumb in her mouth and sucked on it, and as she did, a loud thud made her jump.

Her back was flat against the wall, and she held her breath. More sounds and then something being dragged. It was coming from the ceiling, and she realized she was in a basement.

The sounds stopped, and she felt the warm trickle of urine down her leg. She choked back tears as she realized she'd been kidnapped and continued to run her hands along the wall, looking for a door, though she knew she wouldn't find one. As she made her way to the other side of the room, she felt something hard and loose that jingled. Chains hung from the ceiling.

She collapsed onto the floor, her hand covering her mouth, and began sobbing. She cried and then prayed. She hadn't always been good about going to church, but she prayed harder than she ever had before. She promised that if God took her home, she would start going to church more and stop having sex with Brian.

After what seemed like hours, all the noises upstairs stopped, and she stood up. Slowly, she made her way to the stairs. The steps were wood and creaked loudly as she crawled up.

It took her a long time to get to the top. She looked underneath the door. The crack between the floor and the bottom of the door was wide, and she could see red carpet. A couch was against the back wall. To the right, maybe six or seven feet away, was a door.

Zoe reached up and tried the doorknob. It was heavy and greasy to the touch. She tried turning it one way and then the other, but it wouldn't budge. She put her face back down to the bottom of the door to see if she could see anything.

A pair of boots suddenly appeared in front of the door, making her gasp and pull away.

61

Stanton sat at his desk. He had the pathologist from the Imperial County Medical Examiner's Office on the phone and was discussing the autopsy of Pamela Dallas. He asked if fecal matter had been found in her throat, and the pathologist asked why he would've checked for that. He said he did look to see if it was clear of obstructions, but no scrapings were taken.

From the way the pathologist spoke, Stanton guessed he hadn't actually done the autopsy. Salton City was small, a population of less than a thousand, but Imperial County as a whole had one of the worst epidemics of methamphetamine in the entire nation. The man dealt with plenty of corpses and may just have assumed Pamela was some junkie before giving the project to an unqualified assistant.

Stanton's desktop dinged, indicating a new email. Anderson had sent a scanned file of a missing persons report with a note that said, "You may want to check this out."

Stanton opened the file, and his heart almost stopped. He told the pathologist he would call back and stared at the photo on his computer screen. It was Tami Jacobs, but not quite. The girl was younger, but the resemblance was striking—same color eyes, same height, big breasts. They even styled their hair the same. Her name was Zoe Kelly.

He read the report quickly, as it was only a page and a half. The investigating detective had written that the boyfriend grew hostile and seemed unconcerned about the girl's disappearance. Stanton checked to make sure the email had also been sent to his phone and then left.

He saw Jessica in the hallway. "You're going to want to come with me."

"What is it?" she asked.

"Might be nothing."

"Hang on. Let me get my badge." She met him at the elevators a few minutes later. "What's this about?"

"Missing person." He pulled up the file on his phone and let her read the report.

"Looks just like—"

"I know."

"We going to pay Brian a visit?"

"Yes."

Stanton got on the elevator. She followed and pressed the button for the first floor.

"I called you last night," she said.

"Yeah, I saw. Sorry, I meant to get back to you. What was it?"

"Nothing important. I just wanted to talk."

"About the case?"

"No, just… talk." She cleared her throat. "I saw George Young today."

"Oh yeah? What did he say?"

The elevator stopped, and they got off. "Nothing much. He got off of his suspension today, so he's back at his desk. They didn't find any misconduct, just that he had identified the wrong witness. He did mention you, though. He said for me to tell you to keep the hell away from him."

"No problem there."

They climbed into Jessica's Jeep Wrangler and pulled out of the parking lot.

Jessica turned onto the interstate and sped past another car on the on-ramp.

"You sure Zoe is one of ours? I thought we had our guy and he's under surveillance."

"I checked on that this morning. He hasn't left his house. Surveillance hasn't even seen him to snap a photo. If he has her, she could be in his house. Brian may know something."

They took the Maple Drive exit, and Stanton directed her through a residential neighborhood and then up a hill. Near the top of the hill were a convenience store and a gun store, and across the street was a barbershop. They parked in front of the convenience store and then walked down to the gun store.

The first thing they saw when they entered the place was a giant poster of the Statue of Liberty with a holster and a gun and a huge stamp across the bottom that read, *Second Amendment: Use It or Lose It.* An older man was at the counter, showing some handguns to a family.

Stanton flashed his badge. "I need to speak to Brian, please."

"I'm his father. What's this about?"

"We just have a couple of questions about his girlfriend."

He looked between them and then went in back and came out with a young man following him. Brian appeared malnourished he was so skinny, and he had the floppy, disheveled haircut of a stoner.

"Are you Brian Newman?" Stanton asked.

"Yeah."

"I'm Jon. We're from the San Diego Police Department. We just need to ask you a few questions about Zoe."

"I already talked to the cops."

"I know, but we have some follow-up we'd like to talk to you about. Won't take more than a minute or two."

"I think you guys can talk to my lawyer."

Stanton grinned cordially. "No, I wouldn't do that. What I would do is search your pockets and that backpack I saw you put down in back. I'm guessing I'd find some weed, maybe even a grinder. Might be able to bump it up to distribution for that unless you have a medical license for the weed."

Brian looked to his father, who was helping a customer. "Let's talk in back."

They followed him through a door to the back area. It was filled with boxes and firearms. A few deer and moose heads adorned the walls, and two other people were there cleaning pistols and rifles on a metal table.

"So whaddya need?" he said, folding his arms.

"The night she disappeared, you said she ran out to her car in the parking lot."

"Yeah."

"Could you see her from where you were?"

"No, I was inside the mall."

"How long did you wait for her?"

Brian shrugged. "I dunno, like, five or ten minutes, maybe."

"And I think you said you were in a hurry to get to a friend's house."

"Yeah, we was way late, and she was taking forever. So I went out there."

"Did you go to her car?"

"Yeah. I didn't see nothin', though."

"Well, was there anything or anyone around her car or nearby, maybe farther down the parking lot?"

"Nope. There wasn't nothin'. I thought maybe she'd gone back inside."

"Where was her car parked?"

"Near a light in the back'a Macy's."

"Were there any cars around hers?"

"Yeah, like, some van and a—"

"Where was the van?"

"Um, like, right next to her car."

Stanton took out his notepad and began writing. "What kind of van was it?"

"Blue. Had, like, rust all over it. Looked like a piece'a shit."

"Did you see anyone in it or anyone that got into it later?"

"No."

"Did you see the license plate?"

The boy shook his head. "I don't remember."

"Were the windows tinted?"

"Yeah. Yeah, I think so."

"Brian, this is really important. Do you remember anything else about the van that could help me identify it if I saw it?"

"Um, no. No, I don't think so."

"All right." Stanton asked Jessica for a card, and she passed one to Brian. "If you think of anything else, you call this number and ask for Jon or Jessica, okay?"

"Okay. You're not searching me now, right? I cooperated."

“No, I’m not searching you. But just get a medical license for the weed and you won’t have to worry about it.”

When they were back on the road, Stanton called Chin Ho.

He answered on the second ring and sounded out of breath. “What’s up, Jon?”

“You at the office?”

“Yeah, yeah, just took the stairs. What’s going on?”

“I need you to log in to the statewide and check on a car for me.”

“Okay, one sec… All right, whose car?”

“Our boy’s mother.”

“You know her name?”

“Debra Rattigan. She’d have a birthday in the forties.”

“All right, hang tight a sec… Okay, three Debra Rattigans, one with a birthday of August eleven, forty-eight. Same address as our boy.”

“That’s it. What kind of car?”

“She has a Chevy Express cargo van.”

“What color?”

“Um… blue.”

62

Stanton pulled to a stop in front of Hunter Royal's house. The reporter had been released on $250,000 bail. Within hours, his mug shot and the probable cause statement for his case were online on six blogs and a local paper. He had a lot of competition excited to see him fall.

Stanton knew Hunter wasn't stupid and would not drift silently away. He was, in fact, one of the cleverest people Stanton had ever known. People underestimated him because of the profession he had chosen, but he could easily have been behind a surgeon's scalpel or at a lectern, lecturing about medieval philosophy.

Stanton rang the doorbell.

Hunter answered in shorts and a T-shirt. He hadn't shaved, and dark, patchy stubble covered his face.

Hunter turned and went over to the couch. Stanton came inside and shut the door behind him. The house was messy, with plates covered in dried food on the coffee table and cigarette ash all over the carpet.

"I didn't think you would take it this hard," Stanton said.

"I'm going to be a registered sex offender, Jon. How am I supposed to take that?"

"I thought you would use your notoriety. Make it a part of your persona."

"If I had robbed a bank, yeah. But people with my charges aren't treated that way. I actually have to move out of this house 'cause of the neighbors. They got kids."

Stanton sat down on a tan leather ottoman. "I need your help."

"For what?" he scoffed. "I gave you all I got."

"Your lawyer told the ADA that you threw away all the letters."

"I did."

"I don't believe you."

"Search my house then if you don't believe me."

"You wouldn't throw them away, Hunter. We both know that. Which means either you still have them or you're lying about them."

He turned his attention to the television, which was turned low. "I gave you all I got. Now get outta my house or arrest me."

"Do you believe in evil, Hunter?" He didn't wait for a response. "I do. I think there's real evil in the world. People, for some reason, even people that don't believe in God, still believe in a devil. Why do you think that is?"

"Am I supposed to give a shit?"

"They believe in him because what they see for most of their lives is evil. Good is far rarer, and most people only get glimpses of it. But evil is all around us. Everywhere. You're evil, Hunter."

"Fuck you, Jon."

"You may not want to say it out loud, but I know you think it. Especially when you're alone—at night in those moments before you go to bed and the cocaine and the booze have worn off and the woman you slept with isn't there... I know."

"What do you want from me? I don't have anything left."

"That's not true. You have your soul, Hunter. Even someone as evil as you still has their soul, and you can redeem it. Not all the way, but a little. Help me catch this guy. Give me everything you've got. Don't play me. We're past that. Just give me what you got. It'll stay between us. Besides, if you're telling the truth, he tried to blame you. You don't owe any loyalty to him. Your reporter's integrity will stay intact."

Hunter sat silently, staring at the television. He looked like someone just settling into a long illness. His skin was pale, dark circles under his eyes. "He would email me," he finally said. "I got the emails. He was following you. That's how he got that note into Francisco's apartment. He said he went in after the *eses* popped him, and he dragged the body into the living room and tried to clean up 'cause he didn't want anyone else to find the note. I don't know how he knows who you are, but he does."

"Can I have the emails?"

"Yeah." He left and came back a few minutes later with a stack of pages. They were printed copies of emails dating back nearly two years. "He wanted to be featured in some stories but with his name taken out. I did one piece when Tami was killed, but that was it. But he didn't stop emailing me."

"I need you to email him."

"And say what?"

"I'll draft it," he said.

Hunter led him into the bedroom. The floor was covered in empty beer bottles, and the nightstand held an assortment of imported liquors. A half-eaten jar of peanuts stood on the nightstand, and many of them had spilled over the covers and pillows. Hunter sat down at the desk in the corner and logged in to his email account.

"I thought they got a warrant to search your email."

"They did. But I got other accounts. Got one through an offshore IP address. The President couldn't get to it if he wanted to," he said proudly. He stood up and pointed at the computer. "All yours."

Stanton sat in the chair and began to type:

Police have something. Need to talk to you right away. Don't call from your number. Call me from a pay phone. I want one interview. Call me tonight as soon as possible. I'll be home at seven.

Stanton listed his own cell phone number and then sent the email.

When Stanton had left, Hunter lay on the bed and waited for the reply email. It came within the hour, asking what was wrong and what the police knew. He replied only that he couldn't talk and to call him at seven. Then he shut his computer off and went out the back door to the pool.

A small act—a drop of goodness in an ocean of misery and wickedness. His life had been short and evil. Stanton was right about that. He had committed acts that he had blocked out and not thought about for years. The Percocet and oxycodone he had taken that morning had numbed him but were now wearing off. His mind flooded with images and sensations and sounds—as if a dam of putrid acts had broken and he was drowning. He sat in a lounge chair and threw an empty can into the pool to watch the ripples as they scattered and disappeared into the concrete perimeter.

Hunter rose from his chair, walked to the edge of the pool, and stripped. He pissed into the pool from the side and then went inside the house to the den. He unlocked his safe and pulled out his revolver.

He put the barrel in his mouth and pulled the trigger.

63

Colby Lashowe sat in a surveillance vehicle, munching on pork rinds. The day had been hot, and his underarms were ringed with sweat. It had soaked through his undershirt, leaving his chest and belly pockmarked with dark splotches. Though it was evening, the sun hadn't gone down yet. The sky appeared that odd gray before nightfall, and he watched the stars beginning to shine in the sky.

His partner, Chad Eldridge, was asleep in the backseat. Chad was at least fifteen years his senior and was close to retirement. Surveillance to him was boring, painful work. He would always tell Colby that it made his ass and his mind flat.

Colby pulled out a copy of the *Times* and flipped through until he found the crossword section. He folded the paper neatly into a rectangle and pressed it against the steering wheel. The first line asked for a five-letter word that meant "hard to stir." A car engine started, and Colby's head jerked up. The subject was in his van and pulling out of the driveway and into the road.

"Shit! Wake up, Chad!"

Colby started the car as his partner jumped up in the backseat. He waited until the van had passed before pulling away from the curb and following him. "He's on the move."

"Shit. Did you call it in?"

"No."

Chad dialed a number on his phone and reported that the subject was on the move and they were following northbound. The van drove under the speed limit and obeyed all the traffic laws —almost to the point that Colby thought the man might have memorized the traffic code. He signaled for three seconds before changing lanes and didn't stop the signal halfway through. He came to a complete stop at every stop sign and, instead of going around, waited behind a school bus that was letting kids off.

"Did you get a photo?" Chad asked.

"No, I missed him. The fucker popped out of nowhere."

The van got onto the 405, and Colby counted four cars before he hopped on and pursued him. He let another two cars in between them and then fell back about sixty feet. The van was going the speed limit, exactly the speed limit, in the far-right lane.

Chad wasn't paying attention when Colby suddenly hit the brakes, throwing him forward. "What the hell?"

"Sorry," Colby said. "He's gettin' off."

They took the 28 exit, and the van drove for another fifteen minutes before parking in a convenience-store lot. Colby parked at a Mexican restaurant across the street as Chad got out the camera and began snapping photos.

The subject was huge, around six feet two and maybe three hundred to three hundred twenty pounds. His face was clean-shaven except for a mustache, and he wore glasses. A large belly hung over his belt, and he glanced around before going to a pay phone.

Stanton received a call from an unknown number at exactly 7:02. He waited three rings, wondering if there was any way the man had heard Hunter's voice before. "Hello?"

A silence on the line except for the sound of passing traffic in the background.

"Hello? Is someone there?"

"What do the police have?"

The voice made Stanton's heart drop. Until now, the killer had been a shadow, a conglomeration of images and theories. Suddenly, he was a living, breathing person, and it hit Stanton that those images of Tami and Pamela, which had burned into his brain, were caused by another human being. Not an animal or a demon, but a man. "I have a copy of what they have. But I want something in exchange."

"What?"

"An interview. Exclusive, which means you can't give anyone else interviews if you ever get caught. I'm gonna have you sign a contract, and if you ever give another interview, they won't be able to use any—"

"Fuck your interview. What do they have?"

"That's the deal. A copy of the police file in exchange for one interview. Recorded."

Silence again. Stanton thought that perhaps he had pushed him too fast. The man needed to feel in control, and if he didn't, he would run. "Look," Stanton said, "I'm risking my ass by giving you anything. It's not fair if I don't get a lot in return."

"One interview. Tonight."

"Where?"

"Your house."

"No."

"Take it or leave it."

Stanton knew he had to stand his ground. Hunter would never have agreed to that. "Then I leave it. And you can go it on your own. I'll find the next story of the week. See ya."

"Wait. Where do you want to meet?"

"Somewhere public but not too public. Like a library or something."

"Mission Hills Library. It's on Washington Street."

"It'll take me half an hour to get there."

"That's where I want to do it."

"Fine. How will I find you?" Stanton asked.

"I'll find you."

Colby watched as the man hung up the phone and then went inside the convenience store. He looked around for what seemed like a long time then purchased a fountain drink and a package of doughnuts before going back to the van.

"Did you see the number he dialed?" Chad asked.

"What am I, a fucking hawk?"

"You can see what numbers he dials from where his hand moves. It's called police work, kiddo."

Colby shook his head. "Go back to sleep, Chad."

They waited half a minute before getting on the road and following him again. The van moved slowly and in a circle. It went down into a residential neighborhood, stopped near a liquor store, and then started again. As it was passing a busy intersection, the van began to slow, and then out of nowhere, it sped through the intersection on a red light. A motorcyclist had to swerve and lay down his bike to avoid hitting him.

"Shit!" Colby shouted.

He tried to follow, but without his red-and-blues, none of the cars stopped, and a Dodge truck hammered into his right side. The impact swung his car around sideways. A Saturn slammed on its brakes and narrowly avoided smashing into them head-on.

Colby was dazed and realized he'd hit his head against the window, cutting it and causing it to bleed. He looked back at Chad, who was holding his mouth, blood cascading over his hand.

"Hang on." Colby called into dispatch and requested an ambulance. Then he called Tommy and told him they had lost the van. "He's heading east on Sandy Boulevard. Get a unit down there now."

"How did you lose a van?" Tommy said.

Colby hung up and turned to his partner. He took Chad's hand away from his mouth to look at the wound and saw that he had bitten into his tongue.

"They're on their way."

Chad wrapped his fingers around his tongue and pressed hard to stop the bleeding. "I 'ucking 'ate surweilance."

64

Stanton turned his cell phone off. He pulled to a stop a block away and put the phone and his wallet in the glove compartment. The street was quiet and empty, the type of place where neighbors could live ten feet from each other for thirty years and never know each others' names. Last he had checked, the surveillance team was following the van.

After Brady Rattigan realized Hunter wasn't coming, it would take him about forty minutes to get home. The variable was how long he would wait there without Hunter answering his phone. Stanton's guess was not long. He probably had somewhere between seventy to ninety minutes in the house.

He stepped out of the car. The air was warm, no breeze, the trees still as glass. From the cars in the driveways, the neighborhood was lower-middle class. At the far end of the street, two kids were playing on the sidewalk.

The house appeared old, and the windows were tinted so dark it was difficult to see through them. Stanton went to the front porch. The mother, he had been told, was bedridden in a room on the top floor. The surveillance team had seen her come to the window only once to empty an ashtray onto the driveway. He guessed she wouldn't be a problem.

The lock was a simple pin and tumbler. None of the windows had alarm stickers. Stanton had checked all the major alarm companies, and none had listed this address as a client. Stanton took out a pin and a tension wrench. He inserted the pin until he heard a click and then put the tension wrench into the bottom portion of the lock. The problem was that he didn't know which way to turn the cylinder, so he had to try both directions several times before it clicked and turned over. He got inside and shut the door behind him.

The house was cool, and he could hear an air conditioner running. There were stairs just to his left. Past those was the living room. To the other side a hallway led into the kitchen.

The walls were decorated with plants, the long vines strung up with thumbtacks. It reminded him of an abandoned house in a jungle that nature had overtaken. He glanced into the living room and saw a large velvet Elvis painting. The sofa and love seat were wrapped in plastic, and a basket filled with yarn and crocheting needles sat in the corner. The television, outdated by at least twenty years, had a dial channel knob and bunny-ear antennas.

The shag carpet muting his footsteps, Stanton walked to the kitchen. The table had only two chairs, and placemats with silverware were laid out. The centerpiece was a bowl of plastic fruit with a thick layer of dust.

The linoleum was clean, but the sink was filled with dirty dishes. Food-encrusted bowls, plates and glasses covered the countertops, and the garbage can was overflowing. A large butcher knife lay on a cutting board by the sink.

Past the kitchen was another small hallway. He saw a bathroom on the left. It was filled with men's products: shaving cream, aftershave and hard, unscented soap. He continued down the hallway and came to a bedroom that stank of body odor and sweat. He looked under the bed first. A dresser was against the wall, and he began to open the individual drawers. Socks, underwear, loose change... but in the far right drawer was a stack of pornographic magazines.

Stanton flipped through them. Some dated back to the eighties. They all depicted some sort of sexual violence, whether bondage, beatings or staged rape. He put them back and closed the drawer. Research showed that violent pornography didn't make people violent, but if they had a predisposition to violence, it was like throwing gasoline on a fire.

On the nightstand next to the bed were a lamp and an alarm clock. Some envelopes were tucked underneath the alarm clock. The return address on all of them: Pelican Bay State Prison.

65

Stanton read through the first letter twice. There were five total: three from Eli Sherman and two from "BLR" to Sherman. The first letter was from Sherman, introducing himself and telling Rattigan how Sherman knew of him. Tami Jacobs's boyfriend had told Sherman about the manager of her building and how he had let him in to her apartment. The responding officers had taken a statement from the manager and then never followed up.

But something had never sat right with Sherman. The boyfriend said the manager vomited in the bathroom. The manager had given the same story and said he had flushed the vomit and washed out his mouth before leaving and calling the police. Sherman had checked under the toilet seat and the surrounding floor, and none was there. Vomit, no matter how hard a person tried to prevent it, always got underneath the toilet seat or on the floor around the toilet.

Sherman investigated and discovered that the managers were not allowed to have keys to the apartments in that building. He pulled a criminal history and saw several burglaries and minor sex offenses for Brady Louis Rattigan. Many rapists began as burglars that stumbled upon vulnerable women when they were burglarizing a home. They would develop a taste for sexual violence and continue down that path. Rattigan had gotten the job from an uncle who owned the apartment complex.

You had him and you let him go. Damn you to hell, Eli.

As he was about to turn to the second letter, he heard a sound. He held his breath and waited. It happened again, a scraping sound, like a pen being dragged across concrete. Dropping the letters on the bed, he stood and drew his firearm. He kept his gun at chest height as he moved toward the door. Leaning against the wall, he peered down the hallway. There was nothing but air shooting down on his forehead from a vent in the ceiling.

Stanton stepped into the hallway and made his way into the kitchen. He went past the table to a sliding glass door, thinking that maybe Rattigan had a dog surveillance had missed.

The scraping sounded again, coming from near the stairs. Stanton turned toward that way and realized the noise was coming from behind a door. He leaned against the wall, the gun at shoulder height.

The sound occurred again. The doorknob twisted slightly to the right and then to the left. He noticed a massive gap underneath the door. Either it wasn't part of the original home design or it had been replaced with a wrong-size door. Fingers appeared in the gap, then the knob turned again. The fingers retracted, and he heard thumping, as if someone were walking down a set of wooden stairs.

The fingers had long nails painted with sparkles.

Stanton lowered his weapon. "This is the police. Who's down there?"

"Holy shit! Help me! Please help me!" The young girl started sobbing.

His first instinct was to kick the door down, but he remained calm. He put his firearm away and took out his pin and tension wrench. He had the door open in less than a minute. The space was dark, but Stanton could see the first few steps leading down into a basement. Near the middle of the staircase was a girl, her blonde hair covering her face, her feet bound.

Stanton jumped down to her. "Are you hurt?"

"No. Please, we have to go. He's going to come back. We have to go."

"Okay, okay, calm down. We're going to get out of here, okay?" Stanton tried to loosen the plastic wraps around her ankles, but they were too tight. "Wait here."

"No! Don't leave me!"

"I'll be right back. Hold on."

He sprinted to the kitchen and grabbed the butcher knife off the cutting board. He ran back to the girl, who screamed when she saw him.

"It's okay, I'm just going to cut these wraps, okay? Don't move for just a second." He placed the blade between the ties and sawed into them. The plastic was hard, and he could feel bits of it flying off over his arms. He cut through and removed them. "Come on."

He helped her up the stairs and turned toward the front door. As he pulled out his phone, he remembered that he had no reason to be there. No warrant. Everything found in this house would be suppressed in court, including the statements made by the girl.

"Can you walk?" he asked.

"Yeah. Come on. Let's go." She pushed for the door.

"Hold on. I need you to do something for me. I need you to go to the neighbor's house and call the police. When you do, you're going to tell them that you found that knife in the basement and you cut yourself loose and got out. Say that the door wasn't locked and you got out on your own. I'm going to leave, and you can't mention me."

"No, we have to go." She was crying and beginning to get hysterical. "We have to go. We have to go, please."

Stanton put his palms on her cheeks and brought her eyes to his. "Listen to me. They can't know that I helped you. If they find out about me, the man that kidnapped you will be set free. Do you understand? I'm going to leave, and you're going to tell them that you found that knife in the basement, and you cut yourself loose. Please."

"Okay."

"What are you going to tell them?"

"I... I found the knife, and I cut myself loose."

"Okay. Now, I need you to be strong for me just a little bit longer, Zoe. Okay, just a little bit longer."

She nodded, and they hurried to the door. Stanton opened it and watched as she ran to the neighbor's house and knocked on the door. He ran back into the bedroom to grab the stack of letters. Shoving them into his pocket, he dashed out to his car. Zoe was speaking to the neighbors on their front porch. When the woman pulled a cell phone out, Stanton drove away.

He stopped near a small neighborhood park. Sweat poured out of him, and his heart pounded like a fist against his chest. He tried to relax, but tension coursed through his body, tickling his stomach and bladder, and he had the sensation of needing to urinate. He got out and went to the public bathroom at the park. Nothing came, so he went back to his car, flipped on an overhead light, and read the other letters. The second, third, and fourth missives were just the two men praising each other and talking about their conquests. It reminded Stanton of a school yard pissing contest.

The last letter was dated two days ago.

Jon Stanton's address is 2312 New Haven.

Stanton thought Sherman had given Rattigan the wrong address, and then recognition pounded in his head like a hammer against steel.

That was Melissa's address.

66

Stanton raced down the interstate, weaving between cars. He cut off a semi, and its loud horn startled him. He fumbled for his cell phone and cursed as he waited for it to turn on. As soon as it showed bars, he called Jessica.

"Hey," she said, "what's up?"

"He's going after Melissa. Call dispatch, and tell them an officer needs assistance immediately and get them to 2312 New Haven. Tell them the suspect is armed and hostile."

"Shit. I'm on it."

He dialed Melissa's number, but his call went straight to voicemail. A second try gave the same result. Stanton glanced down at his speedometer. He was going nearly ninety miles an hour, disrupted only by the frequent braking he had to do before passing slower vehicles.

By the time he got to the exit, fifteen minutes had passed. He knew he was closer than any responding officers and would probably be the first one there.

The street was quiet, and no vehicles were parked in the driveway. Leaving the car on, Stanton jumped out and ran to the front door. It was locked. He pounded and rang the doorbell while shouting for Melissa. He took a step back, raised his right leg, and smashed his heel by the doorknob. He did it again and again and again. The door began to splinter, and he did it twice more with the other leg before switching back.

With a thunderous crash, the door swung open, bits of wood flying everywhere. Stanton pulled out his firearm and entered the house. The place was darkened except for a television's blue light coming from the living room. He flipped a switch on the wall, but nothing happened. Pushing his back against the wall, he slid along it, heading for the living room.

When he turned the corner, he spotted a figure slouched on

the sofa. "On the ground!"

No movement. Stanton reached out and flipped a light switch, and a lamp turned on. Lance's head was leaned back against the leather sofa. A small hole in his forehead drizzled blood down his face. The back of his head was blown out, and brain matter and blood caked the wall behind him.

Screaming erupted farther down the hallway, the shrieks of young children. Stanton sprinted down the hall. The gun was in his hand, but it was lowered, and he couldn't think. There was only the instinct to run toward the voices and destroy anything else in front of him.

The screaming was coming from the bathroom. The door was locked. Stanton rammed his shoulder into it, and it flew open. His boys were on the floor, their faces covered in tears and sweat, their eyes swollen. But they were alive. They ran to him.

He wrapped his arms around them. "Where's your mom?"

"I don't know," Matt said.

Stanton glanced around the bathroom. "Come on. Let's go."

He took them outside and shouted for help. A neighbor came out, an older woman in gym clothes. Stanton told her to take his boys to her home, lock the doors, and wait for the police. She looked frightened and confused but did what he asked without a word.

Stanton ran back inside the house. His heart was pounding so hard he didn't think he could hear anything else. He checked the two rooms farther down the hallway. They were empty. He ran to the stairs leading to the second floor. On the first few steps were dirty boot prints.

Stanton climbed the stairs slowly, straining to hear any sounds. He got to the top and stood for a moment, listening. A muffled cry was coming from the room immediately to his left. He twisted around the other side of the door and ducked low. He took a deep breath and reached for the doorknob.

He twisted the doorknob and pushed the door open. Tied to the bed with plastic cuffs, Melissa wore only a bra and panties. Her makeup was running down her face, and she was hysterical, fighting against the straps as her wrists bled.

Stanton pushed the door open farther and then went deaf.

A shotgun blast tore through the wood just above his head, where his chest would have been had he been standing. He fell to his stomach as another blast went off, his ears ringing so loudly he couldn't hear anything else.

He crawled along the floor away from the room as another blast tore through the wall, blowing fragments of wood and drywall over the hallway and on top of him. Another blast blew a hole just above him.

Stanton climbed to his knees and crawled to the end of the hall, but then he heard Melissa scream. He stood and ran toward the bedroom. Rattigan was at the door and fired. The spray mostly hit the wall behind Stanton as he fell to his stomach and fired up at the figure in front of him.

As Stanton squeezed the trigger, he felt the impact against his wrist and shoulder. Another shotgun blast caught Stanton and tore chunks out of his shoulder.

Rattigan was hit once in the face. His jaw shattered into pieces, revealing his tongue and pink throat, and he stumbled backward. Stanton steadied his hand and fired again.

A single shot went into Rattigan's cheek just underneath the eye. He fell to his knees as Stanton stood up and fired two more rounds into his head, knocking the corpse over onto its back. A handgun was in Rattigan's other hand, and Stanton kicked it away. He stood over the body and fired his last round into the heart.

He ran over to Melissa and tugged on the straps. They weren't tightened all the way; Rattigan had been interrupted. Stanton ripped them off and wrapped his arms around his wife and kissed her forehead as she wept onto his chest.

He looked to Rattigan's body, which was nothing more than motionless meat and bone now.

67

Not until five weeks after Rattigan's death did Stanton have the strength to sit there.

The glass partition was dirtier than Stanton remembered. Fingerprints were smeared across it, small fingerprints about the size of a child's.

Stanton didn't want to be there. He would have preferred to be on the beach with the ocean foaming around his ankles. But he felt that if he didn't come, questions would always nag at him. And he needed to look Sherman in the eyes and tell him he had lost. He felt acute pain from the wounds the buckshot had caused and hoped Sherman couldn't see his agony.

Sherman, the man who sent Rattigan to murder his wife, was brought in by a guard. Once seated, he picked up the phone. "So, Johnny gets his man. I'm humbled that you came to see me. Heard you spent some more time in the hospital?"

"Were you ever going to turn him in?"

"I enjoyed his work. He was progressing, Jon. Tami wasn't the first."

"How many were there?"

"His first one was when he was fourteen. Such an early age to begin, isn't it? I wonder how far he would've gotten if you hadn't murdered him." Sherman bit off a long piece of his thumbnail and spit it out. "I saw on the news that you retired after this case."

"I have."

"Retirement's an odd thing. Actually decreases your life span. I'm dying to know something, Jon. What'd they find in his house? Any trophies?"

"They found Mike's cash he'd been paying for blackmail. I take it you found out Mike was sleeping with Tami and had him follow them around for photos?"

"Mm, part of that money is mine. Such a shame. What else did they find?"

"His mother. She had her head bashed in with a hammer."

He chuckled. "A little going-away present. He was going to go away, you know. Right after he killed you and tortured that little woman of yours. He would've had fun with her. She's a fighter."

Stanton leaned in close to the glass. "I came here to tell you that you lost, Eli. I'm still here, and you're still in there. Have fun. I hear their retirement plan is a good one."

He hung up and left without looking back.

Stanton sat in hot sand and let the sunshine warm his body. The beach was nearly empty, since it was a Wednesday afternoon, but a few people were out playing hooky from work and yelling and laughing in the water.

Melissa was farther down the beach, playing in the surf with the boys, the water foaming at her ankles. She looked beautiful, her hair wet and touching the tops of her shoulders. The smile on her face was genuine, and her tan made her appear young.

Stanton looked out over the water and saw a seagull land near shore, dip underneath the water, come back up, and take flight with something glistening in its mouth. He watched it a long time as it glided effortlessly through the air and landed on a secluded part of the beach farther up, near the parking lot.

"Helluva life you got."

Stanton turned as Philip lumbered up to him and sat down on the sand. He still wore his suit coat and loafers and appeared uncomfortable, sweat glistening on his forehead.

"I love the ocean," Stanton said. "It doesn't care who you are or what you do. It treats everyone the same. Our bodies have the same percentage of salinity as the ocean. We have a deep link to it."

Philip shrugged. "Never appealed to me. So, what'd you want to talk to me about?"

Stanton reached underneath a towel that lay next to him and pulled out a manila envelope. It contained a digital recorder and a CD. He handed it to Philip.

"I know why you left the FBI, Phil. And I know you don't want to be on loan to the San Diego PD. This"—he pointed at the envelope—"is the biggest police corruption case of your career. Make it count."

"What is it?"

"Listen to it in your car on the way back."

Philip stood up and wiped the sand off his ass. "Guess you heard Eli tried to hang himself in his cell."

"No, I hadn't heard that."

"He survived. Don't know what's worse, killing yourself or wanting to kill yourself and failing."

Stanton stood up. "Listen to that CD."

"I will." Philip began to walk away.

"Phil?"

"Yeah?"

"Where's Eli now?"

"At the hospital, I think."

"Not the prison infirmary?"

"No, I think he's too messed up for that. He's in a coma."

"They only assign one guard as an escort to the hospital, don't they?"

"I don't know. I guess. Look, I gotta run, I'll see ya."

Stanton watched as he walked back to his car. Philip waved once as he pulled out of the parking lot, and Stanton waved back.

"Daddy! There's a turtle!"

He turned and watched his children as they ran over to show him their find. He grinned and took them in his arms. For the first time in his life, he couldn't think of a single other place he wanted to be.

Made in the USA
Monee, IL
21 May 2024

58750922R00148